WHAT'S LEFT TO LEARN

Al Landwehr

STEPHEN F. AUSTIN STATE UNIVERSITY PRESS

For more information:
Stephen F. Austin State University Press
P.O. Box 13007 SFA Station
Nacogdoches, Texas 75962
sfapress@sfasu.edu
www.sfasu.edu/sfapress

Managing Editor: Kimberly Verhines
Book Design: Emily Williams
Cover Art: Lynn Greyling
Cover Design: Emily Williams
Distributed by Texas A&M Consortium
www.tamupress.com

ISBN: 978-1-62288-234-2

Contents

Chapter 1 ❧ 9

Chapter 2 ❧ 18

Chapter 3 ❧ 26

Chapter 4 ❧ 29

Chapter 5 ❧ 35

Chapter 6 ❧ 49

Chapter 7 ❧ 54

Chapter 8 ❧ 63

Chapter 9 ❧ 72

Chapter 10 ❧ 87

Chapter 11 ❧ 99

Chapter 12 ❧ 106

Chapter 13 ❧ 119

Chapter 14 ❧ 129

Chapter 15 ❧ 136

Chapter 16 ❧ 146

Chapter 17 ❧ 160

Chapter 18 ❧ 173

Chapter 19 ❧ 181

Dedicated to the memory of Tom McAfee
Who, more than anyone else,
Taught me how to read fiction and how to write fiction.

Chapter 1
Tuesday

Ahead, Cold Canyon Creek Road cut through a grove of eucalyptus trees that created a tunnel of shade. The spot triggered a memory in Drayton's mind, and he took his foot off the gas pedal and let his Fiat drift into the oasis of darkness. Drayton restored Italian sports cars from the 1970s and earlier, and an old friend, Barlow, had told him about an abandoned car he'd found near this turn in the road. Barlow said he had stopped at the spot to let his pleading Labrador out to wet down the slick, white trunks of a few trees, and no more than fifty or sixty yards into the trees lurked an abandoned Alfa Romeo, a car that Drayton might be interested in.

Drayton killed his Fiat's engine and stepped out onto the pea gravel shoulder. He was always interested in Italian cars, for restoration or for parts. He reached back into the car for his straw hat, put it on his shaved head, and glanced around. The hills were still tinged by green, but not for long because it was October and the hot Santa Ana winds had started to blow in from the desert. Drayton looked back along the twisting residential road that had almost no traffic. Each side of the road had a narrow gravel shoulder bordered by a deep ditch covered by heavy brush which gave way to the eucalyptus forest. The only sound was the buzz of a single-engine plane droning like some great slow-moving hornet high in the hazy, blue sky.

Drayton stood looking into the dim light and darkness of the grove of trees, smiled, and mumbled: "Whose woods are these, I think I know," but had no idea whose trees or land this was. Drawn, he worked his way through the brush, across the deep ditch and into the darkness, where he expected the air to be cooler, but he was wrong. Not even a breeze. His tee shirt was already starting to stick to his back and his jeans felt heavy, but he was glad he wasn't wearing shorts because the area was heavy with poison oak. He reached a sharp rise and took a few steps beyond it, moving down an incline and deeper into the trees. The ashen white of the trunks of the trees twisted upwards, shaggy bark hanging down in strips. The branches and leaves were still. Dead still. No Santa Ana winds now except at the tops of trees where branches creaked and leaves fluttered.

Barlow had said fifty or sixty yards. Drayton was well beyond that. He looked behind him but couldn't see the road. He paused and stared into the half- light. In a hollow crouched a dark shape, a shape too rectangular to be part of nature. He took a step toward it, then another. Barlow had been right—it was a car. How the hell, Drayton asked himself, did it get into the middle of the woods? He stopped and looked around. No houses. Nothing. The trees. Him. The car. Trees surrounded the car. He could see no way to get it in or out. Then he saw that he was wrong. A passageway angled toward a dirt and gravel road that led from Cold Canyon Creek Road and deeper into the eucalyptus grove. Only a sapling stood in the way. Fifteen minutes with a chain saw and he'd have a passageway to the dirt and gravel road—and no doubt—to somebody's hidden house.

Great purple-black ravens reeled above the tops of the trees and roosted among the high branches. They screamed down at him. On the road behind him, a car hissed past, distant, more like a memory than a sound. Insects began to buzz around his head. He waved them away with his hat and wiped the sweat off his forehead and the top of his shaved head. The car sat deep in the natural mulch of the woods. Had the car been there so long that the sapling had grown and blocked the exit? Sunken in the musty mulch, the tires were either flat, or buried, or both. The floor pan was probably rusted out. He stopped a few yards short of the car and looked at it: a strange derelict. The canvas top hung in shreds from the cross-frames. The entire car was covered with surface rust, and each panel was riddled with rust holes as big as a man's fist. Otherwise, the body was complete and straight. No major damage. A car that had had a good body when it had been abandoned, but time and rain and rust had done their jobs: the body was worthless. Were the car in the condition it had been left, and assuming it was a good runner, it would be worth thirty thousand, but in its present rusted out condition, it wasn't worth much.

Standing ten feet from the car, Drayton wondered what he'd find in the passenger cabin. The driver's window was almost all the way down, so the car had been left in the middle of the woods with the window down. Someone had left in a hurry. Drayton hesitated before stepping closer to the car and peering in the driver's window. Nothing. *No skeleton, Drayton*, he said to himself and smiled. He stuck his head through the open window and into a network of spider webs. Two spiders, each the size of his thumb, scuttled for cover. He brushed the spider webs away from his face. The dash and seats, formerly black leather, had turned a chalky gray, and cracks ran across the seats and opened gaping wounds in the dash. Foam spilled out, dry, brittle. The two pods directly in front of the driver's seat held the speedometer and tachometer. He saw a small cylinder that had been pushed up between the two pods. *A tube of lipstick*, he thought, but when he picked it out, he saw that it was a shotgun shell. When he looked more closely at the area around the pods, far in the back, he found another shotgun shell. He stood looking at the two shells cupped in his hand. The caps shone like bronze, and the casings were dark red. Nobody went hunting in an Italian sports car. He looked at the trees and the deep shadows surrounding him. Suddenly, it seemed that the woods had changed. *Something bad has happened here*, he thought, but then laughed at himself.

Still standing with his upper body through the open window, Drayton reached under the dash and pulled the hood release. The cable was stiff, but the hood thunked open. When he pushed up the creaking hood, he grunted with surprise: the engine and transmission were intact. They'd be worth having. The wiring was in shreds, either rotten or eaten. Squirrels. Prairie Dogs. Rats. *Marmot the varmint*, Drayton thought and walked to the other side of the car. The fuel-injection pump was there. He shook his head: *Everything was there.* Clearly, the car had been in decent shape when it had been dumped there, as if someone had driven it into the woods and then walked away and never returned.

What the hell was that smell? He slipped the two shotgun shells into his pocket and walked toward the back of the car. The smell was so putrid Drayton almost gagged. With his hand over his mouth and nose, he looked at the license plate. The last registration was April 1981. Nineteen years ago. Some find.

He went back to the driver's door and tried to open it. The latch released, but the door wouldn't move because the car had sunk so far into the wet mulch. He kicked away at the dirt and rotted leaves until he was able to open the door enough to reach in and pull the release for the trunk. The cable was stiff, and he heard the latch click, but the trunk lid, weighted down by the same droppings that covered the ground, didn't open. Drayton thought that maybe he didn't want to open the trunk because he knew that the smell was coming from there. *If I wanted*, he thought, *I could forget the whole damned thing and walk back to my car.* But curiosity had gotten him by the throat. Curiosity never left him, it always trailed him, and pushed him towards the end—an understanding of some kind.

He tried to pull up the trunk lid, but it was covered by a thick layer of debris from the trees, and he was able to open it only an inch or two. Insects buzzed around his head. The air, warmer and closer now, was harder to breath, and the urge to gag constricted his throat. That damned stench. His shirt stuck to his back. Sweat was in his eyebrows. He stepped forward and pushed most of the debris off the trunk lid. Spiders and earwigs scampered out. His breath short, Drayton pulled open the lid.

Empty, he thought at first.

A few scattered tools. A water pump. The rusted-out trunk floor. An antique oil can. Jammed into the corner was the rotting corpse of an opossum, much of its flesh gone, its head grinning. He guessed it had gnawed through a radiator or heater hose and drunk some of the anti-freeze. Mammals liked it, and it was a killer.

Drayton stepped back and looked around him. The car wouldn't be that hard to get out, and it looked like a good car for mechanical parts. He thought of the registration: 1981. Could it have been left in the woods nineteen years ago? The shotgun shells in his pocket pressed against his leg. Drayton turned and started walking through the woods and back to his car, and again, he thought of driving away, but he knew he'd never do it. Pausing, he looked back at the spot where the Alfa was too hidden by foliage to be seen. Something told him to persevere—maybe the voice of Bonnie, his ex-wife, who had once told him that he was obsessive but without perseverance. That had always seemed like a fine line to Drayton, even if it was wrong;

he was *both* obsessive and persevering. He never let anything go. He followed through.

DRAYTON DROVE SLOWLY UP the road that twisted through the grove of eucalyptus trees and disappeared as it topped a slight ridge. He had to go slowly because the road was rutted, and his car was seven inches off the ground. When he was almost to the crest, he turned to look back for the abandoned car, but he saw only the trees, so it might have been there a long time without anyone seeing it. Maybe he could find someone who could tell him who owned the property the car was on—or maybe even why shotgun shells were stashed in the dash.

The rocky road crested, then dropped into a natural pasture. He had to almost stop his car and ease over a rock crest. Part of the pasture was fenced, and two horses stood in the shade of a tree. Beautiful horses. Appaloosas. Expensive horses. Someone had some cash. The horses used their tails to swish flies off one another. Still no sign of a house or outbuildings. The road dropped down the ridge, flattened out, and curved around an outcropping of granite pushed up on its side. Even though Drayton was probably only a half mile from the main road, there wasn't a hint of its existence. Once around the granite outcropping, he could see a house and barn. The house was old and wood-framed, something out of the beginning of the twentieth century, but the barn was much newer, its corrugated steel roof shining in the hot sun and creaking in the Santa Ana wind. Sycamores carved a line behind the house and barn, which meant that a creek was back there. Drayton looked at the surrounding hills. They were high enough and had some greenness left, so they had springs, which meant the creek probably had water in it most of the year. The place looked profitable. A fairly new Ford Ranger pick-up truck was out front, and a yellow Honda was parked at the side of the house.

A black Labrador and a limping Rotweiller came to meet his car. They barked and howled and sounded horrible, but Drayton had never known a Lab or Rotweiller to hurt anyone. No sign of the residents. He got out of the car, and the dogs circled him, wary, but with their tails low and slowly wagging. He squatted down and made friends with them. Still no sign of anyone. Maybe they'd gone into town. No sound from the house, which was sheltered in the shade by the sycamores and eucalyptus. For a second on the front porch, he hesitated, the pressure of the shotgun shells against his leg. Don't get paranoid, he told himself, then shrugged and knocked on the frame of the wooden screen door. It was latched, which meant somebody was inside, unless they'd left the front door open and gone out the back door. Drayton knocked again. Still no response. He turned and looked down the side of the house.

"Who's there?" A woman's voice. He couldn't see her. All he could see was light and shadows from inside the house. Was the voice young or old?

Drayton took a step back. "Hi, my name's Michael Drayton, and I'm interested in the abandoned Alfa Romeo that you've got out in the woods."

"My husband's asleep," the woman said. Her voice sounded closer, and Drayton thought he'd seen some movement.

"I was just wondering if you wanted to get rid of it? I'm interested in it as a parts car. The body's shot, but I'll give you a couple hundred for it; the mechanical parts may be worth something."

"I don't know what car you mean," she said. "We don't have any old car."

"Back in the woods, just off the main road," Drayton said. "It's hard to see."

She was closer now, "It must be. I've never seen it." Her voice sounded tight.

Drayton nodded, "Well, it's a 1974 Alfa Romeo Spider. Not worth much as is, but I could make good use of it."

She stepped forward but was still in partial shadow. "I know you," she said, her voice different. "You're a prof at the college." She came closer. Her hair was blonde and gray. Drayton guessed that she was about forty-five: wiry and strong looking, as if she did a lot of the work around the place. Maybe the horses were hers.

Drayton didn't respond to the question in her voice.

She was standing close to the screen door now but still hadn't unlatched it. Her face and arms looked tanned, dark for someone with light hair. Drayton guessed from the look of her that she wasn't a sunbather but a hard worker. She said, "I was in one of your classes." She unlatched the screen door and stepped outside. She wore a blue sleeveless blouse, faded jeans, and a pair of cowboy boots.

Drayton put his hand out, "Glad to meet you—"

"Ellie," she filled in for him. "Ellie Boudreau."

"Ellie," Drayton laughed. "I remember you. You were the best student in my Brit Lit class." He laughed, "Last row on the right, second seat back, and I always went to you when I wanted a smart answer."

She laughed. "You're embarrassing me. I wasn't that good."

Drayton nodded, "Oh, yes you were."

He remembered her well. Sometimes she'd stay after class and talk. A couple of times they'd gone outside and sat on one of the benches under the live oaks beside the Humanities building. At the time he'd been drawn to her, but his marriage was coming to pieces, so he'd decided that he had enough trouble already. And who wouldn't be drawn to a woman as smart and good-looking as she was?

"A small town," Ellie said and laughed.

Drayton nodded. He thought of Bonnie and how things about her had gotten back to him. You couldn't hide much in a small town.

Ellie stepped forward on the porch, pointed at his X 1/9 and asked, "What kind of car is that? I don't think I've ever seen a car like that." She was smiling at Drayton, like maybe now she knew something more about him.

Drayton looked over at the car, laughed, and said, "You don't see a lot of them. It's a Fiat, an X 1/9." He hesitated before saying. "It was a mess when I found it, but I restored it, until now it's a better car than when it was first off the line. Closer to the ideal car. Closer to what the manufacturer wanted to make."

She was grinning at him now. "You're full of surprises. An English Professor—Dr. Drayton—with a fancy sports car." Her facial expression changed, and she said, "Fall term must be just starting for you."

"No," Drayton said. "I took an early retirement. A mutual agreement. Better for everybody."

She started and cocked her head. "Really? I'm surprised. Students liked you a lot. You were a good teacher."

Drayton shrugged, "I guess everything gets old after a while." She was lean with small breasts, her hair cropped short. He asked, "Can you tell me anything about the car in the woods?"

Ellie looked past him towards the woods and shook her head, "I never knew there was a car out there. I've lived here a long time, and I've never seen a car there."

"You wouldn't," Drayton said. "Not from the road. You'd have to walk through there."

She nodded, "Nobody ever walks through there. It's a forest of poison oak. What kind of car did you say it was?" she asked.

"An Alfa Romeo," Drayton said. "A little Italian sports car. It's red -*rosso*." She looked at him and then past him again, toward the road and the woods.

The expression on her face made Drayton ask, "Do you know anyone with a red Alfa?"

She shrugged. "I'm sorry, but I'm not sure what one looks like." She shrugged. "It wouldn't make sense to drive a car like that around here."

The two dogs came up onto the porch and, groaning, collapsed onto the dust- covered boards. Drayton smiled, "Maybe your husband might know. When he wakes up, could you ask him to call me?"

Ellie Boudreau shook her head. "I don't have a husband. He's been gone a long time." She smiled at Drayton's confusion. "Out here, when some strange man shows up at the door, I always say that my husband's asleep."

"O.K.," Drayton said. "That makes sense." He nodded, "What about the car?"

"What about it?"

"Do you have any problems with my towing it away? It would probably cost you about a hundred to get it towed away."

Her mouth slipped into a smile that lighted her up, and Drayton suddenly imagined kissing her. The urge was so clear, so pristine, so untroubled, that he had to make an effort to hold himself back. The heat that had run between them when she was in his class came back to him in a rush. Drayton sighed: *What a fool he was when it came to women.* He'd never known a woman who was as foolishly romantic as he was. Bonnie had complained that he treated her like an idealized character in a romance novel. Said it was a little creepy.

Still smiling, Ellie said, "Sure, take it out of there. It's all yours. If I didn't know it was there, I'm sure not going to miss it. Somebody might as well put it to use. I hate to see things go to waste."

Drayton smiled. The way she'd said it made him think that she wasn't only talking about *things*. He felt the two shotguns shells bulging in his pocket and thought of a variant on that old movie line from Mae West: *"Honey, are those shotgun shells or are you just happy to see me?"* Drayton's smile broadened into a grin, and he said. "If I can use your phone, I'll call a tow truck and that old car will be gone in an hour or two."

She hesitated but then held the screen door open for him, "The phone's there in the hall." She paused, "You don't carry a cell phone either?"

Drayton shook his head and answered, "No." He grinned and said, "I know it's a new century—a new millennium—but I didn't like that damned phone bossing me around. It's at my place on the cocktail table in the living room of my mobile home. I think. I've still got the old phone on the wall in the kitchen." They both laughed. Drayton liked her laugh. She could probably put it to good use.

Chapter 2

After Drayton had called for a tow truck and given detailed instructions on how to find the Alfa, Ellie offered him a glass of lemonade against the Santa Ana heat, and they sat at the kitchen table. The room was dark with shade from the sycamores running behind the house. Sitting there with a glass of cold lemonade in the deep shadows of the cool kitchen, Drayton found Ellie easy to talk to. He remembered what she'd been like in class. Quick and funny. One day in class, she'd delighted him when she'd said that Wordsworth's absolute love of nature suggested that he'd never been to Death Valley in August. She loved the literature, she understood that it was about people she knew, and she understood that literature could change her life. She was one of those students who made him think: *This woman is smarter than I am.* After all his years of teaching, he could tell quickly when someone was bright, and Ellie was bright. She also had an edge to her. When Drayton sat down at the kitchen table and took off his straw hat, Ellie's eyebrows went up, and she smiled and said, "When I took your class, you still had some hair."

Drayton ran his hand over his shaved head. "It kept falling out, and then what I had left would stick out in tufts. Sometimes at the end of the day, I'd look at myself in the mirror, and looking back at me was this balding guy with tufts of hair sticking out all over his head, and I'd been walking around like that all day. So," he shrugged, "I shaved it."

"So, I see," she said and smiled.

"For a while, I had to take the jokes. People called me Daddy Warbucks and Mr. Clean, and then for a time I was known as the King of Siam—King for short, and sometimes just Sy."

"What did your family think?" she asked.

"No family," Drayton said, smiling because he felt as if he was being interviewed. Ellie's face was almost perfectly symmetrical. Most people have two very different sides to their face, but not Ellie, which was probably the main reason she was so pretty. Her blue eyes and her smile were lovely, but it was the symmetry that made her so good-looking. Drayton ran his hand over his shaved head and answered her, "My wife ran off with one of my students, and my son—our only kid—is twenty-two and deep into Silicone Valley."

"A son who is twenty-two," Ellie remarked. "You must have started early."

Drayton took a long drink of lemonade and said, "I'll be forty-six in a couple months."

"I've never heard of that," she said, smiling.

"Never heard of what? Being forty-six?" Drayton asked.

"No," she said and laughed. "I thought professors always ran off with their beautiful young students. I've never heard of a professor's student running off with his professor's wife."

Drayton laughed. "I can laugh about it now, but it wasn't so easy to laugh then. I have to say that she had good taste. He was one of the best students I'd ever had, an older guy, a vet, and he was damned good-looking. Lots of hair. Hair everywhere. I thought he looked a little like a mastodon. "Anyway, it's not unheard of. D.H. Lawrence ran off with Freida von Richthofen, the wife of his German professor."

"So, you're in good company?" she asked, the corners of her mouth lifting in a small smile.

"If you like being in the company of Herr Professor von Richthofen," Drayton said and laughed. He hesitated, waiting for her to speak, waiting to hear her voice—the melody and rhythm of it. It had taken him a long time to realize how important a woman's voice was. He'd always been a slow learner when it came to women, but he did learn. He asked Ellie, "Do you run this place yourself? Do you do all the work around here?"

"Yes," she said, "Well, most of it."

"Are the horses yours?"

Ellie nodded. "They're part of my income, the main part of my income. I breed Appaloosas. I rode when I was girl, and helped at a local breeder's." She smiled. "And my former husband was a rancher. His dream was to raise Appaloosas, and we were just starting to develop this spread when our marriage fell apart. He left me with this place, including the horses, as a settlement." She looked at Drayton and sighed, "I didn't want any alimony. We weren't together long enough." After another sigh and a smile, she said, "Child support, yes, that made sense." She laughed to herself and smiled at Drayton, "We *were* together long enough for that." She looked around the kitchen. "It's a nice house, and it stays pretty cool even during the Santa Anas."

"A lot of hard of work," Drayton said. "Who helps you?"

"An old retired guy, Charlie, helps me when I need it," she answered. "Charlie's an old cowboy, originally from the north county, but now he lives here, about a mile back in the hills." She pointed east. "He's always home and easy to get to help me."

"That's all?"

"A neighbor used to help some," she said, smiling, but her eyes told him the smile was ironic. "A neighbor just over the hill—a third generation rancher back in there." She looked out the window, toward the hills in the east. "He'd help me with the heavy stuff." She drank some lemonade and shook her head. "I should have known he was too kind and helpful." She shrugged, "And him with a wife and two kids."

Drayton smiled and nodded. "Sounds like life to me."

She glanced up at him and smiled, "He told me everyone should make love in a haystack once in life."

Drayton laughed and said, "Oh, Jesus."

The smile left her face. "He scared me one night." She shook her head and looked at Drayton. "I don't think that was what he wanted to do." She shook her head again. "Scare me, I mean." She grinned. "Not the haystack."

Drayton didn't say anything, but just waited; she seemed like it was a story she wanted to tell. He'd often seen that in students, the need to tell a story, and when that need was evident, it was best to just wait. He'd learned a lot from students about how to talk to people, but then, students were people.

"I was here one night not too long after I made it clear that I wasn't interested in him—interested that way." She sighed. "It was after dinner, it was winter and dark, and I took the trash out the back door." Her voice softened. "I happened to look over at the sycamores by the creek, and he was standing there in the dark." She shook her head, "I couldn't see his face, but I knew it was him, I knew how big he was and how he stood." Her voice was more urgent. "After the initial scare, I called to him, said 'Ronnie,' but he didn't say anything. I said his name again, and he just turned and walked down by the creek and into the darkness."

Drayton took a deep breath. "Did you ask him about it?"

Ellie shook her head. "No, I knew he'd just deny it. And the truth is that he's a gentle soul. I was just being silly. He kind of had a crush on me, the way a high school kid might." She pursed her lips, "I saw him a couple weeks later downtown and he said hello, as if nothing had ever happened, and now we chat the way neighbors do. Sort of neighbors looking out for neighbors."

Drayton nodded. "We're a strange species."

Ellie smiled and her voice was lighter when she said, "That's why I started being a little more careful, why I started telling men that my husband was asleep."

Drayton laughed softly. "I don't blame you." He looked out toward the hills and said, "But you stay around here? You don't move into town."

Ellie sat up straighter, "I love it here. At first it was hard, but I love it. I'm not going to let somebody scare me off. Men are always scaring women off of something or the other."

"True," Drayton said. "It's true." The way she'd opened up didn't surprise him. Students or ex-students often did that if they felt comfortable. And he'd seen a fair number of women who, like her, were in their forties—good-looking, intelligent—and abandoned by husbands who had left them for a newer version. Often the husbands were doctors or lawyers, and the women were attractive, educated, and accustomed to a good life, and then the rug was pulled out from under them. At forty and not working outside the home for fifteen or twenty years, it was suddenly time to start a new life. Ellie seemed in better shape than many of those women, but he'd have guessed that she'd had a long time to adjust. Drayton sensed that her intelligence was her shield.

Drayton heard a truck and turned. It was too soon for the tow truck, and he was supposed to meet the driver on Cold Canyon Creek Road.

"Speak of the devil," she said, gazing out the window at an extended-cab pick-up truck raising clouds of dust on the road. The pick-up was black and had double rear wheels-a heavy-duty truck. Steer horns were painted on the driver's door, but Drayton couldn't read the lettering. "That's my neighbor," she said. "That's Ronnie." From the cab of his truck, the driver waved. His hair and beard were reddish. Ellie gestured, sat watching the truck and said, "He's headed for his place." Drayton watched the pick-up disappear into the hills, a faint cloud of dust trailing it. Her eyes softened and her voice flattened, "We're sort of friends now. That was a long time ago."

As the last of the cloud of dust from the pick-up settled, Drayton turned back to Ellie, "So you're here alone. A minute ago you said something about child support. How many kids do you have?"

Ellie looked at him. "You ask a lot of questions."

Drayton shrugged. "Just being friendly. I didn't mean to pry." He smiled. "Forget it."

"No," she said. "It's all right. I get a little strange being out here by myself all the time." She sighed and seemed to relax. "Only one child—Cindy, our daughter," she answered. "My husband, Buddy, left when Cindy was just walking. He moved back down to Santa Ynez, where his family ranches." She smiled and sighed, "Cindy stayed with me, except for holidays and so on. She's a senior now at U.C. Santa Cruz." Ellie stood, "How about some more lemonade?"

"Sure," Drayton said. He watched her walk across the room to the refrigerator. Her jeans weren't very tight, but they were tight enough for him to check her out. Ah, Christ, Drayton, he thought, still checking butts like in high school. When was he going to graduate from high school? It occurred to him that life was about to play one of its tricks on him. Something told him to hold back.

Ellie had baggage, he was sure, but who was he to talk? He had a couple of steamer trunks.

As she stood at the sink pouring more lemonade, Ellie asked, "What will you do with the car? Do you have to register it or anything?"

Drayton nodded, "It's a good idea, because somewhere along the line, I'll want to take what's left of it to the junk yard, and they can't take it without a title. The DMV will do a title search. To try to find the owner."

She frowned. "You said the car had been there a long time. Will it be possible to find the owner?"

"Well," Drayton said, "It's easy enough to find who the last owner was." He shook his head. "It's 2000 now, and the car was last licensed nineteen years ago."

She stood looking at him, waiting.

"The license plate is still on the car, and if that's not enough, there's the VIN—the Vehicle Identification Number. They'll probably give me the owner's name and last address, and I'll try to contact him. If I can't, which is likely, the car will be titled to me."

"Is that a long process?"

Drayton laughed, "Not nowadays. They just type the numbers into the computer, and the owner's name and address come from Sacramento."

Ellie stood at the sink, her back to him.

Drayton asked, "Would you like me to call you and tell you what happened? Who owned it? Stuff like that. Maybe we can find out why he left it there."

Ellie came back to the kitchen table with the two glasses of lemonade. "Sure," she said. "I'll give you my number, and you can let me know." Drayton nodded.

Ellie sat down. "The class I took from you was a good one. You must miss teaching. How long had you taught?"

Drayton smiled. "You ask a lot of questions too." He grinned at her.

She shrugged. "Just being friendly, like you. Besides, we have similar likes and dislikes, don't we? Neither of us gets along with cell phones."

Drayton laughed and nodded. "I taught over twenty years, when you count graduate school."

"Do you miss it?"

"I miss almost everything that's gone," he said, looking at her eyes and wondering what she was thinking. This small talk reminded him of a chess game. Maybe he was about to lose his knight.

"Why did you retire so early?"

Stalling, Drayton took a long drink of lemonade and put the glass down on the table. He smiled at her, "It was mutual agreement, best for everybody."

"Now you sound angry," she said.

Drayton quickly looked up, but didn't say anything.

"All right," she said and winced. "Sorry, it's none of my business. Too many questions."

Drayton relaxed, leaned on the table. "It's no secret." He hesitated, and his voice was different when he said, "A student accused me of sexual harassment, an older woman—I mean older than most students. Thirty-five, she was. Very attractive."

Ellie drank from her glass but avoided looking at him.

"It's hard to talk about," he said, "because no matter what I say, people think that I'm lying."

"Why?"

"Because why would she say something like that if it weren't true? What would be the point?"

"What was the point?" Ellie asked.

Drayton looked up. "I think she liked me. I know she liked me. She wrote me some letters, notes—early on—but I ignored them. I should have paid attention." He nodded, "And I should have saved them, but I didn't want to believe any of it. She was bright, a good student. I thought it was some passing thing." In a lower voice, he added, "I didn't want to think she was crazy."

"It wasn't a passing thing?" Ellie asked.

Drayton shook his head, "No. Then she made the accusations. She's a hell of a good writer. She wrote it all out in details, made everything believable." He took a deep breath, "So an investigation started." He shook his head. "There was nothing I could say. You know, a divorced prof, an attractive student. Denials seemed like they were lies. What else would I do but deny?"

"So what happened?"

"It seemed to me that everybody believed her—some colleagues, the dean, all of them. If they didn't exactly believe her, they sure weren't certain about me. I thought I was in a world of intelligent, educated people who wouldn't jump to conclusions, but they proved me wrong." He took a drink of lemonade, the ice clinking against the glass. Without looking at her, he said, "I remember a news story about a guy accused of molesting a child, but it turned out the child had made up the whole thing. When somebody asked him the effect the incident had on him, he said he'd never allow himself to be alone in a room with a child again." Drayton paused. "The funny thing is that he said he'd felt guilty even though he hadn't done anything." Looking up, Drayton said, "I know that feeling. If people treat you as if you're guilty long enough, you start feeling that way."

Ellie shook her head.

Drayton smiled at her. "Anyway. A philosophy prof on another campus heard about my scorned student and me, and wrote a letter to my dean." Drayton looked at Ellie. "She'd done the same thing to him a few years earlier." Drayton shook his head and laughed. "She liked profs, poor woman."

"So you were in the clear, but you weren't?" Ellie said.

Drayton sat looking across the room at empty space and then said, "No, I wasn't in the clear. I was suspect and I was going to remain suspect." He shook his head. "But that wasn't the important thing. The important thing was that I thought I was in a world which worked on intelligence and reason and fairness." Drayton shook his head. "It wasn't the world I thought it was." He shrugged. "Something went out of it. I just didn't want to be there any more. I didn't want to worry about keeping my office door open when a student was there, and I didn't want to walk around being afraid to touch any of the girls—even just a touch on the arm." He shrugged. "And I like change. Twenty years of good teaching were enough." He nodded. "And I'm a working-class guy."

The only sound was the wind moving through the sycamores down by the stream. Drayton thought he heard one of the horses whinny from the pasture. He turned in that direction and listened. Again he heard the sound—a nice sound. He turned to Ellie, "One of your horses?"

She laughed. "You may be bald, but you can still hear."

"A nice sound," Drayton said.

"Maybe you'd like a job helping breed horses? Not much money, lots of hard work, but not much danger of being charged with sexual harassment."

Drayton laughed. "No thanks, it's all right. I'm getting by. And besides, what I know about horses wouldn't do them or you much good."

Ellie's smile faded. "That's pretty hard. I mean, to lose your wife and your work."

Drayton made a serious face before he said, "But most importantly, I lost my hair."

Chapter 3
Wednesday

Drayton jerked awake and looked over at the blinds swinging wildly, now banging, then billowing out into the room, then banging again, the rhythm increasing. The Santa Ana winds were making themselves known. His mobile home was vibrating with the wind. It was the middle of the night and it was hot. Groaning, he swung his feet off onto the warm wood of the floorboards. Standing, he groaned again, and the memory of the car in the woods came back to him before he went over to the blinds and pulled them all the way up. They swayed and continued to tap against the easement. Drayton smiled at the memory of Ellie, her eyes, her laugh. His dog yawned loudly, and his cat curled between his ankles, its fur soft and warm. Drayton stared out the windows until his eyes were accustomed to the darkness and he could see the eucalyptus trees bending in the wind while the live oaks stood solid, except for the twitching of the branches and leaves. The steel covering over the barn door light drummed against the boards and the doors creaked. A thump, thump, thumping started in the kitchen, and Drayton almost stumbled over his cat as he headed toward the noise. The linoleum floor was cool against his feet, and the kitchen was so dark he had to grope past the refrigerator to the blinds over the sink. He pulled the blinds all the way to the top and jerked at the strings to secure them.

The phone rang.

Drayton glanced up at the clock. Just after three.

He hesitated and looked at the phone as if it might explain something. All it did was ring again. Drayton thought of his son in Silicon Valley, thought of too much to drink and of a car sliding off the road into a dark ravine. Then he thought of Bonnie in Florida. It would be five in the morning there. Again the phone rang, and he picked it up: "Hello?'

"Is this Michael Drayton?" The man's voice was friendly, his words passing through the hollow crackling of a cell phone.

"Right," Drayton said. "Who's this?"

The Santa Ana winds howled down the narrow canyons of the hills, the air warm, dry, and hostile: fire weather.

"A friend," the man said, the connection almost breaking up.

Oh, shit, Drayton thought, *some old drunken friend somewhere in the world.* He asked, "What friend?"

"A friend who's going to help you out." The voice was different than it had been seconds earlier. The man was a little drunk; Drayton could tell that. He said, "All right, quit screwing around. It's after three in the morning where I am. What time is it where you are?"

"Same time. Close to you," the man said. Then Drayton was sure it was a cell phone, and he even thought he could hear the Santa Ana wind banging things in the background. The man said, "I'm calling to do you a favor."

Rip, Drayton's cat, sat staring at him, then bored, looked away. A strong blast of wind rattled the glass in the kitchen windows. "What favor?" Drayton asked, and he knew something was wrong.

"A favor," the man said again, his voice lower, almost lost in the hollow crackling on the line, a crackling which echoed the howling of the wind.

"You said that," Drayton replied, a little worried, but also a little angry.

The line was silent except for the distortion of the sound waves. Drayton listened to the moan of the mobile home. The voice said, "Take that old car you towed away, take it apart, do what you want. Just do it in a hurry and then get it to the junkyard and forget about it." The line of sound dipped. "Forget about it and everything will be fine."

"Who the hell is this?"

"Just do what I say, friend. Take it to the junkyard. Forget about it. That way, there won't be any trouble."

"Trouble?"

"A man can get hurt working around a car. Just take the advice of a friend. I'm trying to help you out here."

Before Drayton could respond, the phone went dead, and soon the dial tone buzzed. Drayton stood listening to the buzz, then looked at the phone and hung it up. He watched Rip slip through the window and into the night.

The mobile home creaked in the wind, seeming to sway on its supports. *Close to you*, the voice had said. And it was clearly a cell phone. Drayton looked out the kitchen window into the darkness, but couldn't see anything except shadows evolving into deeper shadows.

"How the hell?" Drayton said aloud, and thought, *I just picked that car up twelve hours ago*. He shook his head. Somebody sure the hell knew there was a car there. Who? But anybody could have seen it being towed away or across town—or even left outside the shop. Ellie had said that she didn't even know it was there. Could he believe that? But it had been buried in those woods, the kind of small patch of woods no one would ever walk through. Drayton stood leaning against the sink. At first the phone call had scared him. And he was still a little scared, but now he was angry too, and curious. He wondered if it was a drug dealer's car, which he'd first thought. But so what? What could be in the car? Why wouldn't whoever was worried clean out the car? Why let it sit there for twenty years and then try to scare him when he found it? He couldn't believe somebody was going to come after him because of that damned car. None of it seemed quite real.

The Santa Ana winds were a howl now. The creaking of trees and the banging of doors were consumed by the screaming of the wind as it bullied its way through the trees and through the quiet air as it pushed westward toward the ocean—the Pacific which would beat it back. Child's play for the ocean.

Chapter 4

The hot Santa Ana winds had retreated, pushed eastward by the cool fog from off the ocean. By mid-morning, the fog had dissipated to a haze as Drayton stood outside the shop he shared with his partner Ben. Drayton was hosing out the trunk of the Alfa to wash away the last remnants of the opossum. The day before, while the tow-truck driver had been linking a chain to the front axle of the abandoned Alfa, Drayton had used a long eucalyptus branch to remove the animal's rotted corpse, but its smell was harder to get rid of. The tow-truck driver had used Ellie's chain saw to cut down a few saplings that were in the way, and there had been no real problem getting the truck out.

The tow-truck driver had left the car outside the shop where Drayton and his friend Ben did restoration work. The building Ben and Drayton leased was one of three that had made up the city yards, which had been built early in the twentieth century. The roof and walls of the building were corrugated—galvanized steel supported by a frame of massive redwood beams. The only running water Drayton and Ben had was outside one of the other buildings, and the wiring was skimpy and a mess. They had a fire extinguisher in each corner of their shop, and another hooked to a massive workbench. Rent was cheap. A few of the tenants used their spaces for storage, one held a contractor's shop, another housed an engraver's studio, and a third was home to a pest exterminator.

Ben, a small smile on his face, stood leaning against the open garage door of the shop and watched Drayton squirting water into the trunk of the car. A couple of years older than Drayton, Ben was tall and thin. In college, he'd played basketball, and he still had the languid movements of an athlete. He'd grown up in L.A., and for years he'd had the second biggest automobile restoration business in southern California. His spray-painting skills were so widely known that the car freaks called him "the best gun in L.A." After fifteen years in the business, and tired of breathing paint fumes, he sold out to the largest restoration shop in the area. Ben was left with enough money that he'd never have to work again. He and his wife and their two kids had headed north for a better environment.

"Hey, man, what's your plan?" Ben asked Drayton. "You're not going to bring that stinking thing in the shop, are you? Even I can still smell it."

Drayton shook his head, "Nope, I'm going to leave it right here and start stripping it—I'll take off everything I might ever need. Then I'll have the carcass dragged off to the junkyard." He added, "I got a phone call about three this morning, warning me to get rid of the car in a hurry."

"A warning?" Ben asked.

"As in *I could get hurt*," Drayton said. He shrugged.

Ben raised his eyebrows, stood chewing on his lower lip and then smiled, "Who'd bother you over an old car?"

Drayton nodded. "But how did anybody know about it so fast? It had only been about twelve hours since I had it towed."

Ben nodded. "Yeah, but it was towed across town, towed through these back streets, and dumped here. Anybody could see that."

Drayton nodded. "Yes, but who'd care?" He shook his head again. "You're probably right." Then, he added, "But it does make you kind of interested, doesn't it?" He walked over to Ben and held up the shotgun shells. "Yesterday, I found these tucked in the dash."

"Really," Ben said. "Whose car was it?"

When Drayton told Ben the story of finding the Alfa roadster and meeting Ellie, Ben circled the car, looking at it carefully. Then he looked over at Drayton and said, "It was in pretty damned good shape when somebody left it there to rust." He stuck his forefinger into one of the gaping holes on the hood. "Man, I wonder why someone would do that? "

Drayton pointed at the rear of the car, "It's got plates on it—last registered in 1981. Nineteen years ago." He nodded. "I'm going down to the DMV and see if they can tell me who owns or owned it."

"Dumped in the woods?" Ben asked.

Drayton nodded, "Not hidden, but hard to see. Hard enough so that nobody saw it for a long time."

When Ben released the catches and pushed back the convertible top, the joints groaned, the canvas shredded and fell away, leaving tatters hanging from the ribs. Ben pulled open the creaking passenger-door and sat in the front seat, years of dust swirling up around him. With his hand on the dash, just over the glove box, he asked, "You been in here?"

Drayton shook his head.

Ben turned the glove box knob, the door fell open, and the contents came sliding out onto the floor. He looked at Drayton, "Nice design, huh, man? The Italians have a good eye for the line of a fender, but they should hire the Germans to make sure things work."

Ben shuffled through the papers that had fallen from the box. Discounts on oil changes. Scribbled notes that didn't mean anything, notes like "Sylvia Tuesday at ten," "Brushes," and "Beer and Wine." Ben glanced over at Drayton. "There's nothing in here with a name on it." He peered into the glove box, reached into it, and his hand came out holding a half-pint whiskey bottle with a swig or two left. He threw it to the side and reached in the glove box again. This time his hand came out with another shotgun shell.

"Christ," Drayton said.

"This guy really liked to hunt ducks," Ben said, "Mallards, sitting ducks, those things." He looked at Drayton. "What was this guy—a drug runner?"

"What else is in there?" Drayton asked. He stood next to the driver's door, watching Ben.

Ben shuffled through the mess that had fallen to the floor. Grumbling, he held up two prophylactics in silver-blue foil packages. He looked over at Drayton, "Fuck a duck?" He turned the packages over and read, "Ribbed for your partner's pleasure." Ben laughed. "Man, this guy's always concerned with his partner's pleasure." He grinned at Drayton, "A sensitive man with shotgun shells."

"Don't be sexist," Drayton said. "The owner could be a woman."

Ben scowled at Drayton. "Right, a woman with rubbers and shotguns shells in her glove box. Just the kind of thing all the women

I've known carry around. Asshole enlightened English professor."

"Retired," Drayton countered.

Ben shook his head and looked into the glove box. He ran his hand through it and said, "Nothing. That's it."

"Check between the seats," Drayton said. "In these cars, anything on the seat slides off between the seats and gets stuck there or goes all the way under the seat."

Ben shook his head again and looked between the seats, and then ran his hand alongside the seat. He looked at Drayton. "Nothing," he said.

"Look under the seat," Drayton said.

"Yes, sir, Professor," Ben said and slid his hand under the seat. He pulled out a photograph, a snapshot wrinkled by time and heat, and he held it up. "Soft porn," he said and handed it to Drayton. It was a photograph of a naked woman who was maybe twenty-five. Her black hair was in a Dutch Boy cut, and she was very tanned. She squinted slightly because of the sun as she faced the camera, her elbows on her knees, her open hands on the sides of her face, and her ankles strategically crossed.

"Pretty sexy," Drayton said. "Her mother didn't teach her to sit like that."

"Not likely," Ben said. "But I don't think it's mom holding the camera."

"Louise Brooks," Drayton said. "Louise Brooks with a suntan."

Ben looked at him.

"She was a movie star from the twenties who wore her hair like this." "Did she sit around like this?"

"Well, that was before the Hays Commission, but she was more subtle than this."

"I don't think this girl wanted to be in that photo," Ben said. "Man, look at her face! If looks could kill.... The guy behind the camera had something she wanted or had something on her."

"Our mystery man," Drayton said. "Shot-gun shells, a car in good shape that he dumped, and a photo of a naked woman." He hesitated. "And a threatening phone call."

Ben slid his hand under the seat, feeling for anything. His hand came out and he held a second photograph between his fingers. "Another one," he said. "Same girl, different pose." He handed it to Drayton.

As Drayton looked at the photo, he was again struck by how evenly tanned the girl was. Women didn't do that anymore. There were no white stripes on her skin where a suit had shielded her from the sun. The same blanket as in the other photo. The same day. Probably seconds apart. She was lying on her stomach, her elbows on the blanket, her fisted hands under her chin. "What a pert little butt," Drayton said. "Damn, she's good looking."

"*Was*," Ben said. "That photo's at least twenty years old. She's forty or forty-five now. Now she probably looks like the mother of the girl in the photo."

"Maybe not," Drayton said. "If she's still around." Drayton looked at Ben.

Ben shrugged and got out of the car. He slammed the door. "It's been at least twenty years. The car's been sitting there for almost twenty years."

Drayton held a photo in each hand and studied them. He handed them to Ben, "Take a look at her. I think I know her. There's something familiar about her."

"Right," Ben said. "I know what you think is familiar about her."

"No. Really."

Ben looked at the photos. "I'll bet you pink slips she came to California to make it in the movies. With those looks, that had to be the reason." He shook his head, "But she doesn't look familiar. I don't think I know her."

"Imagine her older," Drayton said.

"I don't want to, man," Ben said and laughed. "I want her to stay right there." He shook his head. "I don't know her. At least I don't think I do."

"Two of them now," Drayton said. "A mystery man and a mystery woman." He smiled. "Our mystery couple."

"Long gone, probably," Ben said. "I don't think they're solid citizens who are going to be settling down and starting a family and joining the church. I'll bet that not too long after these pictures were taken, your Louise Brooks and her Clark Gable behind the camera left town. He dumped the car and they split." Ben shook his head. "A rosso Alfa Spider is not a good car to slip away in." He leaned back in the car seat. "I wonder who was looking for them." He glanced over at Drayton. "I tell you, somebody was hot on their asses."

"Her car," Drayton said. "They'd probably take her car. Or a bus or a train or a plane."

"Or," Ben laughed. "Clark took these damned pictures of Louise and then some kid stole his car and dumped it. Louise and Clark are good solid citizens driving a Buick Roadmaster."

"Does Buick still make a Roadmaster?" Drayton asked. He shook his head. "I can't see those two in a Buick." He stood thinking before he asked, "Whatever the case—here or gone—why the phone call?"

Ben, who had walked around to the driver's side of the car, was kneeling next to the car and running his hand back and forth under the seat. His fingers came out with cellophane from a cigarette pack, which he flicked away, mumbling under his breath.

Drayton pointed to the area behind the seat.

Ben frowned at him but then pushed the seat toward the steering wheel. Ben squinted. The last of the morning fog had burned off, and the sun was bright, magnified by a thin haze. "Look at this," he said and held up a roll of undeveloped film.

"More pictures of Louise?"

"All right, man." Ben smiled. "It's worth the price of development."

"Who knows what this could develop into," Drayton said.

Ben grimaced and shook his head, "That's enough to make me shudder."

"I get the picture," Drayton countered.

Ben shook his head and slipped the film into the pocket of his jeans. "Are you going to take those to your local drug store to have them developed? What if they're more of the same, or worse? You could get picked up for pornography."

Ben, smiling, shook his head, "I'll take them home, and Lindsey can develop them."

"Won't she think you're into porno or running around with some young woman?"

Ben shook his head, "Nah, I'll explain, and she always says, 'Better old cars than young women.'" He shrugged. "She knows I'm too lazy to do both."

Chapter 5
Thursday

When Drayton looked at the middle-aged clerk at the DMV, her hair and eyes made him wonder if she was Latina, and when he heard her accent, he was sure he was right. Her nails were a pearlescent blue that accented the blue of her jacket. She hit the print button, handed the sheet to Drayton and said, "This car belongs to or belonged to Lester Tremain, 421 Pacific Beach. You need to make an effort to find this person. If you don't, come back here and we'll give you further instructions."

"May I ask you the color of your fingernail polish?"

The woman looked at her long nails as if she had forgotten what color they were that day, and then she looked up and stared at Drayton.

Drayton interpreted her expression to mean that she thought he was about to hit on her, and he shook his head, and said, "No, I just work on cars, and I think that would be a beautiful color to paint a car, not just any car, but the right car."

Her expression changed, but she still didn't say anything, and she looked around as if she were considering calling security. There must have been five uniformed cops there.

Drayton nodded as if to dismiss the subject of her nails and began to scan the printout and asked, "Is there any kind of report that the car was stolen?"

The clerk hit some more keys, her pearlescent nails dancing across the letters as she watched the screen, "No, nothing like that. Last registered to Lester Tremain on April 14, 1981." She looked Drayton in the eye and said, "More than nineteen years ago."

Drayton couldn't help himself and when he thanked her, he gave her a smile and an almost imperceptible wink.

She stared at him, and without moving her eyes from his face, she said, "Next."

DRAYTON DROVE TO "NANA'S," his favorite Mexican restaurant for lunch. The place was a little seedy, but the Mexican food was the best in town. A Mexican restaurant downtown was elaborately decorated with the green, white, and red of Mexico, and a singing guitarist moved from table to table crooning to the guests, but this made Drayton uncomfortable—he didn't feel right continuing to eat while the guy was singing to him. "Nana's" had no singing guitarist, but the food was good and Nana cooked it. He ordered a tamale, an enchilada, and his usual horchata. In a booth, Drayton sat eating and thinking about his next step. He looked at the address he had. He checked the restaurant phone book, but there was no number for a Les Tremain.

He found four Tremains in the county, but the addresses were wrong. Drayton tried information, but they didn't have anything. He went back to his booth and finished his food, washing it down with his horchata. Again, he went to the phone, this time to call Ellie.

A recorded message came on. Drayton waited until it was over and started to leave a message, but Ellie broke in. "Hello, Drayton. I'm here."

"Screening calls?" Drayton asked.

"Sure," Ellie said, "just the way my husband is asleep in the back of the house."

"You're very careful," Drayton said.

"Very careful." Her voice shifted tone, "Don't tell me you already have some info on that car?'

"I do."

"What?"

"This car belongs to or *belonged* to a guy name Les Tremain. Does the name mean anything to you?"

After a few seconds, she said, "Les Tremain." She paused and said, "Sure, sure, everybody knew Les Tremain."

"Who was he?"

"A local artist who was very social." She paused and then added, "Who was also very good looking. A bad boy women loved."

"How did you know him?"

She laughed. "Bad boys have their appeal." She laughed again and said, "Anyway, he was always at parties. I think I might have played tennis with him—mixed doubles." She hesitated and asked, "Are you going to want to know everyone I may have dated twenty years ago?"

"Did you date him?"

"You *are* going to want to know everyone I date a lifetime ago?"

A phone silence was followed by Drayton saying, "I didn't know you played tennis." He wondered if his knee would hold him up for a little mixed singles.

"I don't," Ellie said. "Not anymore. I seem to suffer from a kind of physical dyslexia."

"How long has it been since you last saw this Les Tremain?" Drayton asked.

"God," Ellie answered, "years and years."

"Maybe nineteen years?" Drayton asked.

Ellie paused and then said, "Right. A lifetime ago." Drayton laughed and said, "Figures, doesn't it?"

When Ellie didn't say anything, Drayton said, "Let's get together for a cup of coffee this afternoon, and I'll let you know what's going on."

"I don't drink coffee. But tea would be great." She paused and asked, "Do you have anything else on the car?"

"Photos," Drayton said.

"Photos?"

"Right. A couple of revealing photos of a black-haired woman with a dark tan and nothing else."

"*Revealing?*"

"As in naked," Drayton said.

"Oh! Porno?"

"Some might say yes, some might no," Drayton answered, then added, "but some say yes to any painting or photo of a naked woman."

She laughed and asked, "Where for the coffee and tea?"

Drayton laughed and said, "How about at Human Grounds at

three?"

"O.K.," she said.

"Good," Drayton said, and then added, "By the way did you tell anybody about my picking up that car yesterday?"

After a pause, Ellie said, "I told a girlfriend on the phone. Nobody else. Why?"

"Nothing," Drayton said. "No problem. I'll see you at Human Grounds."

WHEN DRAYTON HAD FINISHED his lunch, he called Ben to see what he'd found on the film. Ben's answering machine came on, and Drayton hung up. A good time to take a run down to 421 Pacific Beach. Maybe Les Tremain had a different phone number or an unlisted one but was still there and was wondering what had happened to his Alfa Spider. Except that he'd never reported it stolen. Why wouldn't somebody report his car stolen? The only thing that Drayton could think of was that maybe Ben was right and Les Tremain had skipped out in a hurry—or that something had happened to him.

Drayton followed Highway 101 as it hugged the coastline that curved south through the shreds of fog that still hadn't burned away. Far out on the horizon was another fog bank waiting for the cool evening and the onshore winds before it rolled inland to cover the first ten or fifteen miles of the central coast. The ocean, the surrounding hills were beautiful, but Highway 101 was not a place to drive his X 1/9, a car meant for curving roads in the mountains and little traffic. Drayton was eager to exit. Ahead, houses on stilts hung on bluffs the color of sand, which made Drayton wonder what would happen during a record-setting rainfall. The rich were on shaky ground.

He took the Pacific Beach exit and followed the curving road as it twisted its way to the top. Ahead was a pink stucco house completely on stilts. A driveway from the street spanned the stilts to a parking space in front of the garage. Drayton checked the number and pulled into the driveway.

When Drayton stepped out of his car, the air seemed thin and the sunlight brilliant and unfiltered. His knock on the door was answered by a woman close to Drayton's age. She wore a long, flowered, loose-fitting dress and a San Francisco Giants baseball cap. It was obvious that she had no hair under the cap. Her face was white and drawn, but although she looked tired and was obviously ill, her eyes were bright, blue and bright, as if something good was definitely going to happen.

"Afternoon," Drayton said. "My name is Drayton, and I'm looking for Les Tremain. This is the last address I have on him."

Her blue and hopeful blue eyes widened, but she said, "There's no Les Tremain at this address." She offered no more.

"But you do know him?" Drayton asked.

"Who are you?"

"Like I said, my name is Drayton."

"But why are you looking for him?"

"So you do know him?"

"Does he owe you money or something?"

Drayton shook his head, "No, I found his car abandoned in the woods on Cold Canyon Creek Road."

The woman's white face flushed, "His car? What car?"

Drayton hesitated, "May I come in?"

"What car?"

"A 1974 Alfa Romeo Spider, a red one with black leather seats."

The woman's body stiffened, and she reached out and put her hand against the doorjamb as a support.

"Are you all right?" Drayton asked.

She didn't answer, but made a motion inviting Drayton in as she turned to walk slowly into the house. She seemed without energy. Drayton followed her into the living room, which had windows on the two sides staring at the ocean. To the north and south, the coastline was edged by Highway 101 and motels and subdivisions. Many of the houses were in what was supposed to be a Mexican style of stuccoed walls and tile roofs, but they all looked as if they'd been completed the day before and nobody had ever lived in them. Houses too nice, too tidy, to let in people. Straight ahead was the blue-green of the ocean, looking like slate, frozen by the distance, and wisps of fog hung around the beaches and grew more dense farther out at sea. To the south, the coastline curved toward the ocean, and sand dunes imitated the rise and fall of the ocean waves.

The woman in the baseball cap motioned for Drayton to sit down. He sat on a white leather sofa in a room of whiteness—white walls, white furniture, and two large abstract paintings done in white with the faintest of blue streaks. The only other color in the room was a vase of dark red velvet roses.

The woman sat in a chair opposite Drayton. The chair was a white wingback. She seemed to be catching her breath and trying to regain her strength. She reached up to check her baseball cap and settled back. "Mister,..." she began and trailed off.

"Drayton," he said, "just call me Drayton."

The woman almost smiled. "Les Tremain," she said, her voice hoarse and thin, "is my brother. My maiden name was Marian Tremain. I'm divorced, but I kept my husband's name. I'm Marian Mosher."

"Does your brother live here with you?" Drayton asked, even though he thought he knew the answer.

Marian Mosher shook her head, "No, but this is his house. It stood empty for many years, and then I moved in after my divorce."

Drayton nodded, "I see, but where's your brother?"

Marian shook her head and smiled. Tears filled her eyes, and she shook her head again. "Les disappeared in 1981."

"Disappeared?"

She nodded, "This is the first I've heard anything of him in a very long time."

Light glinted off the ocean, filled the white room, and made it seem to expand. "I'm sorry," Drayton said. He shrugged, "I found his Alfa. I wanted to take it for the parts. I checked at the DMV, and they told me to try to find the owner. And here I am."

"Where was the car?"

Drayton told her and she thought about that before she said, "No one has seen that car since the day Les disappeared."

Drayton nodded, "The license plate was still on the car, and when I gave the numbers to the DMV, they gave me his name and this address. I tried the phone number, and when that didn't work, I decided to drive down here." He shrugged and smiled, "When I get interested in something, I can't let it go."

Marian Mosher started to cry, and Drayton hesitated. Tears ran down her face and she managed to say, "He's been gone nineteen years and now his car shows up." She brought her hands to face and shook her head.

Drayton grimaced. He'd waded into something deeper than he wanted. It was like swimming in the ocean, everything is fine, and then you're in a rip tide, which starts to take you out to sea. Swim toward the beach all you want, but it would still take you out to sea.

Marian wiped her eyes, stood, and walked over to a desk in the corner of the room. She picked up a framed photograph and walked back to Drayton. "This is Les," she said. "He disappeared on July 5, 1981. That was the last time anybody saw him."

Drayton looked at the photograph of a young man about thirty years old, which meant that now he'd be about the same age as Drayton. His dark hair, which had receded, was pulled back into a ponytail. He grinned at the camera with an easy smile. Dressed in a dark polo shirt and white tennis shorts, he held his racquet where his arms crossed in front of him, and from the way he held it, Drayton knew that he was a decent player. Maybe he and Tremain had played tennis together back then before Drayton's knee blew up, but he didn't recognize him. Tremain looked confident, but not cocky. Drayton thought of the dark- haired woman with the deep tan in the photos; she could be the kind of woman who might be attracted to someone like Tremain whether it was wise or not, and she would have been close to his age.

Drayton looked up to Marian Mosher, "What about the police? What did they do?"

Marian returned to her chair and put the photograph on the table beside her. Les Tremain seemed to be looking at Drayton. She shrugged, "They looked for him." She shook her head. "They think he just ran away." She hesitated and took a ragged breath. "Les had all sorts of trouble, so the police think he just ran away." She looked directly at Drayton. Her jaw was set, "I told them Les would never do that to me, that he'd never leave without telling me, that we were too close and he'd know how I'd worry." She straightened in her chair. "Even if he was in trouble and had to leave, he'd have contacted me later. He'd have let me know that he was all right."

The photograph of Les Tremain stared at Drayton, who asked, "But the police did look?"

"Surely. Yes," she said, "but they didn't spend any time on it. They thought he'd run away. And they didn't like him."

"Didn't like him?"

"No," she shook her head. "He wasn't their kind of man, so they didn't like him."

"*Their* kind of man?"

She looked angry. "He's a painter, a sculptor. These paintings are his." She pointed to the two large oil paintings of white and blue that Drayton had already noticed.

Drayton looked at the paintings and smiled, then asked, "Was he also a photographer?"

"Yes," she said, excited, but then she paused, "How do you know that? I don't think he sold or hung any photographs."

"In the car," Drayton said. "From photographs in the car."

Marian looked at him, as if waiting for him to finish. "Two photographs," Drayton said. "Both of a woman."

"What woman?"

"I don't know," Drayton said. "A woman with very dark hair, cut short, and with a deep tan."

"Nudes?" Marian asked. Drayton nodded.

"That was one of the things that some of the locals didn't like. He did a lot of photographs of women from the area. There were some nasty rumors: husbands, brothers, boyfriends, all misunderstandings, not understanding that these photos were art."

Drayton didn't say anything. He thought about the two photographs that Ben had found in the car. Art maybe, but if that had been his wife or his girlfriend, he might not have thought of art first.

"Les is a free spirit," Marian said. "He lived his life the way he wanted to." Her eyes drifted away and the room fell quiet—nothing but brilliant light and quiet for a long time, until she asked, "Have you notified the police?"

Drayton shook his head, "I had no way of knowing this was a police matter. All I knew was that I'd found an abandoned car."

"So why did you care whose car it was?" She seemed suspicious now. "Why didn't you just take the car?" Behind her in the blue sky rimming the slate ocean, a single-engine plane moved slowly north. The sound didn't reach him.

Everything in that world on the other side of the glass was silent.

"If you take a car to the salvage people, you have to have a title on it. The police want to keep track of as many cars as they can. Besides, it's somebody else's car, not mine."

"Couldn't you just say you found it?"

Before Drayton could respond, she asked, "Was there anything of Les's in the car? Wasn't there something with his name on it?"

"No," Drayton said. "Just those photographs. No registration, nothing personal."

She looked away from Drayton. The bright sunlight reflected off the tears in her eyes. Her voice flat, disinterested, she said, "He's dead, isn't he? I've always known, but I didn't want to admit it to myself." She grimaced and lowered her head. "I always thought that someday I'd get a phone call, and it would be him, and he'd say, 'Hey Sis, I've been down in Mexico. Sorry I haven't kept in touch.'" She shook her head. "But he'd never do that. He'd never go away and not let me know that he was O.K. He'd never do that. He's crazy in some ways, I guess, but he always cared about people, always cared about people he loved." She shook her head. "I guess maybe he loved too many people." Her eyes welled with tears again. "But now with the car found, abandoned, I don't know. God, I don't know what to think."

Drayton was beginning to wish that he'd never found the car. His guess was that she was right—that her brother was dead. Drayton asked himself why he couldn't have just taken the goddamned car, pulled off what he wanted and used a sawz-all to cut up the rest and throw it piece-by-piece into the trash? No, he had to do it the right way. "Obsessive," Bonnie would say. "Have to do it the *right* way. Can't let well enough alone." Now he'd brought all this back to a sick woman, a woman who looked like she could be dying.

"Maybe the police will be able to follow up, now that the car has been found."

"They don't care," Marian said. "They don't follow up on anything."

"How do you mean? What didn't they follow up on? Something specific?"

"Yes," she said. "I told them about a man named Frank Hollis." She shook her head. "Les came by one day." Her eyes were swollen with tears. "His face was a mess. He'd been beaten up."

"What did he say?" Drayton asked.

"He said this man, this Frank Hollis, came by his house. A man he knew." She licked her lips. "I think Les had gotten drugs from him." She stiffened as if she didn't want to believe her brother had anything to do with a drug dealer. "When Les came by that day his face was bad. His eyes were blackened, the whites were red, and his nose was swollen, with tape across the bridge of his nose."

Drayton nodded. "This Frank Hollis had attacked him?"

She nodded and caught her breath. "Yes, he warned Les, told him to stay away from some man's wife or girlfriend or something."

"Whose wife or girlfriend?"

Marian Mosher shook her head. "Les wouldn't say, but he said that this Hollis man warned him there could be worse trouble."

"Did your brother go to the police?"

She shook her head, "No, Les was afraid to do that."

She shook her head again and started crying. Her voice was harsh. "Les said he was going to get a gun."

Drayton sat up straight. "A gun? What kind of gun?"

Marian shook her head. "I don't know. Les doesn't know anything about guns." She spread her hands and said, "Our father had all sorts of guns and tried to get Les to go hunting, but Les wouldn't have anything to do with it." She sighed. "Les was an artist, not a killer."

"Did Les tell you any more about this Hollis?" Drayton asked.

"Nothing more."

Drayton nodded and asked, "How long was all of this before your brother dropped out of sight?"

Marian Mosher was crying now. She took a handkerchief from her pocket and wiped her eyes. She calmed herself, shook her head, and said, "I don't know. At least a year."

Drayton leaned back in his chair, and in an even voice asked, "And you told the police all of this when your brother disappeared?"

She nodded. "Yes. Probably about six weeks after Les disappeared, I went to the police and reported him missing. Over the next few days, I told them everything, but they didn't seem very interested and kept suggesting that maybe he'd just left town. They did talk to some people, and I think they found out he was an artist and lived a life of freedom, and they just didn't care anymore—they thought he'd just left town." She paused, angry. "I'll bet if he was a banker or one of the big businessmen in town, they would have done something."

Drayton nodded. "Any other *specific* thing the police didn't follow up on?"

"Yes," she said, her chin set. She seemed to be defending herself. "One night, a couple of months after Les disappeared, a woman called, a woman with a Mexican accent." She nodded, "She was drunk or something." She looked at Drayton. "She said that if I wanted to know what happened to my brother I should ask a man named Louis Marchand. She was crying."

Drayton started. "Louis Marchand?" he said. "I know him—an old guy—a screenwriter."

Marian Mosher nodded. "Yes, a famous *personage* in our community, the police said." She looked at him, her jaw tense. "*Personage* is my word, but it's what they'd say if they knew the word."

Drayton had known Marchand years earlier. When Drayton had first come to the English department, Marchand was already on the faculty and was generally disliked because he treated everyone as his inferior, and because he seemed to see no barriers when it came to women students. He'd never violated the campus rule which said a faculty member couldn't have any kind of romantic entanglement with a student while the student was in his class. Marchand thought the rule was stupid and referred to the campus administration as "the love police." And he made no bones about seeing a student after the semester ended. By the time Drayton started to play tennis with him, Marchand had sold a couple of screenplays and left the department.

Drayton looked at Marian and asked, "What did the police do?"

"Nothing," she said.

"Nothing?" Drayton asked. "What did they say when you told them?"

She shook her head, "They said they'd gotten the phone call too, and that it was probably a local crazy woman who Marchand had had an affair with ten years earlier. They said she called them every six months with a complaint about Marchand."

"What woman?"

Marian shook her head. "They never said her name."

Drayton nodded. He could imagine someone like that in the trail Marchand had left. One of the reasons Drayton and Marchand had stopped being friends was because of an argument the two of them had had about a student. The student, Gloria, had had three classes from Drayton and had sat crying a number of times in his office. Although she was bright and articulate, she was a psychological mess because of a domineering and relentlessly critical father. Drayton thought that Marchand had treated her no better, had made her even more of a mess. Drayton had confronted Marchand about it. Marchand had listened politely, but what Drayton said seemed to have no effect on him. Later, when Drayton had been charged with harassment, Marchand had left a message on Drayton's phone which said, "Michael, as you see, what people say about other people is not always true. However, no matter what the case, if you want, I'll set you up with my lawyer who will set you free." He'd hesitated for effect and added, "Will set you free with a pile of money from the university." Again, he'd hesitated, his voice changed, and he said, "Don't let those bourgeois bumpkins get the better of you."

Drayton had responded with a short message: "Apples and oranges."

DRAYTON PULLED HIMSELF AWAY from the memory of Marchand and brought himself back to Marian Mosher. "Maybe now," he said to Marian, "with the car showing up, the police will begin their investigation again."

Marian shook her head, "No, they won't care. It's been too long. Almost twenty years. Nobody cares anymore. I doubt if anyone at the police station even knows about it, it's been so long." She wiped her eyes and looked at Drayton, "If you don't find something, nobody will. It'll just be forgotten again."

Drayton stiffened. He knew he'd never leave it alone, but.... He took a deep breath and tried to shift the ground. "When you said that the police didn't like the way your brother lived his life, what did you mean?"

She sighed, "Les was no saint. He's a real free spirit."

Drayton noted how she spoke of her brother in the past tense and then in the present tense. Nodding, he said, "Meaning?"

"As I said," she said, "women. He loves women. I don't mean in just a sexual way. He always said that people had it upside down, that women, not men, should be running the world."

Drayton waited, but she didn't go on. He said, "Loving women wouldn't make the police dislike him."

She shrugged. "There were lots of women. Some young, some not so young, some single, some married." She looked directly at Drayton, "Some were the wives or daughters of men who didn't appreciate the way Les lived. Well, obviously, I guess they had good reason to blame him, but not to hurt him." Her face took on two or three masks in rapid succession, until she found the mask of disapproval. She took a long and deep sigh, "I resented the degree to which those women took Les from his art. They were terrible distractions."

Drayton tried to bring her closer to reality, "Were there other distractions—like drugs?"

Putting on her passive mask, she looked at him, and in a flat voice, said, "There was some of that."

"Some?"

"Les likes to explore the world. He likes to try everything. He thought the limits society puts on us were ridiculous." She seemed very proud of her renegade brother. "He called them, 'mind-forged manacles.'" She began to cough and couldn't seem to stop. The coughs racked her, but finally subsided. "I don't know where he got that."

"Got what?" Drayton asked.

"That phrase," she said. "Mind-forged manacles."

Drayton smiled, "Blake. That line of poetry is from William Blake. From his poem 'London.'"

Her eyebrows raised, as if her opinion of Drayton had improved.

"I used to be an English teacher," Drayton explained.

Her eyes were wet from her coughing. "Les always said that society had no right to tell him what to ingest." She laughed. "He thought the limits of marriage were ridiculous."

Drayton smiled, "I can see how that might get him in trouble."

"He said that he'd never signed a contract with anyone."

"A contract?"

"Yes," she said, gesturing, "His words, those are. That he'd never signed any kind of social contract agreeing that he'd live as society demanded. He said that society just assumed that he would agree, and there were times when he definitely didn't agree." She nodded. "I heard him say that many times."

Marian sat up straight, her face stern, her lips tight, and she began to cough again. This time the coughing lasted even longer, until she drank from a glass of water next to the photograph of her brother on the table. When she finally stopped coughing, she said, "I have to rest in a moment. I'll have to rest soon."

Never before had Drayton seen anyone look so exhausted, as if she might collapse right there in front of him. He felt bad because he'd pushed her to this with his damned snooping. He stood up, "I'd better be going, let you get some rest, see what I can find."

She used her arms to help her legs lift her from the chair. She swayed, stiffened up, and said, "You have to see his work. He was a wonderful artist."

Drayton nodded, "I'd like to sometime."

"Now," she almost demanded. "Why not now? Much of it is downstairs." Her hands were trembling.

"Downstairs?"

"Yes, of course," she said, her voice elevated. "Everything had to be moved out of his studio when he disappeared. There was room here. This was the logical place to keep it, and I wanted to keep it for him so that when he came back he'd have it."

"I don't want to tire you," Drayton said.

Her hands no longer trembling, Marian shook her head, "No. Not at all. You've caught me on a good day. Tomorrow's my next chemo, so I'm at my best today. We don't know if I'll feel this good again. Please."

Drayton knew that he couldn't refuse now, so when Marian Mosher, at the top of the stairs, flicked on a light switch and started down, he was right behind her. She gripped the handrail for support, taking each step with care, and hesitating every few steps, until Drayton began to wonder what he'd do if she couldn't make it back up the stairs. Carry her up? She was thin enough, just skin, a light layer of weakened muscle, and bone, so he followed her downstairs.

Chapter 6

The downstairs consisted of two large rooms with floors of oak and with no furniture except for another long white leather sofa facing west. Heavy curtains allowed only slivers of sunlight through the glass walls which gave a view of the ocean. The indirect lighting was perfect for examining the art objects. On the wall alongside of each work was a white plaque with black lettering that gave the title of the work, Les Tremain's name, and the date of completion. Drayton felt as if he had just entered a museum consisting of only the works of Les Tremain: The Les Tremain Gallery. He estimated that on the walls of the two rooms were thirty or forty paintings in oil or acrylic, and although the paintings were on diversely dramatic subjects, it was clear that they'd been done by the same person. Many of the paintings were either single portraits or scenes with a group of people, sometimes in a landscape but more often, inside of rooms. Human figures were in all of the paintings, and although they were rendered in geometric forms—planes—rectangles—trapezoids—they always remained recognizable as human beings. The foreground colors were bright and vivid, the whole effect being one of a tensely simplified reality—or what Tremain must have seen as reality.

Marian Mosher said, "He never really gave himself over to the abstract." Drayton nodded and she continued to comment on her brother's work, but Drayton heard only bits and pieces of what she said. Tremain's art wouldn't be easily translated into language—not easily translated into words—and even then his work wasn't something that would gain much from analysis. Drayton could imagine some of his colleagues at the university trying to analyze Tremain's work—putting him in schools and categories and boxes and subdivisions.

Marian had paused and stood coughing, coughing so violently Drayton thought that she would bring up blood or faint. Her face was suffused with blood, her eyes were watering, and her hand was at her chest as if to hold off the pain.

Drayton suggested, "Maybe we should stop; I should come back another time."

Marian held up her hand to stop him, and finally was able to end her coughing and say, "It's all right. I'm doing a little better now, and I want you to see my brother's art. I want you to have some sense of who he was." She gathered herself. "I feel as if perhaps you're my last hope to find out what became of him."

She took a deep breath. "I'm afraid of what you might find, but I want to know. I can't just let him vanish. He is—or was—an artist with some talent, and I want that to be recognized."

Drayton was convinced by her, and he did want to see more of Tremain's work. He thought she was probably right: something had been cut short, and he, Drayton, had come a long way from that abandoned rosso Alfa he'd found in the woods only a short time ago. He stopped in front of an oil painting that he estimated to be six feet tall and four feet wide. The plate next to the painting read, "Supper," and a family of four sat a dinner table, a perfectly respectable family, an upper middle class American family that Norman Rockwell might have painted, except that something had gone wrong. The painting, done in primary colors, consisted of angles and planes, which distorted their faces and bodies in a way that Drayton had to think of as grotesque, yet through the window behind the family was a blue sky with puffy white clouds. Drayton thought about what Tremain's sister had said only moments earlier about her brother's view of marriage. Drayton stood looking at the painting and smiled because he almost expected a Buick Roadmaster to be parked at the curb.

"Les didn't like to be labeled," Marian said, "but people who knew his work said that he was an expressionist." She coughed, caught her breath, and went on. "An artist he thought was wonderful was Max Beckmann, who the Nazis ran out of the country in the late 1930's." She laughed, "Maybe that's what has happened to Les: he's been run out of the county by the local Nazis who disapprove of the naked human body." She flushed with anger, then paid the price for her anger as she began to cough, at one point putting her hand on his arm as if she needed help standing.

Drayton looked at her, and she smiled, her lips curving but her eyes flat and without vitality. She turned slightly and focused on the next painting. Drayton followed the line of her eyes to a painting of young woman who wore no clothes and whose skin was a translucent white, the white of alabaster. Drayton thought of one of the spirits in Homer's underworld. The woman stood beneath the branches of a tree that were a blackened green, and her arms reached up to the lower branches, her breasts stretched and flattened to triangles similar to the triangle of her face. Drayton thought he recognized her, at least the dark hair and eyes, and he looked quickly back to the painting called "The Supper," and saw that it was the same woman, or what appeared to be the same woman, except that when he looked closely he saw that he was wrong: It wasn't the same woman but a different woman seen in the same way. As he stared at "The Supper" a second time, he perceived that, of the four faces of the family members, only her face registered anything close to sympathy or love.

The third painting was titled "Self-Portrait," and was of a lone figure with a trapezoidal rendering of Tremain's face and head. The figure wore the clothes of a court jester, and his face had been painted in variously colored planes that made him look ridiculous, but tragic and dangerous.

In the open spaces of the room were four sculptures of human figures, but again figures of geometric shapes of sharp and dark angles. Three of the sculptures were of women, their postures turned and twisted, as if they were struggling to resist something or escape something. The fourth sculpture was of a man and a woman who clung to each other, their bodies at such an angle that they looked as if in the next second they would fall into space.

Tremain was a spoiled romantic, Drayton thought. A man who could see the possibility of human development and was dismayed at what humans had done. Drayton thought of the poet Shelley, who in the nineteenth century had once hoped for something like the perfectibility of man, and had finally sailed into the teeth of a storm on the Mediterranean Sea. Had Les Tremain sailed into a storm, or had he simply sailed south of the border? Or had someone scuttled his ship?

One thing that Drayton felt now was that Tremain was not some phony who behaved as an artist but created little or no art. You might like or hate his work, but Tremain had worked. He'd worked like hell. If that kind of talent and that kind of work structured your life, how many of society's rules would you embrace?

Drayton turned to Marian and said, "Your brother's work is wonderful. No wonder you're so proud of him and what he did."

She put her hand on Drayton's arm, her face softened, but it was a face etched by exhaustion and pain. "Mrs. Mosher," Drayton said, "none of his photographs are here. Why is that? Where are they?"

Marian Mosher shook her head. "Les didn't want to make his photographs public, didn't want the critics *gawking* at them, because they were just for him." She hesitated and took a deep breath. "And besides, if I hung them, there would be no room for anything else. He must have matted a hundred of them."

"Where are they?" Drayton asked, wanting to see who else Tremain had photographed, wanting to see which women had angered their husbands or boyfriends.

She pointed to a door at the north end of the two rooms and said, "They're in the storeroom. I have boxes of them. Would you like to look at them too?"

Drayton nodded. "I would because maybe they'd help me try to find out what happened to your brother."

She brightened and started to speak, but then she hesitated, growing even more pale, as white as the alabaster woman in Tremain's painting, and she tottered as if she might fall. Drayton stepped toward her and she reached out and grabbed his arm to steady herself. After a minute, she sat on the white sofa. Drayton asked her if he could get her anything, but she shook her head. Finally, she looked up at him and smiled, "I think we can go on now."

"Maybe we shouldn't," Drayton said. "Another time. You should lie down."

She shook her head, but after a few seconds of hesitation, she nodded. "I'm not sure I can find them now. I'm confused." She put her hand to her eyes, "I'm so confused. Oh, damn it."

"Another day," Drayton said. "I'll go now and let you rest. You find them when you feel stronger, and I'll come back. Just telephone me."

Again she tried to protest, but not even her love of her brother could push her body another step. Finally, her head came up. "I'm not feeling as well as I did earlier. I probably should rest." A wan smile touched her lips and her eyes glittered.   Drayton stepped toward her. She rose from the sofa, and let him take her arm and help her up the stairs. The climbing of the stairs became a journey, but at the top of the stairs, she insisted that she walk him to the front door, and once there, she stood with her hand against the jamb, as if she hoped the posture might be mistaken for a kind of elegance rather than simply support. "Please," she said. "Give me your phone number so that I can call you when I find the photographs." She pointed to a table next to the door. Beside the phone on the table lay a pad and ball point. Drayton wrote his name and number.

At the open door she said, "I should inform you that I've offered a $10,000 reward to anyone who brings evidence that leads to the whereabouts of my brother. Please remember, if you find anything, please call me at once. I won't be very strong for the next three or four days, but please call anyway, please let me know. I have to know what happened to Les. I'll call you as soon as I find the photographs and feel better." She closed the door, and Drayton turned back to the outside world, where his eyes were dazzled by the brilliant sunlight filtered but magnified through a thin layer of fog which was only to the east. The wind had picked up and the air was warmer.

Chapter 7

Drayton was early at the coffee shop where he was to meet Ellie. At mid-afternoon, only a few customers sat at tables, sipping coffee or reading. In the background, B.B. King was wailing the blues, which seemed out of place now that the fog had completely burned away and the sky was bright with sunshine. Drayton kept looking out the window for Ellie, but his mind wouldn't let go of the disappearance of Les Tremain. At first, his interest had been mild, and it had been because of the car, but now he was caught up in it. Tremain's art work had moved him—impressed him in some ways. He hadn't expected it. Maybe Tremain didn't have the kind of morals that society demanded, but sometimes society had to give a little—especially in the face of such talent. He thought of Linda Loman's line in *Death of a Salesman*: "Attention must be paid." Somebody had to pay attention to what had happened to Les Tremain. As Marian Mosher had said: if Tremain had been a rich real estate agent or a lawyer, the police and the town would have been all over it. Because "society" didn't approve of his personal behavior and attitudes, he could be ignored. No wonder Van Gogh had cut off his ear. Drayton smiled to himself: on this he was right with Tremain.

Twenty years is a long time, but not enough, if he should rattle the wrong cage. If someone had killed Les Tremain, it could be someone still in town, it could be someone Drayton passed every day on the street, or someone he knew. That would account for the phone call he'd gotten in the middle of the night. Maybe somebody had thought about that car every day for the last twenty years. Drayton scrutinized the other three customers in the coffee shop, but they didn't look as if they could kill time. How about the guy who made the coffee—the guy with tattoos covering his arms and crawling out from the collar of his shirt to snake up the back of his neck? Except, and Drayton smiled at himself, that guy still had his baby fat and would have to have been only five or ten years old when he killed Tremain. Drayton sipped his coffee. No need to get carried away. Les Tremain was an artist, clearly a man who put his art above everything, a man who probably could have simply slipped away. His sister could be wrong; maybe Tremain could leave without a word to her. She'd want to believe that he wouldn't do that, but she could be wrong. Maybe Tremain was somewhere down in Latin America, drawing and photographing dark-skinned women with black hair. Drayton thought of the Louise Brooks in the photographs Ben had found in the car. Drayton took the photographs out of his pocket and looked at them. She *was* fetching.

Through the large windows of the coffee shop, Drayton saw Ellie crossing the street. She wasn't hurrying. Drayton didn't look at his watch. He'd learned not to do that. Against the glaring sunshine and building heat, Ellie wore sunglasses, a sleeveless blouse, shorts and sandals. Her arms were lovely, and he thought, *arms that are braceleted and white and bare, but in the lamplight, downed with light brown hair.* Remembering that line made him laugh at himself. As he'd guessed, her knees were very straight, meaning that she wasn't even slightly knocked-kneed or bow-legged, but he didn't know any lines of poetry about a woman's knees. He smiled. He did, however, know a poem about how a woman moves: *When in silks my Julia goes, then, then, methinks, how sweetly flows that liquefaction of her clothes.* As Ellie approached, he brooded on her liquefaction. She saw him looking at her and she smiled but then her eyes changed, her smile faded, and something like sadness crossed over her face. The shift in her face made something click in Drayton's head, and sadness swept over him, sadness for Les Tremain's death, because now Drayton was sure that Tremain's sister was right, her brother *was* dead. No more delight in disorder, no more liquefaction.

"What's wrong?" Ellie asked, standing next to the table and looking at his face.

"Wrong?" Drayton asked as he stood and motioned to a chair. "You don't exactly look happy to see me," she said and laughed.

"Les Tremain was on my mind," he said. "And I'm very happy to see you."

She smiled again and sat down. Drayton did the same and said, "Les Tremain was on my mind, and for some reason, it seemed clear to me that he was dead. His sister told me that she thought he was dead, and I'm afraid that she's right. It's the only thing that makes sense."

Ellie's face stiffened and she looked older. Small lines radiated from the corners of her mouth and crow's feet edged her eyes. She stared at him, and for an instant, he thought she was going to get up and leave. After a deep breath, she said, "You make me feel like someone just walked on my grave. Is that part of your technique with women?"

Drayton shrugged, "Sorry. This car business—the car and Les Tremain—have me by the throat, and I can't help but feeling that something is going on—and it's not good."

"What tells you this?"

"Intuition, I guess."

"I thought women were the ones who had intuition?"

"We all have it," Drayton said and laughed, "but women aren't afraid to admit it and use it. I've learned how, from women."

"God, you carry on," Ellie said and shook her head and stood up again. Turning, she walked to the counter where a great silver coffeemaker stood. The way she put her weight on one leg, with her hip jutted out, made her look younger, and he could imagine her younger. God, she had a wonderful butt. Back in Victorian England, Dante Gabrielle Rossetti would have called her a *stunner*, would have painted her portrait in those rich colors he used, or he might have written a poem about her, in his lush sensual language. Les Tremain would have known about Rossetti.

Although Drayton couldn't make out Ellie's words as she placed her order, he could hear the pitch and tone of her voice—the melody of it, and he sighed, thinking about all that had been started because he'd stopped by the side of the road. Ellie glanced over at him but didn't smile; it was more as if she were trying to figure out what she wanted to do with him. Young, Drayton thought, she would have been one of those women who is so attractive that it is difficult to believe that they are less than perfect. At least it would have been difficult *for him*. It was better to know her now, when time had taken away the patina of perfection. Time had humanized her.

When she had her tea, she came back, sat down, and looked across the table at him. As she poured cream into her tea, she said, "*Intuition*. What happened to make you feel like this? What's given you this *intuition*?"

Drayton sighed. He loved the way her mind clicked along. He loved smart women. He answered, "Too much imagination, I guess, too much time on my hands." He looked at his hands as if they were the guilty ones. Around the fingernails, they were battered and dark from his car work. Car work was his disguise that separated him from the academic world that he'd been a part of for too long. With his mechanic's coveralls on and wearing a cap, he could walk by one of his old colleagues and not be recognized.

Ellie eyed his hands, then reached out and touched a burn on the back of his left hand.

Her first time to touch him, and he felt the old, eternal, tingle. He looked at the burn on his hand and said, "Hot exhaust manifold."

"And carelessness," Ellie answered.

"And carelessness," he agreed.

"Are you a careless man?"

"I don't care any less than I always have. I care more."

Ellie rolled her eyes and asked, "A punster?"

"That one's a steal from John Donne," Drayton said and closed his eyes to remember. A smile crossed his lips, he looked at Ellie and recited: "inter-assured of the mind, *care less*, eyes, lips, and hands to miss."

The lines hung in the air. Ellie looked at him without saying anything for a long time. Finally, with a broad smile, she cocked her head and asked, "Are you wooing me?"

"How could I not?" he answered and drank from his coffee.

She laughed, "If you are, you certainly know where to go for help."

"Help?"

Ellie shook her head. "Forget it. Let's go back to where we were before you started stealing from John Donne."

"Where were we?" Drayton asked, smiling slightly because she was off balance.

"Puns," she said. "I'd asked you if you were a punster?"

"Ah, puns," Drayton said. "Sometimes. I drive my partner Ben nuts. I tell him it's the punishment he deserves," Drayton said, smiling, waiting.

Ellie shook her head, "*Pun*ishment. You have no shame."

"No shame, isn't that a band?"

"Do you always shift the subject so well?" she asked.

"No, but I am good at it. You don't teach for twenty years without developing some skills at directing a conversation."

Mentioning Ben had made him think of the pictures, and after a second of hesitation, he reached into his shirt pocket and pulled them out.

Ellie straightened and asked, "Are those the pictures you told me about? The ones you found in the car?"

Drayton nodded, handed them to her, and asked, "Do you know her?"

Ellie looked at them and raised her eyebrows. "God, is anybody ever that young and beautiful?" She studied them and said, "What a beautiful girl. She's luminous. She sort of looks like that silent movie actress who had hair like that."

"Louise Brooks."

Ellie smiled, "Yes, that's her name. Christ, do you know movies as well as you know literature?"

Drayton said, "They're part of literature." He touched the photograph with his forefinger. "Does she look familiar?"

Ellie's eyes clouded, she looked away as if trying to remember, and then glanced at the pictures again. Although she shook her head, she answered, "Yes, she does look familiar, but it could just be that she looks like Louise Brooks." As she stared at the pictures, Ellie's face changed, but Drayton couldn't read the changes. She looked up at him and said, "She could be very different now. We could know her here in town and not have any idea that she was the woman in the picture." She handed the photographs back to Drayton.

He glanced at the pictures, slipped them back into his pocket, drank from his coffee and shrugged. "Well, something will pop up, somebody will know her—or something." Drayton sighed. "Unless, of course, she wasn't from around here. My garage partner Ben said that with her looks she must have been trying to make it in the movies. Tremain could have met her down south. The pictures could have been taken in Griffith Park in L.A." He laughed to himself, smiled, and said to Ellie, "Well, anyway, I went to visit Les Tremain's house— or what used to be his house."

"And?"

Drayton shook his head, "Long gone. Twenty years gone. His sister lives there now."

"His sister?" Ellie asked. "Did she tell you anything?"

Drayton nodded, "She said he knew just about everybody in town. You said you knew him."

Ellie nodded, "I did know him some. He was a kind of spoiled artist. He'd always be invited to the gala parties given by the fundraisers for the arts." The corner of her mouth curled slightly, as if she were describing an adolescent. "And he almost always insulted one of the rich donors."

"Insulted them?"

"Yes," she nodded. "He played the insolent artist, and the patrons of the arts played the wounded party. A small play in which everybody had their roles."

"You sound as if you knew him pretty well."

Ellie hesitated and then shook her head. "You didn't have to know him well to know that about him."

"So you didn't know him very well?"

Ellie bristled. "Am I part of your investigation? Do you always grill people when you ask them to have coffee—tea—with you?"

"Sorry," Drayton said. "You're right. I'm obnoxious. But the visit to his house was...well. It shook me."

Ellie raised her eyebrows, "What did his sister tell you?"

"She said he'd disappeared almost twenty years ago, and the police didn't look very hard. The house is his. A nice place up on Pacific Beach." Drayton shrugged. "Too nice for me." Drayton shrugged again. "He must have been doing pretty well as an artist."

"Maybe," Ellie said, "but he also had some aces in the hole."

Drayton took a drink of his coffee. It had turned cold. On the sound system, B.B. King had given way to Eric Clapton, who was singing about cocaine. "What aces in the hole?" Drayton asked.

"He had family money, and he had *patrons*. I don't think he had a lot of either. He lived like he had a lot of both."

"Patrons?" Drayton asked.

Ellie sipped her tea and took her time before she said, "Supporters of the arts who gave him money."

"Women?"

"Mostly."

"You make him sound like a male prostitute. A gigolo." Drayton smiled and began to softly sing the song lyric, "I'm just a gigolo, everywhere I go, people know the part I'm playing."

Ellie smiled at him. "So you sing as well as quote love poems." She shook her head and went on. "It wasn't as bad as that. He'd just happen to be friendly with people, maybe draw them, or promise to draw them, and they'd happen to support him financially."

"A thin line," Drayton said.

Ellie sighed. "What else did his sister say?"

"She told me that not too long after her brother disappeared, a woman called her and told her that if she wanted to know what had happened to her brother, she should call Louis Marchand."

Ellie started and furrowed her forehead. "The old guy with that place on the hill?"

Drayton nodded.

Ellie shrugged. "He must be dead by now."

Drayton shook his head. "No, I don't think so. I would have heard."

"Do you know him?

Drayton nodded, "Used to. Used to teach with him. Used to play tennis with him."

Ellie shrugged again. "Did anything else happen at the house?"

Drayton pursed his lips and looked at the cold coffee in his cup. Eric Clapton was doing wonders on his guitar. Drayton looked at Ellie, "His sister, whose name is Marian Mosher, has cancer. She's bald and wearing a baseball cap."

Ellie closed her eyes and took a deep breath. "Does she have a theory about what happened to her brother?"

"All she's really sure of is that he disappeared twenty years ago and hasn't been heard from since."

Ellie nodded, "I remember. Everybody knew he wasn't around any more." She shrugged, "But I think most people thought he'd gone to New York to make it big in the art world."

"Then why leave his car parked—hidden, really—among the trees at your place? Why not sell it and use the cash as travelling money?"

"Maybe he had reasons to leave in a hurry."

"Maybe so," Drayton said. "But, after all is said and done, his sister thinks he's dead."

"Why?"

"Intuition, I think."

"That again."

"I think she's probably right." Drayton hesitated, shrugged, and said, "I think he's probably dead."

Ellie didn't say anything, seeming to wait for Drayton to go on.

"People don't disappear for twenty years without a trace, not unless they're dead."

Ellie shook her head. She seemed edgy, and took her time responding to Drayton. "That's not true. Some people do disappear for twenty years, even more. How about all those war protesters who went underground in the sixties and seventies?"

"They had a network."

"They also had the FBI. *looking* for them," Ellie said, her eyes flashing at him.

"Maybe Les Tremain didn't have anybody looking for him."

"Why do you say that?"

"His sister says the police didn't like him very much. They might have been happy that he was gone."

Ellie leaned back in her chair and smiled. Drayton could tell she didn't mean the smile. She asked, "Do you always talk like this when you invite a woman to coffee?"

"If at all possible," Drayton replied. "They find it fascinating. Aren't you fascinated?"

Ellie sipped from her tea and looked around the coffee shop as if she might need a witness. To Drayton she said, "Only curious." She laughed, "But you, you're fascinated."

"*You, you're fascinated,*" Drayton repeated and said, "That sounds like a Cole Porter song."

Ellie raised her eyebrows, a small smile on her face. "You're nuts."

Drayton sat quietly. Eric Clapton was still singing, when Drayton said, "Something's not right. I want to know what happened to Les Tremain."

"We're back where we started." Outside, tree branches were moving in the wind.

"And his sister is offering a $10,000 reward."

Ellie laughed, "Now I'm beginning to understand your fascination."

"Why don't we consider this discussion at dinner some night soon?"

Ellie laughed out loud, her head back, her throat beautiful. "Now that you've quoted love poems to me, sung love songs to me, and tried to fascinate me, you think I can't resist a dinner date?"

She sat smiling at him. Thin lines made parentheses at the corners of her mouth. The tip of one of her eye teeth was chipped off—a perfection imperfection. He thought about the men she may have known in her life—and how they'd cause her to see him in a way he'd never see himself. He wondered how Les Tremain saw her. Wouldn't he have been fascinated by Ellie in her early twenties?

"I'll behave," Drayton said. "I'll be more charming."

"Does that mean you won't talk about the mystery car and the disappearing artist?"

"I'll do my best."

Ellie sighed, "All right." She shook her head, "As long as you keep me up on your investigation."

Drayton nodded, "Wonderful." Then he asked, "Was Les Tremain handsome?"

"Who?" Ellie laughed, widening her eyes, and asking "Who is Les Tremain?"

Chapter 8
Friday

The Santa Ana winds had dropped during the night, and the next morning the heat was less intense. Drayton stopped by the shop to see if Ben was there with the developed roll of film, but the sliding doors of the garage were both closed, and there was no sign of Ben's yellow Lotus Seven. After spending a moment walking around Tremain's rosso Alfa, Drayton tried to imagine the artist behind the wheel, tried to see him as all those fathers, husbands, and boyfriends might have. The mere fact that Tremain drove such a car would piss some men off, men who would see the car as too showy, and men who saw the car as a magnet for women—views that Drayton didn't have much patience for. He dialed the combination to the lock on his side of the shop and slid back the garage door.

Trapped heat poured out the open door and the local feral cats scattered, startling Drayton as they always did. At first, he and Ben had thought of trapping the cats and taking them to the pound, but then Ben figured out that the cats were eating the mice and rats that might gnaw on parts of the cars, so a truce was formed, and the two men left small amounts of food for the cats. The shop was dark except for the light from the high windows across the back. Two cars were up on jackstands. One was a '53 Jaguar XK120 that Ben was working on, its body off and hanging by cables from the rafters, its chassis under a cover. On Drayton's side was a FIAT Dino, its body stripped of paint, the bare steel reflecting light from the windows. Ben leaned toward working on English cars, and Drayton favored the Italian models. Each worked on only one or two cars at a time, restoration often taking more than a year, because for both of them, restoration work was as much an art form as it was a business. Each of them was supplementing his primary income, but as slow as they were, they had a waiting list.

Drayton went to the phone that was screwed to one of the redwood pillars. He dialed Ben's number, and Ben's wife answered. She explained that Ben had had to make a run to L.A. because his eighty-four-year-old widowed father had escaped his nursing home and been arrested while driving the wrong way on the Harbor freeway. There were no fatalities, but Ben wouldn't be back for a couple days.

DRAYTON CLOSED THE SHOP, drove to the police station, and found a parking spot a couple of blocks away. He didn't know whether anyone would be willing to tell him anything, but it was worth a try. The woman at the reception desk had long pearlescent nails like the Latina at the DMV, and Drayton waited patiently until she had stopped tapping at the keys on her computer. When he told her what he wanted, she nodded to herself, said nothing to Drayton, and made a phone call.

After Drayton had waited ten minutes, a man in his late forties came from the back of the station and introduced himself as Detective Madsen. Madsen wore a short-sleeved white shirt and a tie, both of which looked as if they were too tight for him. His face was thin, contrasting with his glasses, which were so thick that they tended to magnify his eyes. Drayton's first take on the man was that he could have easily passed as one of the professors in the English Department.

In Madsen's office, Drayton repeated what he'd told the desk clerk. Madsen sat at his desk, cleaning his glasses as Drayton talked. When Drayton was done, Madsen rubbed his eyes, which seemed deep in his skull. "Where's the car now?"

"Over at my shop."

Madsen put on his glasses, adjusting them to his head, and then picked up a manila folder from his desk. "Have you done anything with it?"

Drayton nodded, "My partner Ben and I have started to dismantle it, but we haven't gotten very far." As Madsen watched him, Drayton felt he'd been wrong about the detective looking like somebody from the English department. His magnified eyes were all wrong. Drayton felt that Madsen was examining him and the way he moved, as much as he was listening to his words. It would probably be a mistake to ever lie to Madsen.

"How'd you get Tremain's name and address?"

"Went to the DMV."

Madsen scowled. "I didn't know they gave out that information to just anyone." The window behind him opened onto the parking lot, and a black and white patrol car rolled into a parking space.

"They gave it to me."

Madsen cocked his head to the side. "What did you do with that?" He seemed as if he might be thinking about something else, some other police work, or something else entirely different.

"I tried to phone him, but there was no listing. I went down to his house on the bluffs." Drayton shook his head. "He wasn't there, but his sister was."

"Marian?" Madsen asked.

"You know her?"

Madsen nodded. "I used to date her in high school. Les was just a pain in the ass then." He smiled and shook his head. "Her daddy didn't like me."

"So you know all about Tremain's disappearance?"

Madsen shrugged. "When he took off, I was still a uniformed officer. Everybody knew something about it. Old Sam Hawkins was the detective on the case. He's retired now. He was close to retirement when Tremain disappeared."

"What happened?" Drayton asked.

Madsen fingered the folder on his desk. It held two or three sheets at the most. "Not a lot happened really. Tremain was an ass bandit. He'd chase anything in a skirt." Madsen chuckled. "And I think he usually caught them." He shook his head. "I don't know what they saw in him. Good looking, I guess." Madsen sighed, "Trouble in some ways. A pain in the ass, at least."

"How so?" Drayton asked. Madsen was a talker, seemed to Drayton to be a guy who liked playing the detective. Maybe the thing to do was keep quiet and let him talk.

"Like I said, he was an ass bandit. I think he tried to stick it to every woman in town." Madsen shook his head and took off his glasses again. "Some of them had husbands or brothers or boyfriends who didn't like it. A couple of those guys went after him."

"After him?"

Madsen held up his glasses to the light and said, "Nothing real serious. You know, they'd take a poke at him or something."

"Fight?"

"No, not really," Madsen said and shook his head. "Tremain was a lover, not a fighter." He put his glasses on again.

Drayton waited, but Madsen shrugged and asked, "What else did you find in the car?"

"Not much, really." Drayton asked himself why he was holding back. He added, "A couple of shotgun shells."

Madsen raised his eyebrows, "Shotgun shells? In Tremain's car? That's funny. I'd bet the farm that Tremain never hunted a day in his life."

"Maybe it was to protect him from one of those angry boyfriends or husbands."

Madsen stared at Drayton. "Did you find a shotgun?" Drayton shook his head.

"Well, the shells wouldn't do him a lot of good, then, would they? Unless he was going to throw them at somebody."

Drayton nodded. Two uniformed cops had stopped to talk outside the window behind Madsen's head.

"What else?" Madsen asked. "What else did you find?"

"Well," Drayton said, then without hesitating, lied. "I didn't find anything else, but I did get an interesting phone call."

Madsen turned and tapped on the window behind him. The two cops looked up and walked away. Madsen turned back to Drayton and asked, "What kind of phone call?"

"A middle-of-the-night kind of phone call," Drayton answered. "A *friend*. A friend who warned me that I should strip the car and then forget about it. He also implied that sometimes it's dangerous to be around cars."

Madsen sat looking at Drayton. "Any idea who it was?"

Drayton answered, "No idea. I'd only picked the car up the day before."

Madsen sat thinking. He looked at the folder again. Then he shrugged. "You got me. If anything else like that happens, be sure to let me know."

Like what? Drayton thought. *Like when I get flattened by a car falling off jack stands? What will it take for you to be interested?* At that point, Drayton became absolutely certain that he wasn't going to tell Madsen about the photos and the roll of undeveloped film he had found. If Madsen wasn't going to offer more, the hell with him.

Drayton said, "I've got a couple questions."

Madsen smiled and said, "Sure. Shoot."

"Tremain's sister said that a man named Frank Hollis might know something about her brother's disappearance. She said that Hollis confronted her brother about some woman and beat him up. She said her brother was afraid to report it to the police. She suggested Hollis was a drug dealer."

Madsen looked in the file and laughed. "Right. Detective Hawkins questioned him." Madsen shook his head, "But no results. I could have told him that. He probably knew it before he talked to Hollis." Madsen laughed. "Frank Hollis." He eased back in his chair, a smile on his face. "Now, there's a familiar name. Marian was right, Hollis was a drug dealer, and notice that I say *was*." He leaned forward in his chair. "He was put away about fifteen years ago." He nodded, "Hollis might have helped Tremain disappear. Maybe he could do that. He'd have advice anyway." He shook his head. "But I'm guessing that Marian thinks Hollis did her brother terminal damage." He shook his head again, slowly, "No way that Hollis could do that. He was a real shithead who got hooked on drugs, and the only way he could find to pay for his habit was dealing and knocking around some painter, but kill somebody? No, he never had the balls for that."

When Drayton just nodded, Madsen asked, "What's the other one?"

"The other one?" Drayton asked.

"The other question," Madsen answered. He rubbed his eyes with his thumb and forefinger. "You said you had two."

"Right," Drayton said. "Marian Mosher also said she got a phone call from a woman—a woman she said was drunk and crying—and the woman said that if Marian wanted to know about what happened to her brother, she should talk to Louis Marchand."

Madsen looked surprised, "Louis Marchand? The guy up on top of Taylor Hill? That old guy must be ninety."

Drayton shook his head. "Well, maybe not that old, and for sure he wasn't that old when Tremain disappeared."

"Granted, but...." Madsen trailed off and opened the folder again. "O.K., Hawkins has written here that he followed up on that." Madsen hesitated, "He talked to the old guy, and he asked around." Madsen laughed. "Nothing to it. It was probably some woman who Marchand had done dirty or something. She just wanted to cause Marchand any trouble she could."

"What's her name?" Drayton asked.

Madsen looked up and closed the folder. "Hawkins says he investigated and found nothing." He dropped the folder onto his desk and shifted in his chair as if the meeting was about to end. "So that's about all there is." He closed his eyes, thinking, then said, "Why don't you leave the car alone for a while. Maybe we'll send somebody out there to check it out."

Maybe? Drayton thought. *Maybe?* He asked, "Does this change your investigation?"

Madsen pursed his lips and sighed, "Twenty years is a long time."

"His sister thinks he's dead," Drayton said.

"Dead?" Madsen asked.

"Right. Dead."

Madsen, his eyes huge behind his glasses, stared at Drayton. "Because he's never contacted her? Because she knows that he'd never be gone this long without contacting her?"

Drayton nodded.

Madsen smiled, "Did he contact her the other times?"

"The other times?" Drayton asked.

"She didn't mention those?"

Drayton shook his head.

Madsen looked at the file. "Tremain disappeared twice before. Once for—let's see—for about a month." Without looking up, he went on, "And again later for almost six months." He looked up and smiled. "She didn't tell you about those times."

Drayton shook his head. "Where was he?"

Madsen shrugged. "Nobody knows." He paused and added, "And he didn't contact his sister."

Drayton nodded.

"Maybe," Madsen said, "things got a little warm for him here. Women. Husbands. The police. It's a small town. Every time he'd turn the corner, he'd run into a ghost." Madsen shook his head. "If something had happened to him, if somebody had dug him a hole, we'd have heard something in all this time."

"Was there much of an investigation when he disappeared?"

Madsen shook his head, "No. I don't think so." He tapped the folder in front of him and then opened it flat on his desk. Drayton had been right. It only held two or three sheets of paper. Madsen looked at Drayton. "You can see that there's not much here." He turned in his chair and looked out the window, where a police car was backing out of a parking space. "If you act like a jerk, people don't get too upset if you leave town." He smiled at Drayton, "A lot of people were glad to have him out of their hair." Madsen checked his watch and stood up. "I've got to be in a meeting at City Hall in about ten minutes." He smiled. "Just hang on to the car. If nobody comes around within a week or so, forget it. The car's all yours."

Drayton stood up too. "I wonder if I could talk to the detective who handled his disappearance? Hawkins, you said his name was."

Madsen looked surprised, "Sure. Nobody can stop you if you want to. I don't know if he'll want to talk to you. He's an old guy now. In his eighties. A lot of health problems." He shook his head, "I don't know that I like the idea of you bothering the old guy. Let him have his peace."

"Could you give me his phone number or address?"

Madsen hesitated. "I would, but we can't do that. Too many people out there with grudges."

"What's his full name?" Drayton asked. Madsen had started toward the door.

Drayton turned but didn't move, waiting for Madsen to answer his question.

Madsen hesitated, closed his eyes as if he was trying to be patient, and said, "Sam. Sam Hawkins. A nice old guy who deserves to be left alone." He sighed, "You know, the police can take care of this."

Drayton nodded. Sure they could.

OUTSIDE, DRAYTON WALKED THE two blocks to his car. When he was four or five steps from it, he stopped. "Shit," he said under his breath. Someone had keyed the passenger door and the front fender. Drayton checked his temper. He walked to the car and ran his fingers along the scratch. Along the door, the scratch was really a gouge. He'd have to do some bodywork and repaint that section.

The scratch along the fender was light, and he thought he might be able to rub it out. He still had plenty of paint.

Drayton stood still and began looking around. He felt as if someone was watching him. Trying to remain calm and patient, he looked along the opposite side of the street for a block in each direction. A couple of kids with stacks of books were pushing against each other and laughing. They weren't old enough to key a car. A woman dressed in a pin-striped suit was struggling to get a box out of the trunk of her car. Keying a car would never occur to her. In the other direction, a bus had stopped, and after some passengers got off, some more went on, but nobody looked suspicious, although he wasn't sure what *suspicious* was. What was he looking for?

After a minute more of examining the keyed area, he shrugged and got into his car. Sitting there, he thought, *What are the chances that this is a coincidence? Not likely. Somebody was really pissed—or worried—about me moving that car.* Whoever had done it hadn't discouraged him but had made him that much more curious and determined. He tried to forget about the car and focus on what he'd learned from Madsen. Not much. The tie with Louis Marchand was thin. Drayton and Marchand had played tennis together, and had even gotten drunk together—laughing together about the English department. They'd talked about writers and books. Marchand said that James Joyce was the most overrated writer of the twentieth century. No way Marchand would kill anybody. He was too smart for that. He might find some way to run a person out of town, but it would all be legal. Marchand was too smart to take a chance on going to prison. Morality or ethics wouldn't stop him, but the thought of prison would.

Drayton started his car. Still, it had been a long time since he'd talked to Marchand. It would be good to see him, see how he was getting on. Drayton remembered then that someone had told him Marchand was sick. That had been six or seven months ago. Imagining Marchand sick was hard to do. Maybe he could learn something talking to the old bastard, the smart old bastard. He might see something that Drayton hadn't. It was worth a trip up Taylor Hill. Drayton turned off the key and killed the engine. The courthouse was only a couple of blocks away, and in there was a public phone he could use to call Louis Marchand to see if it was all right to pay a visit.

As he walked toward the courthouse, Drayton remembered Bonnie's reaction to Marchand: One night after a party at Marchand's house, she'd said that every time he'd looked at her, she'd felt as if he had undressed her and was starting to do things to her that she didn't like. Drayton had told her that that seemed more like her imagination than Marchand's, but she hadn't laughed. Drayton had then told her that he was trying to think what it was that she didn't like. She'd laughed this time and said that with Drayton there wasn't anything she didn't like. Drayton smiled as he pulled open one of the courthouse's massive doors. That night, they'd surprised the babysitter with an early return home. Oh, Bonnie, oh, Bonnie, he thought, and remembered some lines from Turgenev: *Moments of gladness, hours of glee, Like torrents of spring, they flee, they flee.* Get out of the past, he told himself. Call Marchand, he thought, but what a trip into the past that would be.

Chapter 9

Marchand's estate, high on the northern edge of town, was hidden at the end of a curving road that ascended until a sharp turn opened to a view of the house, the pool, and the tennis court. Marchand had added the pool and tennis court, but the house had been there for over a century, built in the New England style of white frame with a long porch that gave a view of the mountains to the north and the ocean ten miles to the west. The house had been built by Rawlings Taylor, an Easterner who had come west and married fourteen-year-old Anita Suarez, whose Mexican family owned forty-thousand acres from a Mexican land grant. Rawlings Taylor and Anita Suarez had seven children, only three of them reaching adulthood, and Rawlings Taylor became a land baron. Over the last one hundred years, the ranch had been parceled out by Taylor's descendants, and Louis Marchand had bought the house and four or five acres surrounding it from the last of the Taylor line. The place was still called Taylor Hill.

As Drayton drove up the hill, he had a sense of time lost, because nearly twenty years earlier, he'd driven up that hill almost every Sunday to play tennis with Louis Marchand and two other guests. Drayton was always Marchand's doubles partner, and Marchand picked their opponents. Drayton and Marchand had gotten to the point that each knew what the other was thinking on the tennis court, and they became a formidable doubles team. After their argument over Marchand's "friendship" with a student, and when Marchand's back completely gave out, they quit playing together. That last Sunday,

Marchand had jumped up and scissors-kicked to hit an overhead, a perfect shot—in the center of the court and deep. When Marchand came down, he'd stood, his head lowered for a long time, clearly in pain, clearly in a rage, and then he'd limped over and sat down on one of the two green canvas chairs at the side of the court. Their opponents had made some jokes about age and fragility, but Drayton walked over and put his hand on Marchand's shoulder. Marchand looked up at him, his face defiant and disdainful.

During that long string of Sundays before Marchand had injured his back, he and Drayton would have drinks after the match. Their opponents would drive down Taylor Hill, back to what Marchand only half-jokingly called the "lowlands," and, although Marchand never invited Drayton into his house, the two would sit in the deep shade of a live oak and drink gin and tonics while they discussed the match they had just won, the continuing gossip in the English Department, literature, and ultimately, they'd talk about writing. By then Marchand was only teaching part of the time; the rest of the time he was writing scripts, first at home, sometimes followed by re-writes on the set of the movie. Sitting in the shade of that live oak, they would drink until they were woozy, and woozy not only from their drinks, but from the brilliant and dazzling California sunshine that lighted and heated the range of low mountains to the north and to the east.

As Drayton drove up the curving road to Taylor Hill, the trees changed to scrub and cactus, vegetation that seemed to better fit the heat of the Santa Ana winds. The trees at the top of the hill were those planted by Rawlings Taylor and his descendents. Marchand and his first wife had divorced, and she had taken their two children to northern California, but by then the boy was a senior in high school and the girl a junior. When Marchand was in his early sixties, he had married again, but no one knew the woman. The guess was that she had come from the movie world and that Marchand had brought her north. The town buzzed because the woman was barely more than a girl, something like forty years younger than Marchand.

Drayton had seen her only once. It had been after the Sundays of tennis, and Drayton had driven up the hill to return a pile of Marchand's books. Marchand, a youthful sixty, erect, straight, with white hair combed straight back, and with that same dazzling smile, had come to meet Drayton on the front lawn. In spite of the back surgery he'd had, Marchand still walked like a young man, light on his feet and with a quickness of movement that had served him well on the tennis courts.

As they'd stood there on the lawn, a young woman came from the pool area. Still in her blue, two-piece swimsuit, she had a white towel draped over the back of her neck and the tops of her shoulders. The first thing that Drayton had thought was that she looked like a swimmer—leggy, with developed shoulders, and strong lats. Her hair, clipped short and bleached, was a combination of blonde and dark brown or black. Drayton understood why people had guessed that she was from the movie world because she was so beautiful as to bring to his mind goddesses like Helen, Aphrodite, Athena. No wonder, he'd mused, that the Greeks imagined extraordinarily beautiful women were goddesses; divinity had to be invented to account for that kind of beauty. As she'd walked by, Drayton's gaze had followed her, and Marchand turned, saw her, and turned back to Drayton and said, "Remember in Yeats when he prays that his daughter doesn't become too beautiful, because great beauty makes a woman suffer from pride?"

Drayton had looked at Marchand and said, "And also that it makes men do foolish things."

Marchand chuckled and said, "It's easy to make men do foolish things."

That was the last time that Drayton had been to the top of Taylor Hill.

HOW LONG, HE WONDERED. Fifteen years? More, he thought to himself as he followed the last curve and the house came into view, white and splendid, like something from another world. As he pulled into the drive, the water in the pool glistened and the tennis court reflected a pure white light laden with memories.

As he walked up the flagstones to the front door, it struck Drayton that he was about to enter the house for the first time. Marchand was a very private man. When Drayton knocked on the door, a barefoot woman in shorts and a gray sweatshirt two sizes too big answered the door. Her hair, cropped short, was a deep brown lightened by gray tips, and looked damp; Drayton could smell chlorine. It was Marchand's girl bride, and although close to twenty years had passed, she seemed little changed. This woman was showing some effects of time, but only barely. She had to be in her late thirties. Her eyes were an even deeper brown than her hair, and her face was lightly tanned, but her legs were dark. Drayton knew that look: a face protected from the damaging sun but legs tanned enough to hide imperfections. Drayton guessed that somewhere in her past there was Mexican or Indian blood, or both.

"Yes," she said, having guessed his question, and put out her hand, a smile on her lips, "I'm Louis's wife. I'm Andrea." They shook hands and she said, "And you're Michael Drayton, an old friend of Louis's. You just called? He told me you were coming."

Her darkness made Drayton think of the phone call that Marian Mosher had described, and he listened for an accent or even a rhythm, but couldn't hear even a trace. He said, "Glad to meet you. I heard Louis was sick."

Her facial expression shifted, and she closed the front door. "Yes. He's been sick for a long time."

"We used to play tennis years ago. As a matter of fact, I think I was his partner the last time he played." Drayton gestured toward the court. "Right here on your court."

She nodded, "Louis urged me to take lessons, and I did. Sometimes friends and I would play out here, and Louis would sit and watch." She smiled. "He'd cheer us on, and he'd coach me during side changes."

Drayton smiled, "And you probably won. Louis always likes to win."

"Of course," she said, pausing, and then added, "He's not strong since his last surgery. Please don't stay too long. He'll want to talk on and on."

Drayton nodded, "Sure. I just had a couple of things I wanted to ask him. I won't stay long."

Drayton followed Andrea toward the back of the house. The interior was like something out of Connecticut. The furniture was formal—dark cabinets, easy chairs with floral upholstery, and wooden floors covered by woolen carpets with subdued floral designs—all hidden from the sunshine by heavy curtains and drapes.

Andrea was a half step ahead of him, and he tried to reconcile her with the young woman he had seen briefly that day years earlier.

Bonnie would have said, "The bloom is off the rose." And she'd be right, he thought. Although Andrea Marchand's fluid walk and trim legs made Drayton guess that she was in good shape, she wasn't quite the goddess he'd seen coming from the pool that late afternoon so long ago. Now she was only a beautiful woman. A different person now, he thought, just as he was a different person than he'd been on those Sunday mornings when Bonnie and he were still in love and their son was a young boy. He knew he'd better prepare himself for what a different man Louis Marchand might be, now a man in his eighties—a sick man in his eighties.

The back porch contrasted with the rest of the house; only a few pieces of scattered furniture punctuated the large space—furniture in either leather and wood or in leather and stainless steel. Whereas the rest of the house was darkened by drapes over narrow windows, on the porch no drapes hindered the white sunlight blazing through the windows, windows that reached from inches above the floor to inches below the ceiling. Each window was separated from the next by no more than five or six inches of light oak. The floor was of the same light oak, free of rugs, and bright with reflected sunlight. Outside the windows, the golden hills of fall rolled on one after another until they disappeared in a sunny haze at the horizon.

Louis Marchand's steel-and-leather chair, turned away from the door, faced the mountains and hid him from sight until Drayton had almost crossed the room. Marchand didn't rise from his chair, but extended his hand. Drayton was not as shocked as he'd expected. Marchand had clearly lost weight, and his skin had a waxen cast, but his head and face seemed much the same, more wrinkled maybe, drawn maybe, but much the same. His head, which had always seemed too large for his body, looked even larger now, and his thinning white hair was combed straight back in his usual style. His eyes were the same as that day on the courts when he'd hurt himself: defiant, even disdainful. He grinned at Drayton, almost as if to say, "Tricked you, didn't I?"

When they shook hands, Drayton gripped Marchand's in both of his, and Marchand said, "You're not going to fucking hug me, are you?" He laughed, half laugh, half cough. He pointed toward a chair opposite himself, and Drayton sat down.

Marchand turned to his wife and said, "Andie, my old friend

Michael Drayton was the only member of the English Department who didn't bore me with some outrageously esoteric and specious knowledge."

"That's some accomplishment," Andrea said, and smiled at Drayton.

Louis Marchand continued, "You may not know—many people don't know—that our Michael Drayton has the same name as a very famous historical figure." Drayton shook his head, and Marchand, smiling, looked toward his wife. "The original Michael Drayton was a renowned English Renaissance writer who had the misfortune to be a poet at the same time as William Shakespeare." He laughed. "A strategical error."

Drayton nodded, "Unfortunately, I think I've inherited his skills at strategy."

Marchand closed his eyes, thinking, and said, "Nay, ye get no more of me...." He looked to Drayton for help with the lines of the poem he was trying to remember.

Drayton smiled, "'Since there's no help, come let us kiss and part; Nay, I have done, you get no more of me.'"

"Of course," Marchand said, "that's it." He turned to his wife and said, "But by the end of the poem, the poor lover makes one more try." He sighed. "As men are wont to do."

"As *people* are wont to do," Andrea said and laughed.

Marchand laughed, smiled at his wife, and then looked at Drayton. "Andrea is my best student. We were in love, she hadn't had a lot of education, she wanted to learn—and I was happy to teach her." He glanced at her. "And she's a quick study."

Andrea looked at Drayton and said, "Henry Higgins's Eliza Doolittle."

"Pygmalion's Galatea," Marchand said and laughed.

Looking at Andrea, Drayton said, "You couldn't ask for a better teacher."

"Exactly," Marchand said with a smile and a laugh. After a long hesitation, he coughed, reached to the table next to his chair, picked up his cigarette, and took a long draw. Drayton smelled it and knew that it was not from one of the major American tobacco companies. Marchand caught Drayton's eye, and extended the joint and asked, "Want a hit?"

Drayton smiled, reached out, took the joint and filled his lungs with the smoke. It had been a long time, and he wondered why he had ever left that pleasure behind. Finally, he exhaled, coughed some, and laughed.

Marchand, also laughing and coughing, said, "You know, I've ingested just about every illegal drug ever conceived of by man, and now I can use this simple weed with society's blessing. Almost." He smiled, "I knew they'd come around to my way of thinking."

Andrea Marchand stood to the side of her husband's chair, a smile on her face. When he looked up at her, she took his raised hand and held it between her hands, the way a mother might hold her son's hand, or the way a young woman might hold her father's hand. Marchand asked Drayton, "Want a gin and tonic for old times' sake?"

Drayton nodded, "For old times' sake." The drag from the joint started to affect him, and he felt calm and pleased.

"Andie," Marchand said and looked up to his wife, "would you get Drayton a gin and tonic? I know this is sexist of me, but damn, I'm incapacitated."

"I'll be back in a few minutes," she said. She looked down at her husband. "You need to take it easy."

"Oh, no, you don't," he said as he watched her leave the room. "I'm not going to take it easy at this late date."

A little grin played on Marchand's face, and he said to Drayton, "I hear through the grapevine that you and the university have parted ways."

"You hear right," Drayton said. "A misunderstanding."

"Those happen at the university, all those people with their proper values, many of them hypocrites who pay a lot of lip service to the notion of teaching students but are really more concerned with their careers."

"That's not exactly a generous view," Drayton said.

Marchand laughed. "Were they generous with you?"

Drayton shook his head. "It's a dull subject. A painful yet dull subject."

Marchand nodded. "That's true; a subject about which I can be very petty. Let's talk about other things." Smiling, he raised his hands, palms up and asked, "Well, what do you say? How the hell do I look? Tell the truth. We always told the truth to each other. You know me."

Drayton knew that Marchand was imitating himself, imitating

the man he had once been before he'd become ill, so he played along, smiled, and said, "You look like shit, Lou."

"At death's door?" Marchand asked.

Drayton smiled and nodded, "You bet."

"Like death warmed over?" Marchand asked.

Drayton nodded again. "And any other cliches you can come up with."

"I'm happy to see you can't stand bullshit any more than you could twenty years ago."

"Less," Drayton said.

Marchand nodded. "I'm glad you came up here. Otherwise, it might have been a long time before we saw one another again, because time's winged chariot is running full out and is right on my ass." Marchand took another hit off his joint and offered it to Drayton. He started to shake his head, but changed his mind and took it. What the hell, it had been a long time, and this might be his last time with Louis. He felt as if he was at Marchand's wake, but with the pleasure of the old man's company.

Marchand asked, "You haven't come here to tell me how sorry you are that I'm dying, have you? I mean, Jesus, look at me. How could anybody be sorry? You'd have to be a mean son-of-a-bitch or have your head wayyyyy up your ass to be sorry, to want me to live much longer. Remember what Yeats said: *I'm tied to this sick and dying animal*, for Christ's sake. I mean, I am out of gas. You see that beautiful woman, my wife, Andie? It's not just that I can't get it up, I can't even remember why I wanted to get it up." He laughed until tears filled his eyes.

Drayton laughed too, closed his eyes, and shook his head. He felt a buzz from the marijuana.

Marchand's voice rose. "Don't shake your head at me with that disapproving look. Not *you*, please. You know me."

Drayton nodded, "You're right. I know you." He took a long hit from the joint and handed it back to Marchand.

"It's not as if I haven't had a good run at it—life I mean," Marchand said. "I was able to write, even if it was for the movies. I live in a beautiful place. I've had a couple of magnificent wives, two of the most beautiful women I've ever seen." He paused to take a breath, and then another hit off his joint. Calmer, he said, "I've got a lot of vices, but I've never been greedy. I've gotten my fair share. It's about time to make room for somebody else."

Drayton sat waiting. The marijuana had kicked in now, and he felt as if he'd somehow stepped into one of his own dreams. A slightly surreal drift colored everything, accompanied by a kind of languidness. He thought of the old slang term *mellow. Mellow Yellow.*

Marchand's laughter brought Drayton back, and the old man was saying, "I'm lecturing, ain't I?" He staged a cough and corrected his grammar. "Am I not? All these years away from teaching, and I still do it."

"It's a hard habit to break," Drayton said. "I hear myself doing it sometimes, and I think: *this guy talking—methinks he thinks he knows something other people need to know.* That's when I quiet down." He smiled, "Somehow the world will get along without what you and I know."

"Sorry," Marchand said, "sorry for my harangue. I think the sick and dying animal took over. He's like that sometimes. He whines."

Drayton took a deep breath, "Well, you'll be happy to know that I didn't come to make my farewells to the sick and dying animal. Not primarily anyway. I'm happy that I've gotten here to say good-bye, no matter what you say, because who gives a damn what you say?" He smiled broadly and thought about the funny ways men express affection for other men, but who said it wasn't as good as the way women express affection? It was just different; everybody knew what it meant. He said to Marchand, "I didn't come here just to see you. That may be part of it. I'm glad I did, but I need to talk to you about something."

Marchand was quiet for a few seconds, and then, his voice lighter, he said, "I'm glad to hear that. If there's something you want to know, that still makes me a part of the process. I'm not dead yet, although I get treated that way a lot."

Drayton just nodded.

"What's up?" Marchand asked, increased energy in his voice, almost an exact imitation of what it had once been.

"I'd like to talk to you about Les Tremain, the artist who disappeared almost twenty years ago. I don't even know if you knew him, or you may not even remember him."

"Les Tremain," Marchand said. "Do I remember him? Christ, he could have been my son."

Andrea came back into the room and handed Drayton his drink.

Marchand said to her, "Andie, you'd better sit down. Drayton has come here about Les Tremain."

She hesitated, looked at her husband and then at Drayton before she pulled a chair closer, a steel-and-leather easy chair that slid lightly across the floor. Settling back in the chair, she gave Drayton the impression of someone struggling to be patient, and he wondered how difficult it was to care for her old and dying husband. Her face broke into a kind of recognition and she said, "You mean that freeloader artist who left town all those years ago?"

"No, Andie," her husband said, "I don't think he left town. That would be nice to think, but my guess is that he's dead. Leave town? No. He had it too good here."

Andrea Marchand's presence made Drayton uneasy. She was unsettling, even though she was in baggy shorts and an oversized sweatshirt. He felt some delight in her disorder. Still, he was bothered that he couldn't seem to get past her beauty, as if that was all there was to her. He felt that in some ways such beauty was like a disability—or like being a freak. This close, she looked as if, as Bonnie would say, she'd "had help," meaning some kind of cosmetic plastic surgery. The corners of her eyes and the corners of her mouth had no deepened wrinkles, and the skin under her eyes was smooth. Her lips were full. Her jaw line was tight. If she'd had help, it was well done, but of course, it would be. Marchand had plenty of money, and she'd have plenty when he was gone. At least twenty years with Marchand. She had probably earned it. Twenty years: there that number was again.

"You're probably right," Drayton said to Marchand. "Tremain probably is dead, but I've found out that he disappeared twice before. Once for about a month, and then again for almost six months."

"Where was he?" Marchand asked. He extended the joint, which was now more than half burned away.

Drayton took it and shook his head, "I don't know. I don't know if anybody knows."

"But what brought him up?" Andrea Marchand asked, "Why have you come here *now*?"

"I found his car," Drayton said and took a long draw off the joint. Holding it with his fingertips, he offered it to Andrea. She hesitated and then took it from him and had two quick hits before she put it in an ash tray on the table next to her.

Drayton was surprised that she'd taken it. He started over. "I found his car in some woods on Cold Canyon Creek Road. I traced it through the DMV because I wanted some parts from it, and that led me to his sister Marian." Drayton paused and looked at Marchand. "That's how I got here. She said that not too long after Tremain disappeared, a woman called her and said to ask you about where he was."

Marchand nodded. "I remember some detective coming up here and asking me about Les, but I didn't know anything then, and obviously, I don't know anything now. But why me?" Marchand asked. "Why would someone phone like that?"

"I don't know," Drayton said.

"Sally Wu," Andrea said and looked at Marchand.

Marchand closed his eyes and nodded. "Christ," he said, "that must be who it was." He sighed, "She's a woman I knew a long time ago." Marchand paused and licked his lips. "She thinks that I did her wrong." He glanced at his wife, "Andie knows all about this. But Sally Wu thinks that I got her pregnant, that her son is mine, but I know I wasn't the only one who…." Marchand paused and chose his words, "who was having an affair with her." Then he suddenly tensed, shook his head and leaned forward, his head down. Andrea put her hand on her husband's hand. She looked at Drayton and grimaced. Marchand grunted as if he'd been hit. When he sat up, he looked like he was already dead, or only minutes from it. "Son of a bitch," he said.

Suddenly, in mid-phrase, Marchand had evolved from a sick man to a dying man, and it was easy for Drayton to see just how little time he had left.

Andrea Marchand looked to Drayton again, "I'm sorry. Sometimes, Louis has some terrible pain in spite of the medicine." She looked to her husband, "Should you use your morphine pump?"

"Not yet," Marchand said, the words two short exclamations. After a few more seconds, he shook his head, "That goddamned Wu woman is going to be with me until my dying day." He laughed and said, "Literally." His face lightened as if the pain had passed, and he was able to sit erect again.

Drayton knew that he wouldn't be able to talk for long to Marchand. The old man had tricked him in that he simply seemed very ill, but it was worse than that, he was hanging on, trying to die with some dignity, which was in keeping with his nature. Drayton said, "Maybe I should come back in a couple days or so when you're feeling better." Stopping it all sounded good to Drayton—good because he was light and lazy, marveling at the rays of the sun on the hardwood floor, motes floating like tiny planets through the light. He thought of those woozy afternoons that he and Marchand had spent drinking gin and tonics under the umbrella of the live oak tree.

Andrea Marchand looked at Drayton, her eyes bright, clearly appreciating what he'd offered, but Louis laughed and said, "If you've got some questions for me, I think you better ask them now, not tomorrow and tomorrow and so forth...."

Andrea Marchand sighed, sat back in her chair, looked at Drayton, and gave a slight shrug. Her face registered fear, love, anger, and resignation, all in a second, and as he often did, Drayton marveled at what the human face could say. Still, Marchand had always done what he wanted to do, and it was clear that he wasn't going to change this late in the day.

"Well," Drayton said, "I'll make it short and let you get some rest." Marchand's head was down again when Drayton asked, "You think Tremain is dead?"

Marchand looked up. Drayton could read the pain in the old man's eyes, pain and that glimmer of vitality that was about to be quenched by time. Marchand nodded, "Think? Shit, I *know.*"

"How?" Drayton asked. "How can you be so sure?" Drayton could feel Andrea Marchand watching him.

"Because," Marchand said, "because Les Tremain and I were friends." He looked to his wife, and while still looking at her, said, "And Andie and Les were friends."

"Louis," she said. "Don't say that." She looked at Drayton, "I knew him from when he came up here to freeload and be around some people who had enough money to buy his paintings." She shook her head. "He was always with a different woman." She looked to her husband. "Some of them were no more than girls."

"Andrea," Marchand said, "you were no more than a girl when you married me." He seemed to feel better now, and a slight smile touched his lips.

"You *married* me, Louis."

"Ah," Marchand said, "my intentions were honorable?" He looked to Drayton. "Andrea believes in old fashioned fairness, fidelity, and loyalty."

"That's right, Louis, I don't believe what you believe in—nothing."

"Nada," Marchand said. "Our nada who art in nada...."

Drayton felt as if he had been dropped into an argument that had been going on between the two of them for a long time. He asked, "Did you know that Tremain was photographing a lot of women?"

"You mean the nude shots, don't you?" Marchand asked.

"Yes, not all, but some nudes," Drayton said. "But it's really the nudes that might have gotten him in trouble."

Louis nodded. "Yes, I knew about those, I even saw some of them, but I don't know why anyone would get too upset unless he had some puritanical perspective—maybe someone from the religious right." He laughed and added, "The worst sinners of all—so presumptuous that they think God speaks through them." When he'd stopped chuckling to himself, he focused, his eyes sharp and free of pain, on Drayton, "The photos I saw were well done, done with the eye of an artist."

"That's not what some women felt," Andrea said. She turned to Drayton, "He photographed a friend of mine who, when she saw the pictures, was really upset." She turned to Marchand, "And Les Tremain left them in an unsealed envelope in her mailbox where anyone might have seen them—her husband, her kids."

"She *did agree* to let him take the pictures," Marchand said, smiling.

His wife ignored him and said, "She thought what he'd done was a kind of blackmail, a blackmail to keep her around."

"Blackmail?" Drayton asked.

"Andrea is exaggerating," Marchand said and took a deep breath, "Les was a free spirit, a man who ignored the 'mind-forged manacles,' as he called them. He wasn't corrupt." He smiled and added, "It's hard not to admire defiance in the face of bullshit."

"Would you tell me who this woman is?" Drayton asked Andrea. She shook her head, "Never. Never."

"See," Marchand said, "I told you that Andie believes in loyalty."

"I will tell you," she said, looking at Drayton, "that she left town, that she convinced her husband to start a new practice in a new place." She turned to Marchand, "That was because of your friend with the free spirit." The tip of her pink tongue flicked out and licked her lips.

Marchand leaned back in his chair. He looked exhausted, but interested.

Drayton knew it was time to leave, but he had a question that he had to ask. He looked to Andrea Marchand. "Did Tremain ever want to take pictures of you?"

Marchand's head was resting against the back of the chair, his eyes closed, but at the question he lowered his head and looked at Drayton.

Andrea Marchand took a long time to answer, "Yes. He did. Right here in my husband's house. He didn't tell me what kind of photographs, but I already knew what kind he took." She hesitated. "He asked me here in the house one day, and a week or so after that he asked me down by the pool." Her voice took on an edge, "He paid me a *compliment*, or what he considered a compliment, and then he asked to photograph me." She smiled, but it was closer to a sneer, and then she did what Drayton knew was an imitation of Tremain. She lowered her voice, grinned, and said, "What would be wrong with taking off the top of your swim suit?" She stayed in character, laughed softly and in mellifluous tones added, "After all, they're just breasts. Mammary glands for babies." She shed her imitation and looked Drayton in the eye. "Bullshit like that."

"What did you say to him?" Drayton asked.

Andrea Marchand looked to her husband and said, "I told him that he was not my husband's friend."

Marchand laughed softly, but he was drained white, whiter than the white light from the sun behind him. He lowered his head slightly, seemed to curl into himself and hissed, "Shit. Shit."

Drayton stepped over to Marchand and put his hand on the dying man's shoulder. He could feel Marchand trembling. Pain? Fear? "I'm glad I came by, Louis," Drayton said. He added, "I'm sorry," even though he wasn't sure what he was sorry for.

Marchand didn't look up, but he shook his head and then nodded. In hardly more than a whisper, he said, "Please see Michael Drayton out, Andrea."

At the front door, Drayton turned to Andrea Marchand. Her cheeks were flushed and her jaw rigid. He asked her, "Do you have any idea what happened to Les Tremain? I felt in there that you had something more to say, but you didn't want to say it in front of Louis. Did anyone you know say anything?"

Her eyes were cold on Drayton. She shook her head slightly, almost imperceptibly, and then she looked down, her hand to her mouth. Her shorts were baggy, she wore no shoes, and her sweatshirt was loose, but Drayton couldn't stop himself from wondering if her body was still as beautiful as on that first day he'd seen her so long ago. He grimaced at the thought of how easy it must have been for

Louis Marchand to say the hell with the conventions of a society which told him that she was much too young for a man his age.

She looked up at Drayton, at his face, and her eyes shifted, grew distant, as if she knew what he was thinking, as if she'd been reading that look on the faces of men for years. How old would a man have to be not to look at her that way? A muscle twitched in her jaw, and she said, barely above a whisper, "Louis is dying," as if maybe Drayton had forgotten.

From the back of the house, Louis Marchand called her name. She looked at Drayton and said, "It's all so long ago." She turned, "I have to get back to Louis."

Drayton stepped outside, and she closed the door behind him. He stood on the porch and looked past the swimming pool to the town below. Being stoned in the bright sunlight was always a strange sensation, but now with the heat of another Santa Ana building, it was even stranger. Sweat was running down his back. What could he believe of what they'd said? He knew Marchand could lie without a problem, and she'd been his student, his Eliza Doolittle. Thinking about Louis and Andrea Marchand, he went back to his car and started the engine. For a moment, he sat there and stared out the window, seeing nothing. He was thinking about what Andrea Marchand had read in his face, and it wasn't pretty. As she'd said: *Louis was dying*, he'd stood there at the door thinking about her body. God, did nature never let up? He was pushing toward fifty goddamned years old, and nature still wanted him to reproduce. And he was a fairly decent man.

Chapter 10
Saturday

Drayton lived in a double-wide mobile home on twenty acres of woods off Squire Canyon Road. He'd helped a friend who had a drug problem, and the friend later gave Drayton the job of being the caretaker of the mobile home and the twenty acres, but all that being caretaker meant was that Drayton lived there. The closest house was a half-mile away. Drayton's mobile home was old and looked it, but it was comfortable enough for Drayton, his black lab, named Rupe, and his cat Ripper, shortened to Rip. Forty yards from the house was a fifty or sixty-year old outbuilding, which Drayton had fixed up to be a garage and workshop. It was the only building left by a fire that had cut through the canyon in the 1950s and burned the house to the ground. The fire skipped the outbuilding but took out almost everything around it. Nobody was home at the time, and after the fire, the family who'd lived there had given up on the place. A year or two after the fire, another couple had the mobile home towed into the spot, and the two of them lived there until the early 1980s.

Drayton moved into the place in 1995. The couple had left most of their furniture, so all Drayton had to do was bring in a bed and some kitchen supplies. When Bonnie left, she had taken their bed. Mission style, red oak, queen-size. He'd made it for them on their fifth anniversary, and he was glad she took it because he knew he didn't want to lie in it alone and thinking of when they had been together there. He wondered if the bed made Bonnie think of him when she and her new husband were making love. *You've got a fat ego*, Drayton thought to himself. When he moved into the mobile home, he bought a new bed at Sears, a cheap and sleazy wrought-iron job.

He sat on the porch he'd built on the front of the mobile home, a porch of scrap redwood which he'd never painted or stained, and which was now turning silver-gray. Drayton liked to sit out there in the mornings and drink his coffee. Each morning, when he got up at six, he'd run the two miles down to the main road and pick up his newspaper. His dog, Rupert, shortened to Rupe, would run with him. On the way back, Rupe, somewhat a hound, would range through the woods and raise hell at anything he saw or smelled. Drayton knew that he could never move back to town while Rupe was still alive because no neighbors would be able to put up with the dog's barking, yapping, and howling. But Drayton liked the sounds, and he liked letting Rupe do what came naturally. Drayton grinned to himself: Rupe and Louis Marchand seemed to have about the same moral code, except that it was easier for Rupe to get away with it. *How bad is Louis's moral code?* Drayton asked himself. *Bad enough for him to kill someone?* Drayton shook his head. Louis was a scoundrel in many ways, but he had a great respect for life. Drayton started to shake his head, but then thought, who knows what a man who is sixty might do if he finds that his wife of twenty was playing around? What about Andrea? Could she do it? Out of jealousy? Maybe Andrea and Tremain were carrying on, and she found out that he was running around with other women. But that could be true about any of the women with whom Tremain had been making the beast with two backs. Then again, it could have been somebody he'd never even heard of.

"That's the way to narrow down the suspects, Drayton," he said aloud to himself and laughed. He was sitting on the porch with his feet up and his coffee on a small table beside him as he sat looking in the direction of the woods, which were starting to close in on the place. "Why don't you tend your own garden?" he said aloud to himself, but actually, the way that the brush and the trees were moving toward the house and gradually filling the clearing, also pleased Drayton—especially its slow relentlessness. At first, he'd tried to grow roses, but it was hopeless because the deer loved to come down out of the hills and bite off the rosebuds as if they were a delicacy intended specifically for them. He'd tried fencing off his garden, but raccoons and coyotes always found a way in, and all the others followed. He imagined that while he was asleep, an army of small wild animals marched in single file into his garden. Nature always found a way. He thought of the poet Robinson Jeffers, who had lived in Carmel in the early part of the century and had planted many of the trees in that area. Jeffers loved nature and was dismayed by what people were doing, not only to themselves but to the natural world. Finally, Jeffers seemed to take some solace in the notion that human beings would probably kill themselves off but that nature would go on. One day at the garage, Ben had said that Jeffers was probably right, but maybe humans killing themselves off was *part* of the natural process rather than outside of it. Small talk at the shop, Drayton thought and smiled.

So Drayton had decided to let nature have its way. It was peaceful sitting there with his feet up, the folded newspaper in his lap, his coffee cup and saucer in his hands. He tried to do a little meditation and keep his mind as clear as he could, but so many thoughts were working to find a way out. That phone call in the middle of the night. Keying his car. What kind of adolescent shit was that? Maybe he was wrong in not taking it seriously; adolescents, whatever their age, were capable of doing harm to people. But who? he wondered. Somebody he'd never met? One of those husbands or boyfriends that Tremain had outraged? But what was of interest in the car? Shotgun shells? The pictures? Maybe the roll of undeveloped film. Yes, maybe the roll of undeveloped film. Would there even be anything there after twenty years? Ben would probably be back soon. Drayton hoped the photos were on that roll of film.

His thoughts jumped. Les Tremain, the mystery man. His women. His sister. His abandoned car. Which led to Ellie Boudreau. Drayton's life had been quiet for a long time, and now the action was furious, and Ellie was a flame.

Ellie? Yes, Ellie and Les Tremain. She'd known him, but just about everybody had, except Drayton, who wondered where the hell he'd been when Tremain had been doing art, chasing women, playing tennis, and disappearing. And Tremain's car had been on Ellie's property, or close to it. Was it really possible for her to never have seen that car in twenty years? Maybe, he thought, maybe, considering the hollow which hid the car. Still.... But if Tremain had left the car, why had he been there? Or maybe he hadn't been there. Maybe somebody else dumped the car for him.

Or maybe Ellie's husband had known Tremain. He hadn't thought of that before. Ellie's husband and Tremain would be about the same age. How long ago had her husband left town? Their daughter had been a baby. Now she was at Santa Cruz—just old enough to fit into the twenty-year pattern.

Then again, maybe the car was there out of sheer chance. Anybody who owned a car like that would almost certainly know that Cold Canyon Creek Road was a great drive. But why leave the car among the goddamned trees for twenty years? Drayton had been thinking that Tremain was either dead or half-way across the world, but it didn't have to be either. He smiled at the thought that Tremain could still be living in the county, maybe down on the Mesa, maybe, maybe, maybe.... And who cared about Les Tremain? His sister. Probably Louis. Anybody else? Andrea? Somebody else. Now Drayton. He nodded to himself: he did *care* about Tremain, especially about what had happened to him, and he'd find out.

Still sitting on the porch with his feet up, Drayton's attention was drawn to a group of live oaks partway up the hillside. Rip, his almost feral black cat, was already staring in that direction. Rupe's ears moved forward, and he now looked a little more wild. Drayton heard a small sound. He straightened in his chair and watched the shadows. His hands gripped the chair arms. What was out there? His eyes were slightly dazzled by the sunlight gleaming and flickering through the trees. Rip and Rupe both shifted. Drayton saw something like movement, and then a guinea hen moved out of the camouflage of the trees, her round body almost comic on her spindly legs. Just as quickly, she disappeared into the oaks again. Elusive, Drayton thought to himself, and laughed at his paranoia.

Rupe had dropped from the porch and, his belly close to the ground, was creeping toward the brush. Drayton watched Rupe's stalking, and then something else bobbed to the surface of his mind. Maybe Les Tremain had disappeared because he didn't fit in very well. Drayton had never seen himself as fitting in very well. Tremain's problem was that he was a good-looking man who carried on with a lot of women and did art in direct defiance of a culture which said he should have a 9-to-5 job. Drayton grunted. Tremain probably could have done all those things if first he'd already made a fortune, but you had to have a fortune *before* you could act like that. You had to be *financially responsible and think of the future.* Drayton shook his head: what did he know about Tremain? Only what Tremain's sister and a few others had told him. He probably had no idea who the man was. *Was?* he thought. Or *had been? Is?*

Drayton sipped from his coffee. Rupe looked up at him without moving his head. Rip was somewhere in the brush—domesticity abandoned. Drayton ran his fingers over his facial whiskers and then over the stubble on top his head. He would have to shave all that before his dinner date with Ellie. When he'd asked her the night before, he was afraid she might say 'no' because of the way he'd acted at the coffee shop, but she didn't hesitate. She said that she'd drive into town and meet him, but he insisted on picking her up. He liked the idea of driving Cold Canyon Creek Road with her in the passenger seat, first in the light when he picked her up, and then later in the dark, the car's headlights creating shadows among the trees. In his imagination, he could see the headlights playing on the woods as he drove the small road back to her place beyond the granite outcropping.

WHEN DRAYTON PICKED UP Ellie that night, she wore a black dress short enough to show off her legs, and her cropped blonde-grayish hair was combed with the kind of part usually found on a man's head. Her dress came up to her neck but her arms were bare, and Drayton wondered when a woman's arms had first become a manifestation of beauty for him in the way which legs always had been.

Their plan had been to go to dinner and see a movie, but the sky had just started to slip into twilight and the air was balmy. As Drayton was removing the fiberglass top and storing it in the front trunk, "What kind of car did you say this was?"

"An X 1/9."

"I love your X 1/9."

Drayton laughed. "Stop trying to impress me with your good taste."

"It's tiny," Ellie said as she slipped into the passenger's seat and reached for the seat belt.

"Pretty small," Drayton said. "But it handles very well."

As they bumped along the dirt and gravel road leading from Ellie's house to the main road, she sat with her head back, looking up through the treetops into the blue sky streaked with traces of night. "God, this is lovely," she said. "I haven't been in a convertible in so long."

"It's not exactly a convertible," Drayton said, "because of the way the top comes off and fits under the hood."

Ellie looked forward. "Where's the engine?"

"Right behind us," Drayton said, nodding toward the back window of the car. "It's a mid-engine car."

"I think it's the smallest car I've ever been in," Ellie said, but it wasn't criticism, just an observation.

Drayton laughed. "It's just over twelve feet long."

She looked at Drayton and nodded. "Anyway, I haven't been in car with no top in a long, long time. I'm getting to be an old lady."

Drayton didn't say anything, but he rolled his eyes in disbelief. Ellie shifted in her seat to look at him and said, "Thanks, Drayton."

Drayton nodded and smiled. "You're right, you're missing something if you don't drive in a convertible around here. The Central Coast is the perfect place for one," Drayton said and shifted into third as the road smoothed out.

He laughed. "When I first got this, a friend asked me if I knew how I looked—an old guy driving a wedge-shaped red car without a top." He laughed again, "It was a good question because the answer told me a lot about myself." He touched the brakes for a curve, "I realized that I had thought about that, but it was also pretty clear that I really didn't care a whole hell of a lot. My car. My business."

When they reached Cold Canyon Creek Road, Ellie said, "Let's forget the dinner and movie plan. Nothing could be as good as this. Let's just go for a ride." She turned to Drayton. They were stopped, ready to pull onto the road. "Is that all right?"

Drayton laughed and said, "Are you trying to woo me?" They both laughed, and he added, "It couldn't be better. I'm not hungry now anyway." He turned right onto the road and, over the sound of the revving engine, suggested, "Maybe a long ride to a late dinner."

"Wonderful," she said, smiled, and put her head back to look up at the twilight sky and the sight of the first stars of the night.

Drayton wondered why she hadn't asked him if he'd found out anything more about the Alfa. Maybe she didn't want to think about it. He didn't either, not on such a lovely night and with her beside him.

They passed that section of the road where Drayton had first parked and found the abandoned car. That seemed like more than a few days ago. He looked into the darkness of the trees and wondered what had happened there twenty years ago. Had Les Tremain driven the car in there and then left in another car driven by a woman? One of the women in his life? Or had something much worse happened?

Darkness already covered the road from the shadows of the eucalyptus trees. Drayton switched on the lights and started pushing the X 1/9 through the gears and into the curves, but not pushing it too much, just enough to feel the weight of the car pulling outward toward the darkness. Ellie gave a mock scream at one very sharp curve, the tires wailing against the asphalt. Drayton looked at her, shook his head, and raised his voice over the engine noise and wind. "Don't encourage me." When she didn't say anything, he said, "This car would hold that curve at twice the speed."

She glanced over at him and laughed. "Let's not find out." In the fading light, her face was different, and he could see her as she must have looked when she was younger. Again, he thought of Dante Gabrielle Rossetti and his group, who called beautiful women "stunners." *Stunner* would have been the right word for the young Ellie. *No doubt*, Drayton thought, *if I had known her then, her beauty would have made me act foolish.* Bonnie had accused him of being a sexist in that he saw women not as human beings, but as ideals. From early on, it had been a sore spot in their relationship. *Forget Bonnie*, he told himself. *Ellie's sitting right next to you.*

"Should I slow down?" Drayton asked.

Ellie shook her head, "No, I trust you." She said a few more words, but they were lost in the sounds of the wind and the singing of the engine. The wind ruffled her short hair as she squinted out at the lighted road, a smile on her lips.

Drayton stayed to the back roads, keeping as far as he could from the freeway that cut north/south through the county. He knew all the roads with the twists and turns followed by straight-aways. His route twisted southward on roads that were like those of the California of fifty years earlier.

After a time, Drayton slowed down and rolled into the hills around Foxen Canyon. As they came to the end of a long straightaway, the road climbed and cut sharply to the south. At the next turn, an old white frame church stood on the knob of a small but abrupt hill. Drayton braked and rolled into the driveway that climbed to the church parking lot. The night was almost completely dark now, traces of light streaking the sky to the west over the Pacific Ocean, where Drayton knew the sun was now a golden ball slipping downward behind light surface fog before sinking into the ocean. The cold ocean seemed to swallow the sun and quench its fire.

Ellie leaned forward, looking at the old church.

"It's the old Foxen Chapel," Drayton said. He pulled to a stop, cut the lights, and killed the engine. Fifty yards to the east was a small frame house where the caretaker and his wife lived. The windows were bright with light.

A small light burned inside the church. Drayton and Ellie got out of the car and followed the path through a rose garden to the entrance to the church, where they stopped and Drayton said, "It'll be locked, but I thought you might like it here." He took the two steps to the front doors of the church, but he was right, they were locked. He turned back to her. "We'll have to be happy with the scenery."

From the knob of the hill they could look out over the fields and ranch land, all of it broken by stands of eucalyptus trees that had been planted as windbreaks. A single live oak stood in the center of most of the fields for lunchtime shade.

"You've been here before," Ellie said.

Drayton was caught off guard. He nodded, "Yes, my ex-wife Bonnie and I used to come up here sometimes when our son was little." He pointed to a gravel road that ran along the base of the hill. "That leads to the Sisquoc Winery. It's a beautiful old place with a white frame house from another age, and it's surrounded by beautiful green lawns."

"It's so quiet," Ellie said.

"Not always," Drayton said. "This is the path that Fremont took when he marched on Santa Barbara." He nodded and gestured toward the south, "And lots of old Mexican ranchos. Lots of gringos marrying senoritas whose families had thousands of acres of land."

They fell silent and stood listening to the soft sounds of the night. Drayton sighed and turned toward the car. He held out his car keys to Ellie and said, "Why don't you drive?"

Ellie stepped back and asked, "Me? I didn't think you'd let anybody else drive your baby."

"My *baby*?"

"What if I hurt it?"

"Don't worry about that," Drayton said. "If you hurt it, that means I'll get to fix it."

She laughed and reached for the keys. Drayton put his left hand on her arm. Her skin was warm, even though the night was turning cool. This was as close as they'd been, and Drayton laughed, "Nice perfume, but I think I can just catch the scent of horse liniment."

"Thanks," she said and snatched the keys. "Just what every woman wants to hear when she's about to be kissed for the first time by a man's she's just met."

"A good honest smell," Drayton said. "I like it." He leaned into her and kissed her. Her hand was on his arm and her fingers tightened as she kissed him back.

When the kiss ended, she sighed and said, "Oh, my. Things just got complicated."

Drayton laughed. "We just kissed. We didn't agree to marry and tie our souls together for eternity and live happily ever after."

She laughed and turned toward the car, taking his hand as they walked along the path.

"Why don't you drive?" Drayton said and held out the dangling keys.

ELLIE WAS TENTATIVE AS she drove the X 1/9, but when she had gotten used to it, Drayton urged her to keep her speed into the curves. At first, she'd brake halfway into the curve, until Drayton said, "Don't brake! Downshift, but keep your speed and don't brake." Two curves later she was able to make the shift down into second gear with only a slight rip of transmission teeth, and she held her speed. As she hit the apex of the curve, Drayton said, "Gas," and as she hit the accelerator, the X 1/9 leaped forward with only a little body roll. The centrifugal force made it seem as if the car were being pushed from the side. Ellie came off the gas, and the rear end of the X 1/9 wobbled. She shrieked and Drayton again shouted "Gas." Ellie went back onto the accelerator, and the X 1/9 pushed forward and straightened out of the curve.

Ahead was the entrance to another winery. Ellie, her eyes wide, pulled the car onto the asphalt drive. They sat quietly for seconds, her eyes bright, reflecting the scattered light from the moon. Finally, she said, "Maybe you'd better drive. I almost killed us."

"No way," Drayton said. "You were fine. You were just starting to get the hang of it." He leaned over and kissed her on the corner of the mouth.

She glanced at him and said, "Nevertheless, you can drive from here. I'll continue my race driving lessons at another time."

Drayton drove through the silhouettes of the hills backlit by the moon, the light so bright and the shadows so dark that the rolling hills looked like part of a movie set. Ahead were the lights of cars travelling a major highway. When they reached it, Drayton waited for his opening, cut across the highway into a side road which he followed for a half mile until it led to a restaurant that looked as if it should have a stagecoach parked in front. The building was made of weathered planks and wooden shingles, and inside, the walls were covered with photos from the 19th century.

Dinner was good, but the restaurant was noisy because of a couple of families with loud children who competed with the drunken shouting of some cowboys at the bar. Ellie and Drayton had a hard time talking, so they ate quickly and left, walking out into the cool night and toward the X 1/9. Ellie asked, "Were you ever like those drunken young men at the bar?"

Drayton laughed and held the car door open for her. He said, "I'd like to say that I was never like that, but the truth is that I was probably worse. I was pretty young and dumb for a very long time. I was not precocious. I don't know how my family and friends put up with me."

"You're being modest," Ellie said.

Drayton started the car and said, "I'm being truthful. I don't think either of us would have liked me as a young man." He drove back toward the main highway, cut across it, and said, "You, I'll bet, were a pretty nice girl."

"Too nice," she said, "to go out with any of those cowboys."

"Or with me," Drayton said, "and you didn't miss much." He pointed the car northward and started retracing their path. Drayton drove slowly, wanting to make the night last. With the car's top still off, the night air was chilly, and Drayton turned on the heater, the warm air on their feet and legs, the cool night across their upper bodies and faces. Ellie lay her head back against the seat and stared up at the sky, the moon still bright, the stars brighter than they had been.

DRAYTON AND ELLIE WERE QUIET as the car bumped over the

dirt and gravel road back to her place. The fog still hadn't moved in, and the moon was high and bright, outlining the craggy outcropping. As they approached the house, her dogs barked until the car came to a stop and she called their names.

Ellie turned to Drayton and said, "I'd like you to come in if you can."

"I'd like that," Drayton said, but he was nervous.

"I have to tell you something," Ellie said. Drayton nodded.

She made sure their eyes met before she said, "I don't know how else to say this: I've had cancer, and I've lost my right breast."

Drayton was breathless for a moment, wanting to say something, but he couldn't.

Ellie shook her head, and her voice was tight as she said, "I was going to have some reconstructive surgery, but I decided against it. I think of the scar as a badge of honor."

Drayton hesitated and then asked, "You're telling me this because...?"

Ellie shrugged, "I didn't want to surprise you, and," she stopped and took a deep breath, "and no one has really seen me like this. You see what I mean?" Her eyes, bright and intense, looked straight into his. The moon cast shadows across her face.

Drayton nodded, "Sure I do. And thanks." He leaned forward and kissed her on the forehead and said, "I want to come in, do you still want me to come in?"

"Yes."

"You know," Drayton said, "one night at a dinner party, Nancy, a friend started talking about the mastectomy she'd had a year earlier. She was still trying to adapt. That night she had too much to drink." Drayton paused, "Anyway, she started talking about it. After a while, one of the women told her that she was still beautiful." He paused again. "Nancy said '*Really?*' Then she pulled up her shirt and showed us her scar."

"Oh, my God," Ellie said. "I can understand why she did that."

"You know," Drayton said, "I don't know what I was expecting. I guess I was kind of scared, but it didn't look bad at all. She sure the hell was still a beautiful woman."

As they started toward the house, Drayton put his arm around Ellie and said in a grave voice, "There's something I'd like to tell you."

Ellie slowed her pace and looked up at him.

Drayton said, "Because of a bicycle accident, I've had to have both testicles removed."

At first her face was stricken, then it stiffened, and she said, "This isn't funny, goddamn it."

"Sure it is," Drayton said. "Just about everything is."

"Cynicism?" Ellie asked.

"No," Drayton answered, "hedonism. Do you really think I'd care any less about you because you've lost a breast?"

Ellie stared at him and coughed a laugh, "Oh, you enlightened man." Her eyes narrowed and she smiled. "What," she asked, "if I'd lost my nose?"

Drayton laughed and threw up his hands, "Not even an Old Testament God could be that cruel or that foolish."

Her smile broadened, and she reached up and kissed him quickly on the mouth. "You're a slick talker. And you're a hedonist. A pagan hedonist."

"Guilty," Drayton said. And their exchange made him think of Louis Marchand and his love of this life as the only heaven any of them were going to get, but he shook the thought away. His hand was on the middle of Ellie's back and he slid it down onto the slope of the small of her back and then to the curve of her hip. Ellie didn't move away, and Drayton took pleasure in the gentle rhythm of her hips as they walked toward the house and the front porch, dusty in the moonlight.

Chapter 11

The next morning, Drayton rolled out of bed, pulled on his clothes, and went into the kitchen. Ellie, wearing a blouse and jeans, sat at the kitchen table. She'd combed her hair and she looked lovely—and a little sleepy or dreamy, as if she hadn't completely let loose of the night before. Drayton realized that there had been a time in his life when he would have grabbed her and made love to her on the kitchen table or against the refrigerator, but now that seemed pretty comic, and he wondered if that was what getting old meant: the dramatic turning into the comic.

"Got any coffee?" he asked.

Ellie shook her head, "No. I don't drink it, remember?"

Drayton leaned down and kissed her on the forehead. She smelled of soap and shampoo. She'd be a shower woman—no time to sit around in the tub. She kissed him in return, but then said, "I've got to get into town."

"Scorned," Drayton said.

"Right," Ellie said. "I really scorned you last night." She shook her head, "I'm a little embarrassed. I don't know what got into me."

Drayton kept the smile from his face and asked, "You don't know what *got into you?*"

Her face was blank for a few seconds and then she closed her eyes and said, "Am I going to have to watch everything I say because you're an English professor?"

"Retired," Drayton said.

"Retired," she said.

"If anybody should be embarrassed, it's me," Drayton said. "What a pathetic performance."

"Maybe we shouldn't spend the morning apologizing to each other," she said, "and besides, it's not as if there weren't impediments."

"Impediments?" Drayton asked.

Ellie looked at him as if to say, "You know what I'm talking about."

Drayton did know what she was talking about. Before they'd gotten into bed the night before, she had, with her back to him, pulled on a tee shirt. He had tried to get her to take off the tee shirt, but she shook her head at him, and the look of pain in her eyes had made him stop.

Drayton walked Ellie to her pick-up truck, and as she climbed in, he touched her hair at her forehead and said, "You're my Amazon woman."

Confusion crossed her face but there was a smile on her lips. "Amazon?" she asked.

Drayton nodded. "The myth is that the Amazon women were beautiful and strong, independent women, and they were great hunters with superhuman skills with a bow and arrow."

The smile slipped from Ellie's face, and she nodded. "I remember now. They were great hunters who had one of their breasts removed so that they could better use the bow and arrow."

Drayton nodded once. "Yes," he said, "but they were still, beautiful, strong, and independent—an ideal for women ever since."

She looked at Drayton. "You're all right, Drayton. And you're a smooth talker."

Drayton shrugged. "Sometimes, it's so damned easy." Ellie fired up the truck's engine.

"I'll call you tonight." Drayton said and stepped back from the truck.

Ellie turned to him again, but now her face was strange, and he asked, "Is something wrong?"

"No," she said and continued to smile, but he hadn't believed her, hadn't believed her smile, and he still didn't believe her.

NOW, BACK HOME ON his own porch, Drayton turned to Rupe

lying in the sun and asked, "What do you think was wrong, Rupe? Was I such a bust as a lover?"

Rupe looked up, and his tail whacked the deck a couple of times. Ripper, the semi-feral cat, still sitting on the deck railing, ignored them both and stared into the woods as if she was expecting the Second Coming but still wasn't too excited about it. Easy come, easy go, Drayton thought. He looked back to Rupe and said, "You know, things were very simple four or five days ago."

Rupe used his tail to whack the deck a couple more times and followed with a moaning groan, which seemed to suggest that he'd considered moving but had decided against it. "What do you make of all this?" Drayton asked Rupe. Rupe whacked his tail once, and Drayton said, "Not much?"

Rupe shifted as if he might move but then thought better of it, and settled back onto the deck, his body seeming to spread even more than before, like jello melting on a hot plate.

"Help me out," Drayton said to Rupe, whose eyes got larger at the plea in his master's voice.

"There's the jerk who phoned me and keyed my car. Maybe the key job wasn't even related to Tremain's car. Still, there's the phone call." He paused and sighed. "And there's old Louis Marchand killing time in his house on top of that mountain, and time is killing him, while his beautiful wife takes care of him and is more than still young enough for passion—and sin," Drayton said and paused, waiting for a response from Rupe. When there was none, Drayton said, "You know, it seemed like Louis knew something that he wasn't telling me. His wife, too."

Rupe whimpered.

"I know," Drayton said. "She does that to me too." He noticed that Ripper still sat quietly on the porch railing ignoring the dog and himself, as if she knew something but thought they were too stupid to understand it. "Ripper," Drayton said, but the cat didn't move. "You know, guys, Louis and his sexy wife both knew Les Tremain." Ripper looked at him. She seemed disdainful, and Drayton said, "You're right, Rip, everyone knew Les Tremain." He nodded, "Everyone but me."

The three of them sat quietly, listening to the late morning breeze evolve into a warm wind that was as dry as the desert. The wind rattled the leaves of the eucalyptus trees. The Santa Ana seemed determined to plague them. Drayton asked Ripper, "What do you think about

Tremain? What do you think happened to him?" Drayton nodded. "His sister thinks he's dead. What do you think, Rupe?" Rupe whacked the deck with his tail and howled like an old hound, and Drayton said, "You're right, I think she's right, too. It doesn't make sense that he'd just disappear for twenty years." Ripper arched her back and stretched, and Drayton said, "You're right, Rip, Marchand thinks he'd dead too. At least that's what he said to his wife, who maybe seemed to think he was alive. Or was that just for my benefit?"

Ripper left her stretch behind and jumped to the floor of the deck, and then from the deck to the dirt floor of the woods. Drayton said, "Thanks for your help, Rip, and thanks for being so polite."

Rupe groaned his way to his feet, his face a little sheepish, and Drayton asked, "Are you leaving too? You're supposed to be my best friend, and you walk out on me?" Drayton nodded. "You're right, all because of that damned car, but I met Ellie because of that car. Why can't I leave it like that?"

Rupe turned and headed toward his food bowl. Soon, Drayton sat listening to Rupe crunch his dog food. His chewing was followed by a terrible slurping, as the dog lapped up water to wash down the dry food. Drayton caught sight of Ripper as she eased among some fallen branches and disappeared into the brush cover to catch a field mouse, the headless remains of which she'd bring to Drayton as a gift to make him feel better. Rip's nod to domestication.

IN THE LATE AFTERNOON, DRAYTON pulled into the shop parking lot. The big doors were wide open, and Ben's yellow Lotus was parked out front, but there was no sign of Ben. Drayton figured that'd he'd probably walked to the nearby deli to get a sandwich.

Les Tremain's rosso Alfa, with its splendid rust holes and jagged edges, sat outside the open doors of the shop. Drayton walked over and stood looking at it, as if it might tell him something. He checked the cabin with care, turning back the floor mats, peering under the seats, feeling up under the dash, but he found nothing but dirt and cobwebs. He had no idea what he was looking for, but then he realized that he'd half-expected to find dried blood or matted bloody hair, or something like that, but there was nothing. He searched again, moving the seats forward and backward to better see under them. It was impossible to see clearly because the seats were so low, so Drayton ran his hand under each seat. Under the driver's seat, he found an empty, crumpled pack of Camels, and under the passenger seat, he found a silver barrette with a broken clasp. He wondered what woman it had belonged to and how she'd lost it and how it had gotten broken. He imagined Tremain's hands in Andrea Marchand's short hair. Maybe back then her hair had been long enough so that she secured it with a barrette. *Why had he thought of Andrea? Intuition? Sexual fantasy?* Again, he fanned his hand under the passenger seat. Nothing on the first pass, but on the second he felt something, and his hand came out with it, the small foil package between his fingers. He stood up and looked at the ripped and empty Trojan wrapper. Drayton stared at the cramped cabin of the car, its sculptured seats, the high shifter on the transmission hump, the center console running from under the dash down to the seats. He looked into the back seat, which might have been big enough for Rupe, if he'd sat sideways. Where the hell did they do it? he wondered. He looked around—*in the road*—like the old song? Maybe on the hood of the car? But it sloped forward at quite a rake. You'd slide off on your ass. Tremain was something. Jesus. What had Madsen, the cop, called him? An *ass bandit*. Drayton turned his attention back to the doorsills and panels, but there was nothing, not even a speck of anything that looked like blood on the upholstery.

"Find anything of interest?" It was Ben, walking with long languid strides toward Drayton.

Drayton held up the torn foil wrapper.

Ben laughed. "This guy was something. How'd he find the time?" Ben laughed, "Maybe he just dropped dead of exhaustion someplace." He shook his head. "What a way to die." His eyes lit up, "Oh, I developed those photos. Our mystery man was no slouch. Wait till you see these pictures. He had no biases about color—dark or fair—you name it."

"He's not so much of a mystery man anymore," Drayton said. "His name is Les Tremain, and he disappeared twenty years ago."

"Oh, the flaky artist," Ben said. "That was before my time, but I think I heard about him. He disappeared, right?"

"Right," Drayton said. "Everybody in town knows about him except me."

"I don't know how good his art work is," Ben said, "but he's a hell of a photographer. This stuff is not just porno. I mean, he could take pictures. These girls have beautiful bodies, and that's how he photographed them. It's hard not to see them as pretty erotic, but it's all in the eye of the beholder, they say." He laughed and said, "And you know how I behold them." Then he rolled his eyes, went over to his Lotus and came back with an envelope of photographs, which he handed to Drayton.

Drayton began looking at the photos. As with the earlier shots, these were black and white; some were nudes, some weren't. The first he looked at was of a young woman, her back to the camera, and she was reaching up toward the branch of a tree. The branch was thick with summer leaves. The photo reminded Drayton of a painting— something about the design. The woman didn't seem real, more like an imagined idea, but in another sense she seemed very real. Just the way you see a woman, he thought: idealized and then real and then idealized, and so on. Her hair was blond and straight, flat and glowing, streaming down her back almost to her waist. In the next photo, her face and shoulders were shadowed, her right hand was at her mouth, and her eyes were wide, as if something had startled her. In the third photo, she was in a tree, and her arms and legs and the limbs of the tree all seemed to be part of the same creature. Her body was young and beautiful, and Drayton sighed with sadness.

In the next photo, the camera was close, only a head shot. The woman's eyes were wide, staring straight into the camera, and a few light freckles were scattered across her nose and cheeks. Her face was so honest and so open that she looked innocent. She looked like both a girl and a woman, leaving one, moving into the other. Drayton's first thought was that it could have been Ellie's daughter Cindy at Santa Cruz, but then he saw that it wasn't Ellie's daughter: it was Ellie, twenty years earlier.

"Beautiful, isn't she?" Ben said. "Or at least looks it, the photos are amazing."

Drayton shuffled the photos and looked at the one showing Ellie's body, and he looked with some mixture of anger, lust, and sadness at her breasts, one of them now gone to a diagonal scar across her chest.

"I know this woman," he said.

"Really?" Ben said. "You lucky bastard."

Drayton checked himself, "Well, she looks familiar, but I can't quite place her."

"Somebody from around here?" Ben asked.

"I think so," Drayton said. He felt like he might cry, but he wasn't sure why.

"You crying?" Ben asked.

"I am," Drayton answered.

Chapter 12

When Drayton pulled up in front of Ellie's, the Santa Anas had grown stronger and the heat was heavy and close, without even a hint of humidity. The day's bright light was beginning to slip into twilight. Ellie came outside and stood on the porch. She was still in the blouse and jeans that she'd been wearing that morning. Her eyes were exactly the same as in the photo, but her hair was short now and had brown in it, and some gray. Time hadn't been that bad to her, actually time had been good to her. She was smiling. "You said you were going to call, but I'm glad you drove out instead."

As she looked at him, her smile faded and she asked, "What, Drayton? What is it? What happened?"

Drayton handed her the envelope of photographs, but she wouldn't take them, and her face changed, as if she were frightened and wanted to run. She shook her head and made a soft keening sound. Drayton extended his arm, the photographs almost touching her. "Please take them," he said.

She looked at the packet holding the photos without moving. Mozart was playing on the radio inside the house—violins and violas tremulous and soaring. She said, "I don't need to look at them. I know what they are; that was a long time ago."

"Go ahead and take them," Drayton said, and her hand was steady when she took the photographs.

He watched her face as she looked at them. Her eyes were glossy with tears, "God, that was a long time ago." She glanced up at

Drayton, "Nobody's that young." She smiled, "I was really pretty."

"You still are," Drayton said.

"Thanks, Drayton," she said and smiled at him.

"Those were on a roll of film in Les Tremain's car."

"I'd know any photos Les took. He was a wonderful photographer, wonderful, although not always a perfect human being. Like the rest of us."

"You told me that you didn't know him very well."

"I know," she said. "I didn't know what to say. I was going to tell you."

Her Labrador pushed the screen door open with his nose and ambled out onto the porch where he sprawled as the door banged shut. The music of Mozart continued to soar inside the house.

Drayton said, "You were going to tell me but you didn't, not last night, not this morning."

"I couldn't last night. Too much was going on. It was such a wonderful night, and I didn't want to ruin it." She turned her face away from the sunlight. "Then this morning I was going to, but I just couldn't. What was I going to do when you came out of my bedroom this morning, look at you and say, 'Oh, by the way, I lied to you about Les Tremain. He and I were involved.'"

"*Involved*," Drayton said, his jaw tight, but then he paused, nodded and sighed. "I guess you couldn't really say anything. I know."

"Let's get out of the sun," she said and turned and started toward the house. When she reached the porch, she said, "Why don't you sit down, and I'll get us some lemonade."

Drayton settled deep into the old sofa that looked as if it might be the main resting place for Ellie's dogs. He looked out to the west and beyond the granite outcropping. Things had been going too well, and what did he expect, was she supposed to tell him her entire life story? He realized that it wasn't so much that she hadn't told him—that was only part of it. But he was jealous, and part of him didn't like the notion of her posing nude for photographs, but he wasn't her father or her brother, and he certainly wasn't her husband, and it didn't make sense to be jealous of something she'd done twenty years ago with a man who was probably dead. Now she was old enough to be the mother of the girl in the photographs. *Stop it*, he told himself. *Think. If you hadn't idealized her, you wouldn't feel this way. You'd know she was flesh and blood.* He made himself remember how unfair everybody had been with him when he'd been accused of having sex with one of his students. Those people had driven him out of the academic world. He didn't want to be like them. *Get hold of yourself, don't say something you'll be sorry for, don't say something that will ruin everything. Bite your goddamned tongue. Act like you're pushing fifty—not fifteen.*

Drayton, looking down at Ellie's Lab lying on the porch, smiled and then laughed softly. The Lab whacked his tail on the weathered boards, and a puff of dust rose up. Drayton laughed again, saying to him, "I've got a dog you'd get along with. You both have something of the same personality."

The Lab swished his tail across the porch. "Sure, I'll introduce you," Drayton said.

"Are you having a conversation with Henry?" Ellie asked as she came out the door with two glasses of lemonade. She gave one to Drayton and sat in a rocker facing him. "Are you sure you want to hear this?"

Drayton smiled, "I'm trying not to be an asshole. I'm listening if you want to tell me." He shook his head. "It's your life. You don't have to tell me anything."

She nodded and took a deep breath. "I'll tell. God. I have to tell somebody." She paused. "Buddy and I had been married about three years." She shook her head. "Things weren't going well. I took care of the baby. Buddy had to travel a lot." She paused and looked at Drayton. "This is hard because I've never told anybody about it." She checked herself. "Well, one person knows a little, but no one knows all of what I'm telling you." She shook her head.

Ellie's gaze shifted to the dirt and gravel road that traveled past her place and into the hills to the east. She looked back to Drayton, and he saw it in her eyes.

"You told your neighbor? Ronnie?" Drayton asked. "You told him?"

Ellie looked close to crying. "Ronnie found the car years ago. I can't remember why he went in there, but he did, and he found the car."

"The car you said you didn't know was there? The car you'd never seen?"

Ellie sat looking at floor. "I've never seen it there. I didn't want to go out there." Her eyes were wide as she looked at him, and she was talking more quickly. "As soon as he described it, I knew it was Les's car. I didn't need to see it. I didn't want to see it." She hesitated and looked out in the direction of where the car had been for twenty years. "Ronnie had a terrible crush on me."

"A crush?" Drayton asked.

"Yes, like a boy would have." She was nodding her head. "We'd been friends for a while when he found the car. We'd sit out here and talk, and I told him a little of it." She shook her head. "Nothing ever happened between us."

Drayton stared at her.

"I'd been alone with it for ten years, not a word to anybody." She put her hands to her mouth, her eyes on him. She glared at Drayton, clearly angry. "I know it sounds stupid, but I had to say something to somebody."

"Why him?"

Ellie looked down and took a deep breath. "I told you, because he found Les's car and asked me about it." Her eyes were wet. "I just told him that it belonged to a guy I'd had an affair with it, and that it was what wrecked my marriage."

"And?" Drayton asked. His voice had lost its edge.

"And he wanted to know more, but I wouldn't tell him." She looked down to her hands, their interlocked fingers. "I don't know what he guessed, but enough, probably."

"Probably," Drayton said and sighed with resignation. "That means that he's probably my friend?"

Ellie looked at him: "Friend?"

Drayton nodded. "Remember on the phone when I asked you if you'd told anybody about me taking the car?"

Ellie nodded.

"Well, I asked because I got a phone call the night that I took the car, Tuesday night." He hesitated. "Actually, it was Wednesday morning."

"Phone call?"

"About three in the morning, the phone rang. The caller said he was a friend." Drayton smiled. "He said that he wanted to tell me to get rid of that car as soon as possible."

Ellie was hugging herself, and her head was down. She looked up and said, "I know that he sees himself as my protector, but I don't think that...." Her sentence trailed off.

"That same day, after I went to the police," Drayton said, "somebody keyed my car." Drayton shook his head. "Five will get you ten it's your *friend* Ronnie."

Ellie sat looking at him.

"Women can sure choose strange friends," Drayton said.

Ellie's eyes flared. "And men don't?"

Drayton sighed. "Who else would it be but Ronnie?"

"I don't know," Ellie said. "I just can't believe he'd do that. He's really very gentle. Boyish. He's always treated me as if I were a movie star."

"Exactly," Drayton said. "Christ, you look like one."

She stopped and she was almost matter of fact when she said, "I'll phone Ronnie. I'll tell him to mind his own business. I'll tell him about you and me."

Drayton looked at her when she said that. He nodded. "Yes. You and me."

They were quiet. She kept her eyes on him. Her eyes were wet, but no tears ran down her face.

Drayton sighed again and nodded. "O.K. O.K. I've got no business judging you, and especially what happened years ago, long before I even knew you existed." He shook his head. "It just caught me by surprise." He shook his head again. "It all happened years ago. It's all your business."

Ellie nodded. "I know it was a shock." Ellie swallowed and she laughed. "Do you want to know about Les?" She nodded. "I did some things that I'm not proud of, but you're right, it's my business."

Drayton nodded. "O.K." He took a deep breath, looked at her, and said, "I still want to find out what happened to him. But it's up to you."

Ellie took a long breath and seemed to compose herself. She looked at Drayton. "Nobody knows what I'm about to tell you. Nobody. I promise."

Drayton looked at her blue eyes, wet with tears, smiled, and said, "I know."

Ellie started. "I took a photography class that Les was teaching. It met one night a week for three hours. There'd be a fifteen-minute break in the middle, and he and I started talking. Then he asked me to have coffee after class one night." She glanced up. "Old story, right?"

Drayton thought about how she had done exactly the same thing with him, so how could he judge her? When she'd met Tremain, she'd been twenty-three or so, about the same age his son was now, and not much older than the students he'd taught for years. God, that seemed young to have a husband, a baby, and a lover. Life started too soon.

"Please remember that I was young," she said, "and my husband wasn't around a lot, and when he was around, he wasn't the warmest person in the world." She paused and wrung her hands. "Actually, he was a cold man. Very judgmental." She looked upward, tears in her eyes. "The truth is that it was a terrible relationship."

Drayton nodded and took a drink of his lemonade. Sour and sweet at the same time.

"Well," Ellie said and shrugged, "Les and I had an affair." She looked at him, her nostrils flared slightly and her eyes were defiant. "I'm not going to say otherwise. It was good for a while. Les was smart and talented. He was a little older, good looking, and he knew how to talk to a woman in a way that most men didn't. Still don't, really." She closed her eyes. "God, he could make me look beautiful in a photograph." She shook her head. "Vanity can be a terrible thing. Almost always is."

Drayton swallowed but said nothing. He smiled at her.

Henry, the lab, yawned. His teeth were yellow, an older dog than Drayton had guessed. Mozart was no longer playing on the radio. Haydn now? Ellie had turned down the sound. Drayton could still hear someone. Harpsichord?

"It went on for more than a year," she said. "I don't remember much else from that time. He told me that I was beautiful and that he wanted to photograph me." She shook her head. "I was pretty. All girls that age want to be pretty."

"You were—are—more than pretty."

Her voice softened. "At first I wouldn't, but then he convinced me. The photographs were beautiful. At first they were mainly of my face, that sort of thing, then one night he convinced me to take off my blouse." She shook her head. "I can't believe how easy it was to convince me. I must have been so vain."

"Cameras are funny things," Drayton said. "They're still magic. We don't really completely believe that pictures are going to happen. Someone is just holding a black box. It's still hard to believe that a camera stops time."

She took a long drink of her lemonade and leaned back slightly in her rocker. "Well, Les started coming out here whenever Buddy was out of town. He'd drive his car down the road and pull it off into the trees and then walk in." Her eyes were wide, "He said nobody would see it."

She looked toward the outcropping. "It's so long ago, but I think about it all the time. It's like a movie that I can't forget." She bit her lower lip. A hot wind drifted across the porch.

The light had shifted and shadows had begun to fall across the hills and over the stunted trees that dotted the slopes. The heat was heavy. He could feel the sweat on his back. Drayton tried to think of all these things happening twenty years ago. He could imagine Les Tremain in his Alfa, driving down that road, hiding his car and then walking to Ellie's house. Drayton asked, "So what happened to Les Tremain?"

Ellie shook her head. She looked tired and miserable. She said, "I don't know what happened to him."

"He didn't just walk out of your life—poof," Drayton said and threw his hands up like a magician.

Ellie shook her head. "Someone sent Buddy a couple of pictures of me that Les had taken."

"Who?" Drayton asked. "Who sent the photographs to your husband?" "I don't know," Ellie said. "I didn't know then and I still don't know. Whoever sent them knew which ones to send." Ellie closed her eyes, "Les and I drank a lot, and we smoked a lot of dope." She paused, "Some of the photographs were less tasteful than others."

Drayton tensed his jaw. He was angry, but he didn't know with whom. With the Les Tremain of twenty years ago? With Ellie when she was so young? It didn't make sense, but he was still angry, and he said, "So art slipped over into porn?"

Ellie looked directly at him and said, "Thanks, Drayton. That's very kind of you." Ellie smiled, "You're acting just the way Buddy did, but he was my husband. All you and I have done was have a nice date and sleep together once." Her jaw tightened.

Drayton sighed. She was right. He knew that he was sounding just the way he had when he and Bonnie had had their troubles. Hadn't he learned anything from that? What was the point of accusations? Especially nasty accusations.

Drayton nodded. "O.K. Yes, you're right. Where do I get off giving you a hard time?"

Ellie didn't respond, but finished the lemonade in her glass.

"Tell me," Drayton said. "Tell me what happened."

Ellie put her glass down on the floor next to the rocker and rubbed her eyes. "At first, Buddy was just stunned. Nothing like that had ever happened in his family." She closed her eyes. "They're a big cattle-raising family down in the Santa Ynez Valley." She shook her head. "They'd treated me like one of the family. His mother treated me as if I were her daughter."

Drayton shook her head.

"I don't know," Ellie said. "I don't think that Buddy ever told his family about what had really happened. I don't think they've ever known that I was unfaithful." She shrugged, "I think partly out of pride on Buddy's part, but also the whole family lives by this strong Christian code, and one thing you do is to avoid casting stones. You know?"

"Do they even know that Les Tremain disappeared?"

Ellie shook her head. "I don't think so. Why would they? They didn't know Les. And I doubt if Buddy ever said anything about the tie between Les and me."

Drayton nodded, "Right." He hesitated and took a long drink of his lemonade. The light was slipping away. The sound of Haydn on the radio was barely perceptible. Everything seemed a little unreal. The air was hot, but the evening light was beautiful, and the story was sad and sordid. He said to Ellie, "You said that *at first* Buddy was stunned. What happened after *at first?*"

Ellie turned her face away from the dust. "He called me a whore and other terms, terms that men like to use for a woman's genitalia to hurt you as much as possible as if all you are is what's between your legs." She took a deep breath. "He asked me if he and Cindy, our child, weren't enough for me."

Drayton just nodded.

Ellie looked at him. "Yes, it was a question I couldn't answer—the question that helped me see what I'd done." She closed her eyes. "I told him I was sorry, that I didn't know why I did it." Ellie put her hands to her mouth, "I'll never forget the look on his face. He didn't have to say anything. It was all in his face."

She leaned back in the rocker and stared off at the light growing less brilliant in the west. Her eyes came back to Drayton. "He told me that he had to leave, that he had to leave and he was afraid that he couldn't come back, that he couldn't ever trust me, and he couldn't come back." She looked at Drayton and grimaced. A paused followed. "He let me keep Cindy." Her eyes were wet and her voice was low.

"He always sees her at holidays, and sometimes in the summer she goes down to Santa Ynez, but he never comes here. He's never been back here since the day he left." Her voice was choked, "I think maybe he thought that Cindy wasn't his, which was crazy, and I'm sure he knew that, but somehow he still thought it, not even thought it really, but just had it somewhere in his mind, you know the way we do."

"So, he and Cindy aren't good together?" Drayton asked.

Ellie laughed at the idea and said, "No, not so good. He's always helped with money and in other ways, but they've never been close. But he's a good man." Ellie shook her head, "I've never told Cindy a lot about this. I mean I told her that the break-up was my fault, that I'd had an affair, but I didn't ever talk to her about Les."

"But she knows?" Drayton asked.

Ellie looked startled, as if maybe she'd never admitted it to herself, but she nodded and said, "This is a small town."

"What a mess," Drayton said. "I'm sorry."

Ellie nodded. "I know. I know. How dumb of me. What a mess."

"So that was it?" Drayton asked. "Your husband just drove away and that was the end of it?"

Ellie shook her head, and her voice was strained, "No, I wish it were. But Buddy's last night here—the day when he told me he was leaving and that he'd never be back—that night was a Tuesday night, the night that Les always came by, parked down the road, and walked in."

Drayton sat up, started to speak, but stopped and waited.

"I didn't know what to do," Ellie said, biting her lower lip. "I think I was really crazy that day. I mean if I had been tested, they might have put me away, I couldn't think about one thing for more than a second, it was just thought after thought, and my head hurt, I was sick. I didn't know what to do." She took a deep breath. She called to Henry, who got up and lumbered over to her. Scratching him behind the ears, she went on, "I tried to call Les, tried to tell him that Buddy would be here, but Les wasn't home, or he wouldn't answer the phone. If he was painting or sculpting, sometimes he wouldn't answer the phone for days." She looked at Drayton, "There were times when I went by his place when he'd be there working and wouldn't have shaved or showered in days, and I don't think he even ate much." She smiled slightly, "I knew he cared about me, but I also knew that when he was working, I was not at the top of his priority list." She closed her eyes, "And I was young and didn't like that, and I tried sometimes to get to the top of the list." She looked at Drayton and smiled, seeming to laugh at herself, and said, "I could have danced naked in front of him, and I think he'd have told me that I was blocking his light." She laughed softly and wrapped her arms around herself as if she were cold. She looked directly at Drayton and smiled. "Les was a man unto himself. His art filled his days. All the rest of us came in second or third or worse." She smiled to herself.

The sun had dropped close to the tops of the nearby hills, but the wind was hot and intense. Drayton waited. He'd finished his lemonade but sipped the water from the melted ice cubes and waited. Early evening quietness had moved in, and Drayton thought he could hear a car pass, or the hiss of a car passing, on the Cold Canyon Creek Road. Violins were still playing from the radio in the house. Ellie's Labrador groaned, but Ellie didn't move, and Drayton said, "I'd like you to tell me what happened that night."

Ellie looked at him. "*That night.* That's how I always think about it. *That night.* I've never told anyone about it, not all of it, not that part of it. I've gone over it so many times now that I'm not sure what happened."

Drayton waited for Ellie to gather herself. She closed her eyes, opened them and began, "Just before ten, which was when Les often came by, I went a little crazy. I decided to go out to the road and see if I could stop Les. Buddy was out in the barn getting some things that he wanted to take with him the next morning." She hesitated, closed her eyes, caught her breath, and went on, "I could see the light in the barn, and I was fairly sure Buddy was in there, and Cindy was asleep, so I started running for the road. I cut through the woods." She shook her head, "I couldn't see, and I fell and hurt my leg, but I kept going." She looked upward, thinking, remembering. "Through the trees I could see headlights on the road. I tried running faster." Trembling, she looked at Drayton, "I was so damned scared. I didn't know what Buddy would do if Les went up to the house." She swallowed, "When I was maybe a hundred yards from the road, I heard a gun go off. I didn't know what direction it came from." She put her hand to her face, "The sound was so loud that I was sure everyone in the county had heard it."

"What kind of gun?" Drayton asked.

"A shotgun," Ellie said.

"Do you know a shotgun blast when you hear it?"

"Yes, I know a shotgun blast," she said, "and this was a shotgun."

Drayton nodded, and Ellie went on, "Then I heard Les, I think it was Les, cursing someone."

"*After* the shot?" Drayton asked.

Ellie nodded, "Yes, after. I stopped and waited. It was quiet. I started walking toward the headlights. Everything was still. The car was stopped. I stopped again and waited and tried to see the car. It looked like Les's car. I started to walk forward again, but I heard a car door slam, so I froze. I was so scared. I could see a car, and I could see someone just to the side of the car, barely lighted by the car, and then whoever it was turned and walked into the woods, coming straight at me. I thought that whoever it was had seen me and was coming for me." She nodded, her jaw tense, her eyes wide. "I just started running, not caring about the noise I made, and I didn't stop running until I got back to the house." She caught her breath, "I ran into the barn to get Buddy, but he wasn't there. His stuff was stacked in the back of his pick-up, but he wasn't there. I didn't know where he was." She looked to Drayton, her eyes wide.

"Where did you think he was?" Drayton asked.

Her voice quavered. "I was afraid that he was out there in the woods," she said. "I was afraid that he'd seen me, and I didn't know what to do. I thought maybe he'd gone straight down the road and gotten there ahead of me. I didn't know. And then all I could think of was Cindy, and I ran into the house." She took a deep breath. "She was fine, asleep in her bed."

"That's it?" Drayton said. "You didn't you call the police?"

She shook her head, "No, I was too afraid. I didn't know what had happened. I didn't know if anything happened. I'm still not sure anything happened."

"You didn't do *any*thing?"

Ellie lowered her head, "It's easy to say I should have done something, but I was so scared, and I was so young."

"What *did* you do?"

"After I'd made sure that Cindy was all right, I looked through the house for Buddy, but he wasn't there." She nodded, "So I went back to the bedroom. I lay down in bed, and just lay there all night." She looked at him, saying, "I must have fallen asleep a little because I can remember suddenly hearing Buddy moving around. I waited, but he didn't do anything, and in a few minutes I heard the springs in the sofa squeak, and I knew he was lying down." She stopped and clasped her hands. She looked at Drayton. "You're the first person I've told the whole story. Nobody knew it all but me. I've been carrying it around all these years, and then you showed up at the door out of the blue and told me you'd seen the car."

"You kept pretty calm when I told you."

"Not inside," Ellie said. "I didn't know what to do."

"What did you think that night?"

"Well," she shrugged. "I thought maybe Buddy *had* done something, even though it wasn't like him." She shook her head. "And I was afraid what he might do. I didn't know what." She laughed and shook her head, "When he left the next day in his truck, I went in and sat at the kitchen table, and I started shaking. I sat there forever." She took a deep breath and looked at Drayton. "I was waiting for him to come and tell me what he'd found in the road, but he didn't come." I just kept sitting there. Finally..." she shook her head. "Finally, in the afternoon, I put Cindy in the truck and started down the road. I could hardly drive I was shaking so much. But when I went around the bend, there was nothing there, no car, nothing, nothing." She raised her hands and said, "I even got out and looked at the sides of the road, looked in the ditches expecting to find I don't know what, but probably Les's body, but there was nothing there, and it was like nothing had happened." She made a small noise in her throat and said, "And I just went on pretending nothing had happened and telling myself that everything was O.K., that I was all right, but then somebody told me that Les had disappeared, then somebody else told me, and I didn't know what to do. I thought maybe Buddy *had* done something—maybe he'd put Les's body in the back of the pick-up truck, covered him up, and driven down to Santa Ynez." Her eyes were wide. "He'd know a thousand places down there where no one would ever find a body. And I didn't want Buddy to have to go prison or anything, when it was partially my fault. I didn't want it to all come out." She stopped, "So I didn't do anything. I didn't do anything for all these years. I made myself not think about it. And then you showed up at my door."

The encroaching darkness seemed to make the night even more quiet, and Drayton and Ellie sat silently, thinking, each with separate thoughts, more removed from each other than the inches between them. Ellie's eyes had been full of tears, but they were dry now as she sat looking at Drayton, who sat with his head down, his elbows on his knees, his back bent from the invisible weight. Finally, he looked up at her and said, "Jesus, Ellie, I'm sorry. I didn't know you were carrying all this around, and then I show up and make it worse."

Ellie shook her head. "You haven't made it worse. I just have to face it. You don't get away with much." She stood looking off into the dark woods.

Chapter 13

Drayton had left Ellie's house and reached the highway at the end of the dirt and gravel road. The car sat unmoving, the engine humming, and Drayton stared straight ahead. The hot winds were steady, and the distant hills were becoming silhouettes.

Drayton switched off the ignition key, and the engine came to a quick halt. The melodic sounds of twilight flooded at him, punctuated by occasional metallic pings from the cooling iron and steel. He had to laugh at himself: had he really believed that Ellie knew nothing about Tremain's Alfa that had been sitting in the woods a half mile from her house for *twenty years*? She'd claimed that she'd never seen it, and maybe that could be true, because the car would be hard to see unless you walked through the area, and she probably avoided ever walking through there.

Drayton shook his head: he was terrible with women. He almost always liked them. *Liked them*? He thought. God, he *adored* them, and when they were intelligent and beautiful, he was really lost. And now he was entangled in a complex web of twenty years of lies and fear.

Drayton leaned his sweating head back against the headrest and looked up at the darkening sky. The woods on both sides of Ellie's road were surrendering to shadows and darkness, and Drayton looked out into them as if they had some answers for him—as if—were he to wander off into those woods, he might, after complete darkness fell, magically stumble onto that night twenty years ago when something had happened to Les Tremain. For Drayton, that night had now taken on images of headlights, voices, a shotgun blast, and someone walking toward Ellie, who stood hiding in the darkness, a pale figure among the bone-white trunks of the eucalyptus trees. Now, the thought of walking into those woods scared Drayton. He could feel the hairs on the back of his neck stand on end, and he shivered.

A low but sudden sound startled him, and he studied the woods. For seconds, he sat staring into the trees, and then he heard the sound again. He laughed at himself when he realized the sound was the gurgle of the coolant in the engine and through the hoses. A van swept by on Cold Canyon Creek Road, its lights illuminating the dark tunnel made by the eucalyptus trees. Drayton sat waiting. Had whoever it was that night *seen* Ellie, or did he just happen to walk toward her? Maybe he had let her escape, or maybe she'd been lucky enough to escape. Whoever it was must not have been able to identify her, or later she would have heard something in some way. That was a frightening thought. If it had been her husband Buddy, he'd have known that it was Ellie among the dark trees, and wouldn't he have said something? Then again, maybe not, depending on what he had seen or done. Was there somebody out there—out there in the world— who thought that Ellie had seen what happened? Drayton paused, listened to the quiet of the night, looked out at the purplish black twilight, and told himself that now that he'd stirred the pot, maybe that person would see Ellie as a threat. Still, there was no reason to think that if someone had killed Tremain, that same someone would go on killing other people. "But a murderer might not think like you, Drayton," he muttered aloud, his words dissolving into the darkness and the hot wind that had kicked up a notch and was rustling leaves. He could think of a few people whom he, in the worst combination of events, might—*perhaps*—*maybe*—kill, but he could not imagine killing someone just for being a witness.

Drayton sighed, looked into the darkness, told himself that he had to get out of there, and he reached out to turn the ignition key, but his thoughts stopped him. Ellie had said that she had heard the shot and then someone's shout, and *Tremain* was the one with the shotgun shells in his car and presumably a shotgun at hand. Tremain was afraid of somebody. Maybe that somebody had stopped him there on the road and, terrified, Tremain had shot that person, whoever it was. Drayton took his fingers off the ignition key and leaned back in his seat. Then Tremain could have driven his Alfa into the woods and taken away the dead body in the murdered man's car. But if so, why had Tremain never come back for his car? That didn't make sense, unless he'd just been so scared he'd kept driving, ditched the body someplace, and kept driving until he abandoned the car. Drayton's hands lay curled around the padded steering wheel. But Tremain was not the man Drayton had once thought he was. He might have been serious about his art, but he also mistreated people who loved him. Drayton thought of Andrea Marchand's story of Tremain leaving photos in the mailbox of a woman with whom he was having an affair. In his mind, Drayton put it into words: *sexual blackmail.* For the first time, Drayton thought of Tremain in the same way that Madsen and Andrea Marchand did—as a son-of-a-bitch. And he shook his head. Maybe Ellie's experience that night had not been the same night Tremain had disappeared. She had obviously been strung out, confused, and frightened. Would she have known that Tremain had a shotgun? Drayton said aloud, "You don't know shit."

Drayton started the engine and released the emergency brake. The car rolled a couple of feet and creaked to a stop. Drayton flicked the switch, and the headlights rose into position. The trees across the road looked grotesque in the two tunnels of light. Lost in the high darkness of the treetops, an owl hooted. Drayton shook his head— none of these thoughts made sense; it was too damned complicated, and Tremain or his corpse should have popped up somewhere in the last twenty years. And still, more and more, Drayton felt certain that Tremain was dead, that he'd been killed that night. And who was there that night? Ellie. But she hadn't shot Tremain. Drayton was certain of that. And her husband Buddy was there—Buddy who had just found out that Ellie was having an affair and who had in his hands some incriminating pictures of her for proof. Finding out that your wife was having an affair would be bad enough, but it would be a lot worse to have explicit pictures. Ellie had said that she was afraid of Buddy when he had found out. He could have seen her leaving the house that night, put two and two together, followed her, and then cut over to the road and met Tremain.

"Nice theory," Drayton muttered aloud, slipping the transmission into first gear and pulling out onto Cold Canyon Creek Road. Shifting into second, Drayton accelerated toward the crest of the hill. It felt good to be in control of the car, if nothing else. What would he do with his theory? Lt. Madsen wouldn't be interested. It was just a theory. Drayton asked himself how much of what Ellie had told him he was willing to pass on to Madsen. Drayton shook his head: *none of it*. Drayton stared at the bright white sheen of his headlights on the road ahead of the car. *Why?* he asked himself. Because Madsen had rubbed him the wrong way. Drayton smiled at his next thought. *And because Ellie had rubbed me the right way.*

The road lay ahead, black asphalt bisected by the centerline, bright white in his headlamps. Drayton could feel the wind pushing against the side of his car. Santa Ana winds at night, in a way the most stifling. Another thought came to him—that maybe whoever it was that Tremain was scared of had waylaid him there. Maybe Tremain had threatened *whoever* with the shotgun, and the guy had taken it away from him and killed him with it. Drayton thought to himself that if he, Drayton, had a shotgun and was in danger, he didn't know if he could shoot someone. Probably not. He realized that he had never performed a violent act. He had never even hit someone. Not in his entire life. This business of possibly dealing with a killer was new territory to him. *No experience*, he thought. *Nothing.*

A pair of headlights swam into his rear view-mirror, making Drayton squint against their glare. The lights rode high on the vehicle—either a pick-up or an S.U.V. The road was isolated. Little traffic at this time of night. Little traffic on this road anytime, he told himself. You could get away with murder on this road. *You're talking yourself into paranoia*, he thought to himself. Nevertheless, he picked up his speed and rushed into a curve, his tires singing. The headlights disappeared. Probably someone who lived in the area had turned off. He turned his thoughts back to what might have happened—back to the gun. Maybe the killer had his—or her—own gun, and Ellie simply didn't know what kind of gun she'd heard. But if Ellie was right and it was a shotgun blast, it didn't make sense that the shooter had been a woman. Ben, at the shop, had been right when he said that a woman wasn't likely to carry around a shotgun or shotgun shells.

Lowering his speed, Drayton drove slowly through the curves, weaving along the shadowed road. Dead quiet. Drayton thought of a shotgun, or of any gun, going off late at night—how loud it would be. But just because a gun had been fired, didn't mean someone had been shot. Maybe someone just scared the hell out of Tremain—maybe he'd run down the road to escape and had never come back. The guy with the gun could have driven Tremain's car into the woods and then driven away in his own car, laughing at the thought of Tremain running down the road. Tremain could still be running.

The road straightened out, and again the headlights glared in Drayton's rear-view mirror. The muscles in his neck and back were tightening. He picked up speed. The headlights seemed to keep pace. Maybe the smart thing to do would be to go to the police with all of this. What else was he going to do—drive down to Santa Ynez and start questioning Buddy? Who the hell was he to start questioning Ellie's ex? And Buddy might not be very happy about being accused of doing something to the man who had wrecked his marriage. Buddy would want to keep all of that behind him. But the police—Madsen—wouldn't do much.

Drayton pushed his little X 1/9 until the car was wallowing in some of the curves, but he knew that the tires were a long way from losing traction. Again, he looked in the rear-view mirror. No headlights now, but he'd gone into a curve and maintained his speed. Maybe it was time for him to act. Drayton leaned into a curve, and the tires squalled. The road leveled out, and Drayton watched the speedometer climb quickly to 90 mph, and then he downshifted into a shallow curve. No damned SUV or pick-up would be able to take the curve at that speed, and no headlights shone in the rear-view mirror. The air was hot and alive, not the kind of night to worry about what had happened twenty years ago to people he didn't even know. But he knew Ellie, and that was the complication—he knew Ellie. What if there was some way to get her out from under all of this? She'd carried it around for twenty years. She didn't deserve that. How to help her? Not the police.

Hawkins, he thought. The retired cop who had investigated the case. Old Hawkins. It was still early enough in the evening, and the old guy was sure to be home. Old guys are always home at night. They can't see to drive. Drayton pulled to a stop at the main highway and sat waiting to see if there were any headlights behind him. None. Just the dark night. Ahead, the moon was a sliver. He pulled out onto the highway and headed toward town and to his shop, which was close, and where there was a phone. The air had turned chilly. He'd stop at the shop and phone Hawkins.

Clouds swept in, the sky became overcast, and Drayton couldn't see the moon or any stars by the time he reached the shop. All the other shops were closed. Ben and Drayton had a motion light over the doors to their shop, but it had broken long ago, and neither of them had climbed up to fix it, so Drayton left his headlights burning. Tremain's Alfa squatted outside the shop in the darkness, looking like nothing more than an abandoned hulk. Drayton dialed the combination to the padlock and pushed the groaning garage door open just wide enough so that he could slip in. When he stepped into the darkness, he heard something run across the shop, by the back doors. He froze and waited. *Paranoid*, he told himself, *you're paranoid*. The noise had to be either a rat or a cat. Feral cats had made the garage their home, and the mice their meals. He'd never opened that door at night without something scurrying around inside. Drayton switched on the lights, shuffled through the phonebook, found what he thought was Hawkins' number, and tried it. When the old man answered the phone, he said that, yes, he was the retired cop, and sure, he remembered Tremain's disappearance, and damned right he'd be willing to talk about it because it was a pain in the ass that it had never been solved, and he thought about it from time to time and always thought it was a stinker, and Drayton should come on over.

As Drayton hung up the phone, he heard tires scuffing on the asphalt-and- gravel parking area, followed by the slight groan of brakes, and then he could hear an engine idling. *A big vehicle*, he thought. *A truck. A V-8 engine.* The engine continued to idle. Next came the closing of the truck door. Still the engine was running. The crunch of footsteps crossed the gravel and asphalt apron. Drayton looked around. A ball-peen hammer lay on the workbench in front of him, but it seemed like a comical weapon. On a hook at the side of the workbench hung a crowbar. Drayton grimaced at the thought of hitting someone with it, and somewhere in the back of his mind, he could hear steel crunch against skull. He looked away from the crowbar. The footsteps were right outside the door. Drayton saw Ben's nail gun and grabbed it. The nail gun felt heavy in his hand as he stood looking at the opening in the sliding doors.

Drayton half-expected the ghost of Tremain, but it was a real man who stepped through the small opening that Drayton had left when he slid back the door. The man, tall and thick, stepped into the light. His face was angular, almost a triangle, his chin pointy, his mouth small. Drayton could see that he was probably in his mid-forties and almost bald on the top, but what hair he had was shaggy and to his shoulders.

Drayton stood with the nail gun at his side. He felt silly. He had fired it only once, and he wasn't even sure it was loaded and ready to fire. In a quick glance, he saw that a row of nails was hanging from it, like shells from a machine gun. Could he really shoot these at the man? Would the nail even go straight? The nail gun had no rifling.

The man, bigger than Drayton, stepped a little closer. "I'm a friend of Ellie's."

"I guessed that," Drayton said. "You're Ronnie, right?" The nail gun was cold and heavy in his hand.

Ronnie flinched, ignored Drayton's question, and said, "I'm trying to watch out for Ellie. She's a special person."

"I know," Drayton said. He tried to remember how the nail gun worked. *Shells?* he thought. *Twenty-two-short shells?*

"She's a good person, and she's been a good friend." His voice was raspy. "I care a lot about her." He took another step toward Drayton.

"I know," Drayton said again. "You're the guy who called me late the other night and tried to scare me—and then you keyed my car because I went to the police station. Right?"

Ronnie stiffened but smiled. "You don't take a hint so good."

"You didn't waste any time getting started," Drayton said.

Ronnie nodded, "I was heading out and saw the tow truck pulling that old car." He reached up and rubbed the back of his neck as if he was trying to release the tension. "I just cut back down and followed the tow truck."

Ronnie seemed young, almost boyish, as Ellie had said, but he was clearly in his forties. Drayton understood how Ellie could have trusted him—at least enough to tell him some things—enough to lighten her load. Ronnie reminded Drayton of one of his students who had gotten into trouble and didn't have a clue about how to get out of it.

Trying to slow everything down, trying to stall, Drayton asked, "What did Ellie tell you about the car?"

The question pulled Ronnie up short, and he hesitated for an instant. "She just told me that it had something to do with her divorce and that it could cause her some trouble. That she just wanted to leave it there. Just wanted to forget about it." He nodded. "And you won't let her do that."

"That's all she said?"

"That was enough for me," Ronnie answered, his jaw set. He stepped forward and saw the nail gun in Drayton's hand. He looked back to Drayton's face and said, "I've never really hurt anyone, but I don't want Ellie to get hurt." Ronnie stepped forward. "She's a special person."

"A special person?" Drayton said.

"Like nobody else I've ever met."

A flutter of noise came from the shadows at the back of the shop. Ronnie glanced that way, his eyes narrowing.

"Cats," Drayton said. "Feral cats after mice." The nail gun felt heavy now, as if he had an anvil in his hand. Drayton didn't think he'd ever be able to shoot the damned thing at Ronnie. Drayton smelled something. What was that? Pissy sweat from fear? Ronnie? Himself? He was scared enough.

Ronnie started forward again.

"Wait. Did Ellie call you?" Drayton asked.

Ronnie grimaced and shook his head.

"Hold it," Drayton said and raised the nail gun. "She was going to call you and explain everything." He gestured toward the phone mounted on the post. "Just call her, she'll explain. I'm trying to help her."

Ronnie looked at the nail gun in Drayton's hand, and hesitated. Drayton watched the two parts of the man struggle against each other. Ronnie's jaw tightened as he took another step toward Drayton.

"Hold it there," Drayton said, and gestured with the nail gun. Ronnie shook his head and took another step.

Drayton shouted, "For Christ's sake, call her! Don't do something we'll both be sorry for. Just call her. It will take a minute."

Ronnie hesitated, looking at Drayton.

"A minute," Drayton said. "Just stop for a minute and listen to me."

Ronnie took a deep breath, picked up the phone, and angled his body toward Drayton so he could watch him.

Ronnie punched in the number, and Drayton thought, *he knows it by heart. But why wouldn't he?* The nail gun felt as heavy as an anchor in his extended arm, and he let the gun drop a few inches.

Watching Drayton, Ronnie stood with the phone to his ear.

Drayton could hear the phone ringing and pictured the hallway in Ellie's house, saw her dippy dogs slipping and sliding on the hardwood floors.

After a few seconds, Ronnie's eyes shifted, and he said, "Ellie." He waited, listening to her talk, before he said, "That's right." Then he asked, "Is this Drayton guy any trouble for you? I know who he is. I know he had that car towed away."

Drayton watched Ronnie and waited. Ronnie seemed more and more like a big boy—not so much slow-witted as naïve. He glanced up at Drayton and then back to the phone. He was listening. "O.K., Ellie. I understand. O.K. I understand. Sure." He listened some more and then said, "O.K., Ellie. Sure. O.K. That's what I'll do." A change came over him. "I didn't mean to be a nosy neighbor. I didn't mean to get into your business." He smiled. "Bye."

Ronnie's expression was pained. He nodded. "Ellie says you're O.K. Like you said, she said you're trying to help her. That you're just trying to help her."

Drayton nodded, "That's right." He lowered the nail gun to his side and sighed loud and long.

For as long as a minute, Ronnie stood unmoved, then looked up. "I'll go." Embarrassed, he started toward the door, in a hurry to leave.

"Hold it," Drayton said. "Sorry about the confusion. I don't blame you for trying to help her. She *is* a good person."

Ronnie stopped, but he shook his head. "No, it's O.K."

Ronnie's shoulders slumped as he looked toward Drayton. "I'm sorry about your car. Let me pay to have it fixed."

Drayton smiled, shook his head, and looked around the shop. "I fix cars all the time. That's what I do. I've got plenty of paint, and it'll be an easy job."

Ronnie sighed and walked away. Drayton watched him step through the open garage door and out into the darkness. Drayton didn't move as he heard the truck transmission thunk into gear—an automatic transmission—followed by the grinding of the tires on the gravel and asphalt, and then the truck was gone. Still, Drayton didn't move. After a minute, his heartbeat returned to normal. *Jesus Christ, poor Ronnie*, he thought. Starry-eyed. *The poor bastard did care about Ellie.* Drayton shook his head. *There are worse things than being dumped by a woman.* He glanced up at the shop clock. There was still time to visit Hawkins. Now, for the first time, he felt like he was getting someplace, but he didn't have a clue why he felt that way.

Before he left the shop, Drayton called Ellie to let her know that he was all right. When he told her what had happened, she said that she didn't think Ronnie would have ever really hurt him. Drayton stared into space, he raised his eyebrows, and said, "We'll talk later."

Chapter 14

Drayton was still arguing with himself fifteen minutes later, when he pulled up in front of the address Hawkins had given him on the phone. The house was a surprise: a big, two-story job of glass and redwood. Drayton had expected Hawkins to live in a white frame house from the twenties, about the same time the old man had been born. This house looked expensive for a cop, but the roar of the freeway was close, and maybe the noise drove the price down.

Hawkins stood waiting at the open front door. "I was watching for you. I'm getting so damned deaf I can't hear the bell ring. Come on in."

When Hawkins closed the front door, the noise from the freeway diminished to a low hum, a sound that Drayton thought could have been mistaken for the ocean's hissing roll. As he shook Hawkins' hand, Drayton noted he was about the same age as Louis Marchand, somewhere in his eighties, the generation of Drayton's father, but Hawkins was in better shape than Marchand. Hawkins' hair was white, his eyes blue, and his movements were those of a much younger man. However, his hearing problems gave him away, and Drayton quickly learned to speak loudly even though Hawkins was wearing two hearing aids. Hawkins motioned Drayton to an easy chair and asked loudly, "I was about to have a cold one, you want one?"

Drayton nodded, "Sounds good." He thought he remembered having seen a younger Hawkins on the news, being interviewed about criminal cases.

Hawkins went into the kitchen and Drayton looked around the room. The furniture was old, but not too worn, just comfortable looking. Drayton guessed that Hawkins and his wife had bought new pieces about twenty years earlier and then had quit forever on trying to upgrade. On the mantle were family pictures. One was of Hawkins and his bride on their wedding day. Drayton could recognize him. He wore a tuxedo, and his bride wore a white wedding gown with a long train. Behind them was a painting of what was supposed to look like a castle wall. Hawkins' wife had long black hair braided in a single rope, which hung over her right shoulder. Her dark hair, eyes, and skin made Drayton guess that her background might be Mexican, and then the nearby pictures of a string of kids, some of them dark like Hawkins' wife, others fair like their father, supported the notion.

"That's Irene and me fifty-two years ago," Hawkins said, handing Drayton a bottle of beer.

Drayton smiled, nodded, and said, "A pretty woman."

"Beautiful," Hawkins said, "but she's even a nicer person, generous, full of love, forgiving. A heart as big as a house." He smiled and shrugged, "I don't know what would have happened to me if she hadn't come along."

"You're lucky," Drayton said.

"I know," Hawkins said. He looked at Drayton, "You're divorced, right?" Drayton nodded, "Right. How'd you know?"

Hawkins smiled, "Well, it's always a good first guess nowadays, and after years of studying people the way I did, you get to know certain things, see certain things."

Drayton asked, "I *look* divorced?"

"To me, you do. Eyes," he said. "Our eyes always give us away." He looked back to the wedding photo, "She's in that new place for people with Alzheimer's." He shook his head, "I couldn't take care of her anymore, so..." And he shrugged.

"Sorry," Drayton said.

Hawkins nodded, "Yeh, it's the shits, but people get old and almost nothing works anymore." He laughed to himself. "A long time ago, when I was about your age, an old guy I knew was retiring, and when I asked him why, he told me, 'Because all the wrong things are stiff in the morning.'"

Drayton laughed and said, "You seem to be doing O.K."

Hawkins smiled, "Well, this house used to hold Irene and me and seven kids." He shook his head. "I don't know how we did it." He smiled, "I can't hear very well anymore, but sometimes when it's real quiet, I think I hear the bunch of them running through the house." He laughed, "Sometimes they drove me crazy, but Irene always said that I was the patient one."

Hawkins eased himself into a recliner, its dark leather creased and cracked. "But you didn't come by to hear an old man piss and moan. You want to talk about that son-of-a-bitch Tremain."

"You didn't like him?"

"Didn't like what I knew," Hawkins said. "Selfish son-of-a-bitch. Thought the sun rose and set on him. Thought he was God's gift to women. He needed to have some kids so he'd know he wasn't the most important person in the world." The old man shook his head, "He never worked, and he went around taking dirty pictures of girls." Hawkins hesitated and shifted his bottle of beer from one hand to the other before he said, "I'm surprised someone didn't take him out of the picture a lot sooner." He gestured toward Drayton with the neck of his beer bottle, "Anyway, what do you need to know?"

Drayton told Hawkins about the Alfa and about some of the rest that he'd found out since, but he left out the last part about Ellie and Tremain, and Ellie's husband. He didn't want to air all of that unless it was absolutely necessary.

"So you found the car," Hawkins said. "That puts a different light on things, I guess."

"That's what I thought," Drayton said, and took a drink of his beer.

"If we'd found the car, we might have looked harder for Tremain," Hawkins said. "I wanted to look harder anyway, but the Chief didn't think it was worth the time or money. Everybody thought the s.o.b. just skipped out of town."

"What did you think?"

"I thought we could get two birds with one stone. I never did think he skipped out. I always thought he was killed—maybe murder, maybe manslaughter—I don't know."

"Why's that?" Drayton asked.

"Christ, nobody skips town and leaves *everything* behind. True, we thought the car was gone, but everything else was there. All his clothes and furniture, almost nine thousand dollars in the bank, and no recent withdrawals. All of his art stuff." Hawkins shook his head, "They always slip up, they always take something."

"So you think he's dead?"

Hawkins laughed, "Sure. Nobody will ever find him, but you can bet that he's dead."

Drayton nodded, "You said a minute ago that you thought that you could have gotten two birds with one stone. What'd you mean? Who was the second bird?"

"A piece of shit named Frank Hollis," Hawkins said. "A thug. A drug-runner." Hawkins paused. "Tremain was afraid of him, scared shitless of him. Hollis roughed him up, but Tremain wouldn't press charges." Hawkins shook his head. "But make no mistake about it: Tremain was scared." He laughed. "He had an old double-barreled shotgun in his car. Sawed off." He laughed. "He was lucky he didn't shoot himself in the ass, much as he knew about guns."

"I asked Madsen about Hollis," Drayton said.

"Drugs," Hawkins said, "Frankie Hollis dealt drugs, a nasty little weasel who had a mean streak."

"Inspector Madsen told me that Frank Hollis could never kill anybody." Hawkins laughed and shook his head, "Madsen thinks that queers...." Hawkins interrupted himself—"Hollis was queerer than a nine-dollar bill." He shrugged and continued, "Madsen thinks that queers don't have whatever it takes to kill somebody." Hawkins laughed. "Madsen doesn't understand people very well. *Any*body can kill somebody." Hawkins gestured toward Drayton and then himself. "You don't have to be mean or some damned thing. Not true. Sometimes they're just desperate, sometimes they just get tired of people shitting on them. Most of us could do it if you pushed us too hard."

"That was Frank Hollis?"

Hawkins closed his eyes. "That was Frankie Hollis, and somebody paid Hollis to put a scare into Tremain."

"Who was that?"

Hawkins shook his head. "Don't know. Didn't really try to find out. No charges were pressed, and there were enough guys who wished Tremain ill. It would have taken the whole police force and we still wouldn't have found out who it was."

"How'd you find out all of this?" Drayton asked.

Hawkins looked surprised. "Hell, I asked Hollis." He shrugged. "And I asked around. This town's got a little world of its own that most people never get a glimpse of."

"Did you follow up on any of that?"

Hawkins took a long drink and then rubbed his left ear and started shaking his head. He looked at Drayton, "Damned ear starts ringing, ringing like hell." He took his hand from his ear and said, "Follow up on that? Yes, sure, as much as I could, but like I said, nobody really gave a damn."

"Tremain's sister gives a damn."

"What?" Hawkins asked, and Drayton repeated himself.

Hawkins frowned at him for a moment, his jaw tight, his eyes focused, and Drayton had a glimpse of what the old guy had been like when he was younger and a cop. Then, he again became the white-haired old man and said, "Sisters always give a damn, more than wives usually. Sisters remember them from when they were kids." He looked at Drayton again. "She's the one who filed the missing person's report."

"How long did you look for him?"

"Honestly?" Hawkins said. "Maybe a week."

"And that was it?"

Hawkins nodded, "And that was it." He shrugged. "Except that about six months after he disappeared, we got a phone call on it."

"A phone call?"

Hawkins nodded, "Yes, some woman." He took a drink of beer. "No name. No number. I heard the tape. She sounded dead drunk to me. God knows, it could have been one of a dozen women Tremain was messing with or who wanted to cause somebody trouble. I thought maybe it was something, but my chief told me to forget the damned case and move on."

"What'd this woman say?"

Hawkins thought for a few seconds. "Like I said, she was drunk, she was hard to understand, and she had an accent, heavier than my Irene's." He nodded, "She said that if we wanted to know what had happened to Les Tremain, we should talk to Georgie Gagne."

"Who's that?" Drayton asked. "I haven't heard that name before."

"He's down on the Mesa, some junk man. Auto salvage yard, they call it."

"Did you talk to him?"

Hawkins nodded, "Sure, I drove down there. A bad guy, I thought, but being a bad guy's not a crime." He shook his head. "I couldn't see him and Tremain knowing each other, unless Gagne had a good-looking wife or daughter."

"Did he?"

"Well," Hawkins said, "he had a wife, but I doubt if she was good looking."

"What did Gagne say?" Drayton asked.

"He said he'd never heard of Les Tremain, but of course he'd have said that even if he had no reason for lying. He was one of those guys who'd lie just to be lying. He said that he didn't know what the hell I was talking about." Hawkins shook his head, "Not a guy you could intimidate."

"That was it?"

"That was it," Hawkins said. "Nobody wanted me to spend any more time on the case. And there was no connection between Gagne and Tremain. Both of them were low lives, but one was dumber and poorer than the other. Meaner too."

Drayton nodded, "Like I said, I haven't heard that name before."

"No reason you should have. It was all police business," Hawkins said. He smiled at Drayton and asked, "What's your interest in this?"

Drayton took a deep breath, "First I just got interested when I stumbled onto the car and found out that nobody knew what had become of Tremain. Later on, it became more personal. He knew a friend of mine."

"A woman," Hawkins said. It was a statement, not a question.

Drayton nodded, "A woman."

"Well," Hawkins said, "that's your business. I know better than to give advice to people in love." He smiled. "Nobody could ever tell me a bad thing about Irene. Not unless he wanted his nose popped." He looked at Drayton and said, "I won't give you any advice on romance, but I will give you some on this Tremain stuff. If you're planning to go down and talk to Georgie Gagne, I'd forget it. I don't think Gagne knows anything about Tremain, so I don't think it would do any good, and I don't think he'd appreciate it." Hawkins watched Drayton drink the last of his beer. "I can tell you're not listening to me. I can tell you're stubborn. Let me tell you this, take this from an old cop: Tremain is dead, and the man who killed him was Frankie Hollis, and Frankie died in prison."

"Wait," Drayton, interrupted. "Hollis died in prison?"

Hawkins sat looking at Drayton, and then said, "Yeh, he was in there for dealing. Died of AIDS, I heard."

"How long ago?"

"Close to fifteen years ago, I'd say," Hawkins said nodding. Drayton nodded and was quiet.

Hawkins smiled, "So, all the scores have been settled." He paused and shrugged, "As much as they ever get settled." He laughed and said, "On television, I think they call it *closure*. Silly bastards, nothing like this ever gets closed. When somebody gets killed, nothing gets closed."

Chapter 15

Monday

Drayton snapped awake at dawn the next morning, his heart thumping. Short of breath, he lay remembering his dream, which had been about Ellie. In the dream, the two of them were again driving through the night in an open car, but this time the car was Les Tremain's Alfa, and as they drove blissfully along, Drayton had the persistent sense that someone or something was in the back seat. Just as he'd turned to look, he awoke with a start. All night he'd slept badly, the worst he had in a couple of years, and he knew he was more depressed than he'd wanted to admit about what had happened with Ellie. Their night in his car, driving south through the hills and through the starry darkness, had had a kind of magic for him, and it had seemed as if the loneliness and aimlessness he'd been feeling since Bonnie left was falling away.

Unable to move, unable to face the day, and exhausted, Drayton lay there feeling old and feeling sorry for himself, and listened to the Santa Ana winds until he finally fell back asleep and didn't awake again until late morning. Rupe was asleep on Drayton's right side, curled up as if he thought he was a puppy, and Rip, on top of the dresser, was a ball of fur with one eye looking around, ready for anything. Drayton sighed: what sleeping partners he had. He gave up trying *not* to think about what had happened in the past couple of days. Ellie hadn't really lied to him, she just didn't tell him how well she knew Les Tremain. And who would expect her to do that? A sin of omission the Catholics called it. What woman in her right mind would say to a man she'd known only a few days: "Oh, by the way, I used to run around with an artist who took some sexy pictures of me and broke up my marriage, and then he disappeared and I don't know what happened, but I've been afraid to think about it for twenty years, let alone say anything to anyone about it, because I was afraid that my ex-husband might have had something to do with it."

He swung his feet out onto the carpeted floor and sat on the edge of the bed. Rupe and Rip both jumped down and headed toward their bowls in the kitchen, ready for breakfast. So much had come at him so fast that he couldn't seem to get any perspective on it, and he felt more confused and uncertain than he had in a long time. Standing there in his boxer shorts, with Rupe and Rip waiting for him in the kitchen, he paused for a second and then told himself that, if he wanted to, he could just walk away and let Les Tremain be history, which was what almost everyone else wanted. Old Hawkins had given him some good advice when he'd said that the case was settled, that Frankie Hollis had killed Les Tremain and then had died of AIDS in prison. End of story. *And so you, Drayton*, he said to himself, *So you go chasing your tail around and making life difficult for the most attractive woman you've met in years, a woman who already had her share of pain—a broken home—carrying a heavy secret for twenty years—having cancer and losing a breast, and up you pop, Drayton, to rattle her cage, to say, "Hey, I want to know what happened to Les Tremain, whom I've never met in my life and who doesn't mean a thing to me."*

Except that wasn't quite true: There was also the fact that Drayton didn't like it that something might have happened to Tremain because of the way he had chosen to live his life. No doubt he had done some things that many people would see as immoral and unethical, but he hadn't done anything that he should die for. Drayton stopped himself because he realized he kept assuming Tremain was dead—but it sure looked that way. If he was dead, and if Frankie Hollis hadn't killed him—as Hawkins thought—then maybe one of the people Drayton had talked to was a murderer. Two big *maybes* in his thinking. And *maybe*, he thought, maybe they have mild winters in hell.

Drayton pulled on a pair of running shorts and slipped on his running shoes for his jog down to the mailbox. He tugged a tee shirt over his head as he walked into the kitchen to feed Rupe and Rip. They looked up at him, Rupe eager, Rip cool. He put their bowls out, and they began to munch as he stepped out onto the deck to stretch. By the time he was finished stretching, Rupe pushed open the screen door with his nose and was ready to go for their morning run. Rip had disappeared into the woods and brush.

The sky was a spotless blue through the branches of the oaks and eucalyptus trees. As Drayton broke into his jog, he began to think of Bonnie, who had always told him not to turn his life into a tragedy. She'd scolded him one day when he said he was getting old, and told him not to rush getting old, it would be there soon enough. "Don't call yourself old," she'd said while she stood in front of the mirror putting on her earrings and checking her hair. They were going to some kind of fundraiser for the arts. The evening was a bore, but when they came home they'd made love on the carpet in front of the fire, the logs crackling in the flames and Bonnie's skin scented and soft— small sighs of pleasure coming from her, followed by throaty chuckles of delight. Those were the last images that he could remember of them making love. He knew there were other times after that, but that was the last one he remembered. At times like this, jogging on a warm morning, troubles all around him, he couldn't believe that she was gone from his life, and gone forever. He hoped she was happy in Florida with her new husband, and he wondered how turning fifty soon would be for her.

After his run, Drayton made coffee and toast and sat eating while he read a week-old newspaper. A wind was blowing through the eucalyptus trees. He wanted to believe Ellie's story. He *did* believe her story. That was the long and the short of it: he *did believe* Ellie's story. He laughed and said aloud, "You've known her a few days and you believe her without question." Bringing the coffee cup to his lips, he sipped it and looked out at the bright sky. What believing Ellie meant to him was that he had to continue to find out what happened that night. That was the only way things could be right between them, and that was the only way she would ever have anything like peace. He laughed at himself because he knew that another big factor driving him was simply that he wanted to *know*—there was something about Les Tremain, there was something about the story that made him want to *know*. Maybe, he thought, it was because the truth had become so blurred and lost for him at the university when he'd been accused of sexual harassment, and maybe it was because of how the truth got lost for a long time, and then when it was found again, there were still people who didn't believe it, people who *wanted* to believe otherwise. It put drama in their lives.

Whether Les Tremain was a womanizing son-of-a-bitch or not, he didn't deserve to be dead and forgotten. Tremain hadn't even gotten the chance to lament being fifty years old. He didn't get to do the creative work he wanted to do. He didn't get to go on loving the women he loved. Drayton sighed. Louis Marchand would say it didn't make much difference in the long run, but Drayton thought it did make a difference. He wasn't even sure that he knew why he thought it made a difference, but he did. To say that it didn't make any difference was the cheap answer, the easy answer, because the truth was that it made a difference to Tremain's sister, it made a difference to Ellie, and it made a difference to him. Who had met Tremain out there that night? What poor bastard had been carrying *that* around for twenty years?

Rupe chomped at his food, eating with such enthusiasm that he pushed his bowl across the floor until it stopped halfway under the refrigerator: now he had it cornered. Drayton laughed at his dog's simple pleasures, then the laughter settled into a smile, the smile faded, and he asked himself where he was in his efforts to find out what had happened to Les Tremain. At least poor Ronnie was out of the picture. Poor Ronnie, who was like a teenage boy about Ellie. Ronnie had acted just like a high school kid. But, Drayton asked himself, what does that mean in terms of trying to find out what happened to Tremain? Closer, he sensed, closer somehow. He didn't *know* it, but he *sensed* it, and he felt his energy returning and his depression lifting. Maybe he wouldn't like the answer when he got it, but he still wanted to find it. What had made it seem as if he was closer? What had his mind pieced together that he didn't know about yet? Ellie had laughed about his sense of intuition, but what intuition meant to him was that his mind had understood something that hadn't reached his consciousness. He thought back to what Hawkins had told him about the phone call from the woman with an accent. Marian Mosher had said that the woman who had called her about her brother's disappearance had a Mexican accent. It was a safe bet it was the same woman.

Louis Marchand and his wife had said that the woman caller was probably Sally Wu. "Rupe," Drayton said, looking at his dog. "Sally Wu ain't got no Mexican accent." Sally Wu with the Mexican accent had led him to Louis Marchand. And she'd led Hawkins to Georgie Gagne, and Hawkins had warned Drayton to stay away from Gagne. Stay away from the junk man. Drayton went to his phone book on the kitchen sink and began to look through it. No number for a George Gagne. No Gagne at all. He checked the junkyards down on the Mesa. None of them had Gagne's name attached to it, but all of the junkyards on the Mesa were lined up on the same road. Finding Georgie Gagne couldn't be too hard. Maybe Gagne could tell him who Sally Wu with the Mexican accent really was.

Drayton had shaved his face and his head and was just getting out of the shower when the phone rang. Normally, he never rushed to the phone, but he thought it might be Ellie, so he ran, bath water dripping from him to the telephone and onto the floor. Wet and chilled, he answered the phone, but the voice on the phone wasn't Ellie's. "Mr. Drayton?"

"Yes, this is Drayton."

"Mr. Drayton, this is Marian Mosher, Les Tremain's sister. You were at my house the other day. You left your number."

"Sure," Drayton said. "Hello, Mrs. Mosher. What is it?" Puddles were forming on the hardwood floor at his feet.

The phone was quiet except for Marian Mosher's breathing, and then, her voice thin and distant, she said, "You said to phone you when I felt like you could look at Les's photographs." She paused, "I have them. I'd like you to come look at them and tell me if you've found out anything about Les."

Drayton shook his head, but he didn't say no, because he felt sorry for her, because he imagined her searching her house like a ghost moving through Les Tremain's past, and because he didn't have the heart to put her off.

"I've recently had my chemo treatment, and I don't have much strength, and I'm pretty sick—but I have to know about Les." She paused before adding, "and I'm hoping this is a good time for you."

Drayton hesitated. His plan had been to drive south to the Mesa and the junkyards, and her house was on the way. Why not stop and see what she had, although he didn't know what he could tell her about his search for her brother.

"Is about a half-hour o.k. for you?" he asked.

"Yes, oh yes," Marian Mosher said, her voice weak but animated. "Please come down as soon as you can." She hesitated and Drayton could barely make out her words as she said, "I'm afraid I won't be very hospitable. I won't be," and she laughed softly, "I won't be my usual charming self. I've just had my therapy, and it really takes it out of me."

"Of course," Drayton said, "all you have to do is point me to the photographs."

AHEAD WAS PACIFIC BLUFFS, and even at that distance, Drayton could see Marian Mosher's house. When he exited the freeway and started climbing the twisting road to the house, he hoped that in those boxes of photographs, there would be none of Ellie. Although he'd already seen some, and although he already knew what had happened, he just didn't need any more concrete reminders. If those photos bothered him this much twenty years later, how much must they have bothered the husbands and boyfriends when they had first seen the photos of the women in their lives? Probably more than one of those men had thought about killing Les Tremain. But thinking about it and doing it were two different things. Even thinking about it and planning it were very different from doing it. If you did it, you'd ignored all those opportunities to think about it and *not* do it. Premeditated was the word all right. *Meditate* on it, think on it, *before* you did it. Anyone could think about killing, but to do it was hard to imagine. Maybe as a reflexive action, maybe under terrible conditions, but not when you had time to think about it.

Marian Mosher's front door was slightly open. Drayton knocked and called her name. Faintly, her voice came back, telling him to come in. Drayton followed her voice into the kitchen, where she sat at a white table, a glass of water before her. In any other situation, she might have looked comic because she wore a white sleeping gown with brocade at the collar, a white duster over it, and her San Francisco Giants baseball cap that looked too big for her, as if she'd forgotten to adjust its Velcro strap. She looked up, and Drayton felt almost frightened. His heart went out to her because she looked so sick and so weak, and he felt some real sense of what all this meant to her. Much of her life had been on hold since her brother had disappeared, and whatever had happened to Les had happened to her as well.

Pulling a chair close to her, Drayton said, "This is not a good time for you, Mrs. Mosher. Let me come back another time."

She glanced up and there was a wan smile on her face as she shook her head. "No, I'll just tell you where the photos are, and I'll go lie down." As she looked at him, her eyes seemed wrong for her face, because they were still bright blue and full of vitality. Drayton remembered what Hawkins had said about our eyes giving us away. She wet her lips and said, "They're downstairs in the storage room that I showed you. Two boxes labeled: 'Photographs.'" The two sentences seemed too much for her, and she sagged.

Drayton reached out and put his hand on her hand. It was cold and smooth, like a sculpture you weren't supposed to touch. She gripped his hand and said, "You take your time. I'm going to lie down on the sofa now." Drayton helped her up, and she leaned against him as they walked into the living room and the white leather sofa. She wore a cologne that smelled of lavender, but beneath that scent was another smell almost like smoke from a smoldering fire. Her white gown and her white skin seemed to blend into the sofa. When she lay down, Drayton took a cream-colored woolen blanket from the end of the sofa and covered her. She pointed to the table and a television remote control. When he gave it to her, she took it in her hand and held it as a child might hold her toy animal.

Drayton stood looking at her for a minute and lost any doubt about trying to find her brother. He'd find out what happened to Tremain, no matter what. *No matter what*, he thought.

Satisfied that Marian Mosher was comfortable, Drayton went down the stairs and into the storage room, where he found the two boxes on the floor next to a table. One box had once held a ream of typing paper, and the other box was half again as big. Drayton put the boxes on the table and sat down in an office chair. He flicked on a lamp that was on the table, removed the top from the smaller box, hesitated, and then took out a group of photographs. Each had been matted. Packed and sealed for so long, they still gave off the acrid smell of the chemicals used for developing film. Again, Drayton hesitated; he prayed that nowhere in the two boxes would he find any photos of Ellie.

The first photos weren't what he'd expected—all images of beautiful women. Instead, some of the pictures were shot so close to the subjects that they lost their identities and became geometric shapes. At first he tried to identify each shape or part, but then he realized that hadn't been the point, and he looked at the shapes and designs. All of the photographs were in black and white. The next group had some colored shots, and they were more realistic. Still, they weren't of people, but of objects and forms that suggested what Les Tremain might have thought of some people, or the way people thought. One photo was of two figures in beautifully but strangely colored light, and the two figures stood next to each other: one of the figures was the Virgin Mary, the other was Dorothy Duck. They both stood bathed in the strange light, both looking like important religious icons. Drayton had to smile. He knew even a little better how Les Tremain must have pissed off people. *He must have loved doing it*, Drayton thought. He flicked through the pictures and had a better sense of Tremain's wit and his creativity, but none of the photos told Drayton anything that might help him figure out what had happened to Tremain.

The second box, the larger box, wasn't full, but contained thirty or so pictures, all matted, and they were what Drayton had at first expected—shots of people—all kinds of people. Again, the light and its shadows did amazing things to the peoples' faces and bodies, distorting them, sometimes making them more beautiful than they could have been in reality, sometimes making them grotesque, like something out of some lower level of Dante's hell. Some of the photos were of naked children playing in a stream, their small curved bodies both beautiful but also distant, so that Drayton found himself looking at them as he might look at photos of other mammals. The children were naked, but only a sicko would think that they were in any way sexual. The photos celebrated the children's bodies but also suggested what they would become, how they were animals evolving into very different shapes.

The next photos were again in black and white, and this time they were of naked men, men sitting in chairs, lounging on sofas, hanging from trees; one striking shot was of a man's white body, his head back, as he floated just below the slick surface of a small mountain pool, his arms extended in almost absolute relaxation. In all there were a dozen photos of men, and Drayton noted for himself that none was in any way sexual. They'd be sexual for him only if society had sent him there with a strange and distorted load of baggage.

He wondered if Tremain had boxed the photographs and placed them in order, because as Drayton went through the two boxes, his perspectives shifted, and he moved away from a tendency to look for the realistic and instead began enjoying the shapes and forms of people and objects that he saw every day. By the time Drayton had reached the photographs of the men, the thought of anything sexual had diminished, and that diminishment told him something about himself—that maybe he wasn't always as enlightened as he thought he was.

Halfway into the second box, he came to the photos he'd been expecting—photos of women, photos of women in clothes, or without clothes, in a variety of settings and situations. The pictures seemed ageless. Nothing about the women seemed to suggest that the photos had been taken twenty or more years earlier.

After eight or nine photos, Drayton came to one that made him take a sharp breath because all along he'd been afraid that he'd come on a photo of Ellie, and he wasn't prepared for what he saw. The woman in the photo wasn't Ellie, but was a young red-haired woman who had a density of freckles on her face and across her white shoulders. She sat behind a gleaming, dark walnut dining room table, her arms folded under her bare breasts, her face in a slight smile, and all was inaccurately reflected in the lustrous gloss of the table. Her smile made her seem happy, which was amazing, because Drayton had known her, and she had never been happy when he knew her. Her name was Sadie Courtland. She'd been one of his students when he'd first begun teaching at the college, which meant that she was now a middle-aged woman, although Drayton wondered if she had gotten that far, because she had been pitifully unhappy. Drayton corrected himself: she hadn't been just unhappy, she'd been mentally ill, often lost in a lake of depression so deep that it was impossible for her to reach the surface. She'd been very bright, wrote well, and loved the literature, but she just couldn't keep her life together. Drayton remembered her well because she was the first student who had confided in him, and he hadn't known how to help her. When he suggested that she see a campus counselor, she laughed and told him that she'd been seeing psychiatrists for ten years and that she understood her illness better than any of them. About a year after that, she'd dropped out of school, and he'd never heard from her again, although he often wondered what had become of her.

He'd been thankful to Sadie because she'd helped him understand how important he could be in the lives of some of his students and had also helped him to understand that sometimes he would fail to teach them, to help them, to know them. That knowledge was one of the reasons that when he'd been charged with sexual harassment and few people had believed him, he'd decided on early retirement.

Drayton leaned back in the chair and looked at the photo. The house was quiet, nothing from Marian Mosher upstairs, and he hoped that she was asleep. He wondered how Les Tremain had come to know Sadie Courtland, but it was a small town, and the artistic people gravitated to one another. Drayton sighed: his images of Les Tremain had become so complex that he could find no clear sense of the man.

In that state of mind, Drayton turned to the next photograph, and when he looked at it, his jaw clenched and then a great sigh escaped him, and he clenched his eyes as if he might begin to cry. When he opened his eyes, the picture was the same. A young woman was walking toward the camera, her eyes on the camera. She was walking through the shallow water of a swimming pool, walking in the light of late afternoon, her nude body glistening, and before he thought of anything else, Drayton again thought of the classical goddesses of ancient Greece.

Drayton thought how blind he had been to what should have been so obvious. He should have known that Tremain would have found a way to photograph Andrea Marchand. Drayton asked himself why, when she had vehemently denied allowing Tremain to photograph her, why hadn't he, Drayton, been thinking: *Methinks she doth protest too much.*

Andrea Marchand had lied. Of course she had lied, just as Ellie had lied, but what else could they do? And was Andrea Marchand supposed to tell him that, yes, she had known Les Tremain and, yes, she had been photographed by him. Was she supposed to tell Drayton that in front of Louis Marchand, her husband? Except as Drayton stared at the photo of Andrea coming out of the pool, looking like Venus rising from the sea, Drayton couldn't help but think that the pool might well be Marchand's, and that Marchand might have known everything.

Chapter 16

On the car seat next to Drayton lay the photograph of Andrea Marchand, which he glanced at as he drove. After finding the photo he'd gone upstairs, where he found Marian Mosher asleep on the sofa and snoring loudly. Drayton walked quietly over to her. She looked peaceful, and he decided it was better not to awaken her because he didn't want to try to explain why he thought the photo might be important, especially since he wasn't sure. He'd picked up the pad of paper on the small table next to the front door, written a note thanking her and then telling her he had a photo that he was taking but would soon bring back. He left the note on the table next to the sofa where Tremain's sister was sleeping. With the photograph in his hand, he'd gone back to his car and sat looking out at the hazy blue sky and the deep blue green of the flat Pacific. He'd left his house at late morning with the intention of going down to the Mesa, and he still wanted to do that. Only now, he had a picture of Andrea Marchand. *Now*, he told himself, *Don't rush to any conclusions, hold back, just keep holding back until all the pieces come together.*

Highway 1 curved south, cutting through a forest of eucalyptus trees growing in sandy soil, the ocean only dunes away. Drayton had seen few cars on the road. He was driving too fast, and he kept glancing over at the photograph of Andrea Marchand, as if it might disappear. He told himself to slow down. No need to rush now. Tremain was long gone. Tremain the outsider, the artist, a man who could photograph a woman and make her look even more lovely than she was, so that each woman could get a glimpse of herself as the ideal. Drayton wondered if Tremain had paid for that talent with his life. The road climbed to the edge of the Mesa and became a series of long sweeping curves cutting through manzanita.

After fifteen minutes, Drayton braked, slowed down, and turned into Saddle Ridge Road, which was covered with gravel that rattled against the bottom of the car. Saddle Ridge Road ran for a half mile and then ended in scrub rooted in sandy soil, which led to the beach. Drayton could smell the salt water and kelp as he drove toward the ocean, the road cutting through a maze of salvage yards, one after another, each butted up against the next one so that he couldn't be sure where one yard ended and another began. Cars were stacked two, three, even four high, a painted wooden sign would mark one of the yards, and close to the sign would be a small clapboard building that served as an office. Alongside the road, an occasional car was parked, a car that looked a day or two away from the salvage yards. All the parked cars were American. These people were patriots. Drayton's gleaming, Italian, low X 1/9 would not only look strange, but it would make him suspect.

Drayton wasn't sure how to find Georgie Gagne. All he had was the name. He made a right down a dirt road that seemed to be a boundary line between two salvage yards. The remains of wooden fences leaned close to the snapping point and were topped with razor wire. Ahead, at the side of the road, two men sat close to one of the fences. One man sat in a wooden rocker, the other in a ratty recliner. They sat there as if they were in a living room rather than at the side of the road. Both men were dressed in khaki work clothes, looking like discards from the military. The man in the recliner looked up when Drayton stopped at the side of the road. Drayton smiled but the man didn't respond. Drayton called out, "Do either one of you know a man named Georgie Gagne?" The two men looked at one another. They both began to laugh to themselves, and Drayton wondered if he had wandered into an area reserved for men suffering from arrested adolescence. He waited, but neither of them said anything, so Drayton said, "Georgie Gagne?"

The one in the easy chair reached down, picked up a soda bottle and drank from it. He said something that Drayton couldn't hear and Drayton said, "What?"

The man seemed impatient with him but said, "Try Maso's."

"Maso's?"

"Maso's Salvage." The man nodded, said, "Just up the road," and pointed in the direction from which Drayton had come.

Kicking up gravel and dust, Drayton made a hard U-turn and headed back toward Saddle Ridge Road. Heading east, Drayton almost missed the sign which said "Maso's." So many washing machines, dryers, and cars were piled up that they almost hid a low-ceilinged frame building. He pulled over and waited, but there was no sign of life. A hot wind kicked up and the cars stacked three or four high creaked and moaned, as if they were pleading to hit the road again. Drayton got out and started toward the building. A sign said *office*. He laughed because *office* seemed like a lot of word for the ramshackle building.

Drayton's laughter cut short when he sensed a sudden movement, a shadow hard to his left, and he threw his arms up to protect himself, but the lunging dog snapped to a stop in mid-air and fell to the dirt, his flight stopped short by a chain on his collar. The chain, attached to the boards of a small tool shed, was taut, and the dog stood growling. It looked like a German Shepherd but was too big for that, and Drayton wondered if it was part Husky—or even part wolf. He'd read in the county paper that on the edges of the county, in the rural areas, some people were breeding wolves and dogs and creating an unpredictable and deadly animal. Drayton was able to breathe again, but his arms were still up, and he still faced the dog. The chain pulled against the plank wall of the shed, and the plank moved with each of the dog's lunges. Reluctant to turn his back on the dog, Drayton edged over to the low frame building, which had a door but no windows.

The inside of the building was as dark as the entrance to an abandoned coal mine, and Drayton had to stop, his eyes unfocused. Slowly, colors and shapes came back, and before him he saw automobile parts stacked on shelves, on counter tops, and on top of each other. Everything seemed covered by a skim of grease, as if someone had come in and sprayed it on. Drayton made out two men sitting on wooden boxes. Both men were dressed in work shirts and coveralls. Neither man said anything. Each looked at Drayton and then looked away, as if Drayton wasn't his problem. A third man, talking on a wall phone, glanced at Drayton but spoke into the phone: "I told you I had to leave, god damn it." He listened and shook his head, "No god damned woman's going to tell me when to come and go," and without another word, he hung up the phone. He turned to Drayton but didn't say anything. Drayton felt like Dante descending into another level of hell.

Drayton nodded but didn't smile. He'd figured out that to smile in this place was a sign of weakness. To Drayton, the man who'd been on the phone looked like a young Abe Lincoln gone bad, or gone mad. He had the long sad face and the dark hair, but his eyes were all wrong. *Wall-eyed*, Drayton thought. *That's what they call wall-eyed.* Drayton realized that he lived in a world where he'd never seen a wall-eyed man. The wall-eyed Abe Lincoln wore an old baseball cap, the beak smudged with grease, the crown stained crusty-white with sweat. He still didn't say anything.

Drayton couldn't take the wait anymore. He surrendered and asked, "Does anyone know Georgie Gagne? I think he works here."

Wall-eyed Abe in the baseball cap looked at the other two men, and while still looking at them said, "Well, you're a little late, mister." His voice wasn't anything like Drayton imagined Abe Lincoln's voice might have been. The wall-eyed man's voice was high and squeaky, comic, ludicrous really, but Drayton didn't think it was a good idea to laugh.

"Late?" Drayton asked. "Late how?" The dog barked, followed by the creaking of wood.

"You'll have to go to hell if you want to talk to Georgie."

Drayton waited, his eye on the doorway, expecting the wolf-dog to come through and go for his throat.

"Georgie goddamned died a few years back."

Outside, the dog was still barking. The chain rattled, followed by another thud as the chain pulled against the plank. "Died?" Drayton asked. "When? How?"

"Well," said the man in the baseball cap. "I guess Georgie was so old and dumb that he died."

Drayton waited.

One man held a sandwich made with white bread. He'd taken one bite of it, and his greasy thumb and fingerprints contrasted with the white of the bread. He put the sandwich down on a transmission beside him before he said, "Close to five years ago. Like a joke. All them years of him drinking like hell, and that ain't what kills him." He paused and shook his head for effect, "Before he got killed, he got religion. Praying. Sprouting the bible. Wouldn't drink nothing."

Sprouting the bible? Drayton thought, but decided that it wouldn't be a good idea to correct him.

Baseball-cap Abe said, "Yeh, he finally got sober and got himself killed." His voice was so squeaky that Drayton almost smiled.

"Killed?" Drayton asked.

"Dumb thing to do." The man pointed to the salvage yard. "See them cars stacked up one on top the other? Three? Four?"

The man waited until Drayton nodded before he said, "Old fuck got in the middle of them, and a whole stack—well, two cars—came down on top him."

The man with the sandwich licked his fingers and said, "I think it was the Buick that got him."

The third man spoke for the first time: "Cadillac got him."

The man in the baseball cap shook his head and looked at Drayton. "Oh, it's easy enough to do, getting yourself crushed like that. Just go on out there and see how rickety those cars are." He turned to the other two men and said, "It was a fucking Ford that got him, a Pinto." He turned to Drayton, "Broke his old goddamned neck. Cracked in his old skull. Took him a long time to die out there."

Outside, the dog was still at it—a low growl like a threatening musical score—determined to get to Drayton. The image came to Drayton's mind of the wooden plank holding the chain splintering, the dog breaking free, running toward the office, dragging the chain and part of the shed behind him. Would these men help him or just sit around smirking?

Drayton asked, "Does he have any family?"

"Got a wife," the baseball cap said.

"Do you know where she lives?"

The baseball cap asked, "Why should I know where she lived? They didn't exactly have me over for supper, and he watched her close cause she had a real nice ass when she was young."

"Capshaw's," the sandwich man said, still chewing.

"Capshaw's?" Drayton asked.

"That trailer park down by the oil fields just south of here."

Drayton looked at him.

The sandwich man added, "That's where his old lady lives."

"How do you know where she lives?" asked the baseball cap.

"Do you know her name?" Drayton asked.

The sandwich man looked at Drayton as if he were stupid, "Well,

Jesus Christ, Gagne, I figure."

"Betty Gagne," the baseball cap said.

"Thanks, guys," Drayton said. "You've been a help." Then he turned, and stepped back into the open yard, where the wolf-dog greeted him. The dog lunged, his bark lowering into a steady growl, the fur along his back standing up, his eyes on Drayton, who swallowed and then tensed his jaw. "Damned Cerberus," he said, and his anger began to bubble out of control for the first time since he'd started looking for Tremain. *Hang on, cool down*, he told himself, but it didn't work. In a pile of parts, a sway bar stuck out at a sharp angle. Drayton pulled the sway bar free. Better than three feet long, the bar had a healthy heft. Holding the sway bar in both hands like a baseball bat, Drayton started forward toward his car, never taking his eye off the dog, whose head was low, his eyes focused on Drayton. When he got to his car, Drayton opened the driver's door, threw the sway bar down in the dirt, and slipped behind the steering wheel.

As Drayton drove south, the shadows among the eucalyptus began to deepen and darken. The sun had started its drop, and Drayton felt tired and hungry, but he didn't want to stop for something to eat. He wanted to talk to the widow, wanted to talk to Betty Gagne. On the western side of the road were miles of oil fields, the pumps looking like giant mechanical grasshoppers, nodding and nodding endlessly. Cars on the road were few and far between, and Drayton felt as if he was lost, as if he was driving through a plateau of nodding oilrigs and creaking abandoned cars. His weariness and his hunger, combined with his trek through the junkyards, had left him almost woozy, a feeling that was heightened as he moved back and forth between the present and the world of twenty years earlier. Time travel was disorienting, and it was intensified by the heat of the sullen Santa Anas.

The Capshaw Mobile Home Park was in better condition than Drayton had expected—the mobile homes were in decent shape and the road through the park was fresh asphalt. Still, the mobile homes were packed close to one another like jail cells, and he thought how sweet *his* mobile home, all alone in the woods, seemed. He wondered how he'd find which place was Gagne's, but it was easy; the name was block-lettered on the side, right on the outside wall. Lights were on inside. A four or five-year-old Camaro was in the driveway. Silver blue. In front of the car was a motorcycle with a tarp thrown over it. Drayton picked up the edge of the tarp and whistled: an Indian in top shape. He wondered if it was Georgie Gagne's and had been sitting there since his death. The Camaro and the Indian were two very expensive vehicles to find in a mobile home park on the Mesa.

At the front door, Drayton could see through the screen door into a living room engorged with furniture, including a large-screen television set which was on—but soundless. The television was in an oak cabinet. A white leather sectional sofa took up a fourth of the room, and a tan vinyl recliner sat pointed toward the television, but nobody was in the chair. The furniture was oversized, as if Betty Gagne thought she lived in a mansion, or maybe that she was going to be moving into a mansion. Drayton thought of Marian Mosher's house and the back porch of Louis Marchand's house, both with little furniture and a great deal of light.

As Drayton raised his hand to knock, a woman's reedy voice said, "Come on in." She stood in the entryway to the kitchen, and the first thing that Drayton thought as he looked at her was that she was an attractive woman, but when he opened the screen door, he saw that although she once may have been pretty, damned pretty, time and other excesses had done their damage.

Once inside the door, he told her, "I'm Michael Drayton."

She smiled and said, "I know. You're looking for me. I'm Betty Gagne." In her pronunciation or in the rhythm of her speech, something suggested to Drayton that she was Latina. As he played her voice over in his head, he understood that the Latino quality was in both the pronunciation and the rhythm of her last three words: *looking for me*. He told himself to go slow because a lot of women had Mexican accents.

"How did you know that I was looking for you?" Drayton asked.

She shrugged, "I got a phone call."

"From?" Drayton thought of the three men at Maso's Salvage. Maybe they knew her better than they had admitted.

"Slow down," she said, and her voice cracked between that of a middle-aged woman and an old woman, as if she'd struggled to keep the younger tone but couldn't. Her blue cotton dress was almost elegant, but it was too young for her, and where it was open at the neck, her skin looked wattled. She smiled at Drayton, and he knew the smile was a wreck of what it had once been. Time and trouble had her by the throat. She said, "I was making myself a vodka tonic." She gestured with a near-empty glass in her hand, "Want one?" The ice in her glass clinked. Her voice had enough of a slur for Drayton to know that she wasn't on her first drink.

"Sure," Drayton said, wanting her to keep drinking, hoping it would loosen her tongue. As she turned to the kitchen, he sat in the vinyl recliner and wondered if it had been old Georgie Gagne's chair before the cars had fallen on him. The Buick or the Cadillac or the Ford. Not an Alfa Romeo or X 1/9.

Ice in a bowl rattled in the kitchen. The room had a musty smell that Drayton couldn't identify. It was like what he used to smell long ago in the homes of friends who used a lot of drugs—a smell of human sweat and chemicals.

Betty Gagne tottered back into the room, leaning against the jamb as she came through the doorway. When she handed Drayton his drink, he noticed that her hands were large, her fingers long and bony. As tall as she was, she seemed almost like a tree as she swayed slightly. A Mexican mother and a tall, thin father? he wondered. Or a tall Mexican father and a thin blonde mother? Now, her face was smeared and blurred, and Drayton knew that if he wanted any information from her, he'd better hurry before she passed out. Maybe, he thought, this was how she spent her days. As she settled onto the sofa, Drayton asked, "Who called? Who said I was coming? "

She ignored him as if he'd said nothing. She took a drink, looked into her glass and said, "I'm drunk." Drayton watched her seem to drift away and then return as she repeated herself, "I'm drunk. That's the only way I'm going to get through this. I want to. I'm pissed. Really pissed."

Drayton nodded, but before he could say anything, she went on, "This has already cost me my darling Georgie."

"What cost you?"

She took another drink and Drayton took his first. The drink was strong with vodka, and he knew that if she'd been drinking them that way, she couldn't last long. A heaviness hung over the room, not just because of the furniture, and not just because of that smell, but because of a sense of trouble, trouble for a long time

"I got a phone call just this afternoon," she said and held up her drink. "I've been drinking ever since. I'm pissed off," she said again, as if she were trying to convince herself. "I wasn't always an old bitch. I can remember what it was like to be treated with respect. By men.

Even by her."

"Her?"

Betty Gagne scowled at him as if he shouldn't interrupt her, and she said, "She cost me my Georgie. Oh, what a lover sweet Georgie was." Off she drifted for a long minute, her gaze seeming to examine the room, and then she came back, looking startled by his presence. "But this is the end of it. I don't care how much money they got. This is the end of it."

"I'm not sure who you mean," Drayton said and waited. On the television screen, a man was talking to a woman, smiling and saying things which must have been sweet, but Drayton couldn't tell because the sound was so faint it was like a memory.

"I got a phone call. He called and told me you'd be coming." She laughed and shook her head. "But it ain't going to work this time. Fuck them and his money. It just buys me grief. I don't care what happened. I don't care whose fault it is. I don't care if it ain't nobody's fault." She brought her glass to her mouth and emptied it. When she looked into it, she closed her eyes, got up and started toward the kitchen. "They're right," she said.

"Who?"

From the kitchen, she said, "They say money can't buy happiness." Her voice was scratchy, hoarse, as if she was going to lose it.

Drayton waited until she came back into the room, her full glass in her hand. Again, she leaned against the doorjamb, and some of her drink sloshed out on her hand. She wiped it on the side of her dress. Drayton remembered the old expression *falling-down drunk*; it was made for her. She shook her head, "Poor Georgie. It killed him, my sweet lover." She smiled, her eyes dreamy, her voice raspy. "He always said that there was nothing as soft as the inside of my thighs."

"Georgie?" Drayton said.

Betty Gagne scowled at him as if he had insulted her, but then she forgot and said, "That's what got it all started. That horny bastard." She smiled as if she had a secret. "He couldn't get enough of me." She looked at Drayton as if he'd been arguing with her, shook her head, and said, "But I'm ending it now. Betty Gagne is ending it now."

Drayton kept his mouth shut. On the television, a young woman was holding up some toothpaste and smiling maniacally. She was insanely happy with her toothpaste; it made her life better.

"If he hadn't been such a horny bastard, this wouldn't of happened.

He wouldn't of done that to her."

"Who called you?"

Betty Gagne stiffened and stared at him. Suddenly, she seemed sober, and she looked frightened and angry. "I'm going to die because of this," she said. She took another drink, as if to fortify herself. "He shouldn't of called me. He shouldn't of threatened me. He should of let her keep talking to me. I felt like I owed her something, but not him. Not him. Not that rich bastard."

"Louis Marchand?" Drayton asked.

She looked at Drayton as if he'd missed something or was slow to get it, and she said, "Sure, that old son-of-a-bitch, Louis Marchand."

Drayton leaned back in the recliner and took a sip of what tasted like straight vodka. He thought of Louis up there on his hilltop, his life oozing away by the minute, his beautiful wife by his side. Faithful to the end? So much for fidelity, he thought, but she would be faithful to the end, knowing that at the end there would be a fortune for her. No matter how it was cut up between her and his kids, she'd be a rich woman. So why do anything?

Betty Gagne sat on the arm of the sofa and then slid down onto the cushions, part of her drink spilling on her dress. She put her head back, her face toward the ceiling, and didn't move. Drayton thought she had passed out, but then she yanked her head upright and started talking. "I told Georgie from the beginning not to get involved. Just stay out of it. I knew it would end like this."

"How did Marchand know your husband? What did Georgie have to do with it?"

She laughed, "You don't know a thing." She shook her head. "He didn't know Georgie. She was the one."

"Andrea Marchand?"

Staring at Drayton, clear eyed, as if she hadn't had a drink, she smiled and said, "She was our love baby."

Drayton bit his tongue, took a drink, and waited.

Taking a deep breath, she said, "He said he was doing it for her. That he owed her."

"Andrea?'

Betty Gagne looked at him as if he annoyed her. She nodded, "She called that night." She dropped that line as if it were nothing. She called *that night*."

On the television, a blue car was sailing off the side of a bridge toward the dark water below, and Drayton asked, "What night?"

"You know what night."

"The night Les Tremain disappeared?"

"Disappeared, shit," she said and laughed.

Drayton let her words hang in the air for a minute and then said, "Was killed?"

Betty Gagne wagged her finger at him, "I knew you knew. He said you were a smart one."

"Why," Drayton asked, "did Andrea call your husband that night?"

She sat smiling at him and then said in a voice that seemed younger. "He was her daddy."

Drayton sighed. "She came from down here? She didn't come from Hollywood?"

"Both," Betty Gagne said. "When she was old enough to make it on her own—fifteen or sixteen—she headed down there. Didn't even finish high school. She wanted out of here." She looked around, "Can't say I blame her." She paused, "She hated it here." She paused again, "She was always a smart kid, right from day one."

"Marchand found her down in Hollywood and brought her back here?"

"Not *here*," she said and looked around. "She didn't come near the Mesa."

Drayton thought of Andrea Marchand, thought of that day he'd first seen her walking away from the pool, and thought of Les Tremain's photograph of her, with her luminous face and stunning legs and breasts. He tried to picture her in this mobile home, but there wasn't a place for her, he couldn't even get her to the front door.

Betty Gagne took another drink. Her glass was almost empty again, but Drayton didn't think she'd be able to get up to mix another. He was about to lose her. He asked, "What happened that night?"

"My love baby," she said and laughed, "*our* love baby was diddling that Tremain guy who was taking pictures of her and diddling her while her husband sat up on that hill."

Drayton didn't move.

She rattled the ice cubes in her glass and finished drinking the last drops of vodka. With the care only a drunk can muster, she placed the glass on the table in front of her. "And that son-of-a-bitch was doing the same thing with that other woman. Another married woman. Out in the country, Georgie said."

"Ellie Boudreau?" Drayton asked.

"Whatever. I don't know her name. Don't want to know. Just another dumb girl taken in by that bastard." She shifted, as if she was going to get up, but nothing happened.

Drayton leaned forward but said nothing, then leaned back in his chair. Betty Gagne blinked and nodded. "She called and asked her daddy for help—the daddy she'd disowned. She wanted him to help her get rid of that bastard."

"Tremain?" Drayton asked.

She looked almost bored with it all and slumped back. After a few seconds, she smiled, "He didn't have no choice. He was already starting to get religion. Starting to pray to Jesus. He had to help her. Had to help make it up to her."

"Make it up?"

Betty Gagne scowled at Drayton as if he wasn't paying attention and said, "What do you think? My God, you seen her?" She shook her head. "I don't know where she come from."

Drayton thought to himself that yes, he'd seen her, and where had she come from?

"You should of seen her at thirteen or fourteen. Georgie didn't have no religion then." She laughed loudly, "No religion. He didn't have much more than a hard-on."

"Christ," Drayton said.

"No. No Jesus," Betty Gagne said, shaking her head. Then she seemed to understand what Drayton meant and said, "Georgie would have told you not to use his name that way. I mean Georgie after he got *saved*."

"What did he do?"

She moved forward again as if she was going to get up, but couldn't, and she lay back against the sofa, her arms and legs splayed. Her voice was tired, as if this were an old story, "He told me part of it. All I know is that after she called, he went out there that night. It was getting close to daylight. He went out there in his pick-up truck." She shrugged, "He said he threw him in the back of the pick-up and threw a tarp over him. It was starting to get light—morning." She shook her head, "Drove right along the highway with everyone driving to work and him with that dead man in the back of his truck, with a tarp over him and a couple of tires to hold it down in the wind."

Drayton too felt tired now. He finished his drink and looked at

Betty Gagne, who sat staring straight ahead in a stupor. When they had both been quiet for a long time, Drayton thought he could now barely hear the voices from the television, which brought him back, and he asked, "What did Georgie do with him?"

She looked up, as if surprised that he was there, and said, "Oh, he told me about that later when he started getting religion." She laughed. "When he got born again. Told me he put him in the trunk of one of those old cars that was going to the crusher and then shipped it out to wherever the hell they ship them out to."

Drayton sat staring at her and trying to imagine how you'd tell your wife that story. Where would you start?

Betty Gagne sat quietly, drifting off. She looked at Drayton. "Money can't buy you much. Marchand sent us a thousand dollars each month. Ten one-hundred-dollar bills in a envelope. Nothing else in the envelope, nothing on the envelope but Georgie's name."

"So you wouldn't say anything," Drayton said.

"I guess," she said and nodded, "but he should of left it alone. He should of. Every month that money came kept reminding Georgie what he'd done." She closed her eyes and said, "And then he found God and decided he wanted to confess. Told Marchand that he wanted to tell the truth."

"When was that?" Drayton asked. "Five, six years ago," she said.

Again, they were quiet, and again Drayton could hear the voices on the television, like someone whispering in the dark shadows at the back of the mobile home. He thought of Georgie Gagne sitting there every night and watching television and pretending that everything was all right. Drayton turned to Betty Gagne and asked, "And then the cars fell on him?"

Betty Gagne had started to cry, but she made no sound, and she didn't bother to wipe away the tears from her eyes or the snot from her nose. "He shouldn't of called. He shouldn't of warned me that you were coming. He shouldn't of told me that he was going to send me a lot of money. He called it a bonus." She shook her head, "That really pissed me off. That was a mistake. He can come down here and do what he wants to me. I don't care no more."

Drayton shook his head. "He won't do anything to you. It's all right. He's very sick and is dying. You're all right." He stopped talking and thought about the mistakes all of them had made, and thought about Georgie Gagne driving out to the salvage yard and taking Tremain's body and stuffing it in the trunk of a car about to be crushed. God, that would make you get religion. He thought about what Andrea Marchand—or Andrea Gagne—had gotten for being so beautiful, so beautiful that she didn't belong in the world of her parents.

Drayton stood up, and Betty Gagne sat staring at him; it was clear that she couldn't get up by herself. Slowly, she raised her hand, gave him her glass, and said, "Please, make me a drink, honey." Drayton took her glass and his to the kitchen and mixed drinks in both glasses. The bottle of vodka was almost empty. He took the glasses back to Betty Gagne and put them on the table in front of the sofa. She smiled and said, "Thank you very much. I hope you have what you wanted." She lowered her eyes and asked, "Did you get what you wanted?"

Chapter 17

The sky was clear, the moon was full, and the Santa Ana winds sang as Drayton cut from the old highway to Highway 101, where he knew he could make better time. Although the heavy and fast traffic would mean his X 19 would take a buffeting from the tractor-trailer trucks, the hour was already late, and he wanted to get to Marchand's house as soon as he could, even though he doubted if the old man was doing much sleeping these days. He'd be trying to squeeze as much as possible out of each minute of life he had left. The number of things which he respected were few, but life was one of them. He had a line from a poem that he loved to quote: "Shall the earth seem all of paradise that we shall know?" Then he'd always smile, but it was a rueful smile.

An open stretch of highway was ahead and Drayton picked up speed, the little X 1/9 reaching eighty, the RPMs heading past 4000. He eased off. How much vodka had he had at Betty Gagne's mobile home? Probably too much. He didn't want to get stopped by the police now; that was a delay he didn't want to endure. What he *did* want was the whole story. The whole story: jealousy? As simple as that? A married couple. An old man and a much younger and beautiful woman. *Cherchez la femme,* Bonnie would say. Add to that couple a young and charming artist, and a volatile mix started to brew. He thought of the photo of Andrea Marchand that Tremain had taken. It was still on the passenger seat, and he glanced over at it, but it was lost in the shadows. It didn't make any difference: he had it memorized. It would always be with him. Her face and her body were full of promise, promises that would cause all sorts of trouble, trouble she had never intended, but which had come about because of the way she looked. Nature wanted reproduction, so created ideal beauty. Drayton couldn't imagine that a young man could resist that look of promise, and he knew that even at his age he'd find it difficult.

For the next twenty minutes, Drayton drove hard, making himself concentrate, because he was exhausted. But he couldn't stop himself from going over the day in his mind: Marian Mosher and the photograph of Andrea Marchand. The junkyard and Gagne dead. Betty Gagne and her story. The day seemed a week long. Maybe he should just go home and sleep on it, crawl into bed with Rupe and Rip, and they could all snore the night away, but he was afraid he would lose his resolve, and, more importantly, because he just wanted to complete the story of Les Tremain. Complete it as much as possible, because he knew it would never be finished. As old Hawkins had said: there would be no *closure*.

Ahead, the town's lights glowed in the dark sky. He'd be at Marchand's in a few minutes. He wondered what this would be like for Louis—old, burned out, and about to leave this world, and now your old friend Drayton was on his way to put a stake in your heart. Drayton made himself not think about it. Trying not to think at all, he exited the freeway.

In a few minutes, Drayton made a left onto the road that curved up Taylor Hill to Marchand's house. In the darkness, everything at the sides of the road was different than it had been in the sunlight. His headlights turned the trees and brush into moving shadows that threatened to jump out onto the road. Drayton tried to imagine the night of Les Tremain's murder off Cold Canyon Creek Road. What exactly had Ellie seen, or heard and seen? The shot and then someone shouting.

Maybe Tremain had been hit and didn't drop right away, maybe he'd just gone down and died there, his body left behind in one of the deep ditches until Georgie Gagne came and then headed back to the Mesa. Drayton didn't know if he had what it would take to live with that kind of guilt, but maybe some people wouldn't feel any guilt. That was hard to imagine. He thought that he'd probably end up a drunken wreck like Betty Gagne.

When Drayton completed the next curve, the house was visible, the drapes all open now, lights flooding every room in the house, as if Louis was trying to stave off the darkness. Even the porch lights were on, as if Louis and Andrea were expecting company. Maybe they were. Louis would know he was coming. Louis was always a step ahead of everybody else. He would have figured out what Betty Gagne would do after he had called her and offered her money. He'd have been able to hear the anger and resignation in her voice. Louis Marchand had always been smart as hell, and it wasn't going to end just because he was dying. To underestimate a person because he was dying was a mistake.

Drayton let his car roll to a stop in the driveway, killed the engine, and sat there for a minute, gathering his strength. The heat was less up on the hill, or the Santa Anas were on the wane. The smell of chlorine wafted up from the swimming pool, which was a lake of reflected moonlight. Crickets and frogs serenaded each other and themselves. Nature was peaceful and calm now. Drayton reached over for the photograph of Andrea Marchand and stepped out of the car into the clear night air. The moon's glow lighted the photograph, and in it Andrea Marchand seemed to be walking toward him through the night. Drayton took a deep breath and hesitated. In a slight breeze, the water in the pool glittered like diamonds. That day when he had first seen Andrea Marchand came back to him, that first glimpse, the same kind of glimpse of her that Louis and Tremain must have gotten, and Drayton felt as if he were swimming in a sea of time, but it was a sea with no shoreline. Frogs were chirping now in a kind of madness. Melodies of love, Drayton thought, and it would get them into all sorts of complexities.

Drayton held the photograph at his side as he stepped onto the front porch and reached out to ring the bell. Before he could ring it, the door opened, and Andrea Marchand stood there in a white terrycloth robe, a robe that looked as if it were fresh from the box and would never have a spot on it. Her skin, tanned and dark, contrasted against the purity of the robe. Why was it, Drayton wondered, that he felt she didn't have anything on under the robe? She was a woman who would sleep naked. His thoughts, he told himself, were the products of lust, late-night lust, which always hit him about this time of night—especially when a beautiful woman was standing in front of him.

"Good evening," Andrea Marchand said. "Come in. Louis said

162

it would be you. He said that you'd want to talk. He's at the back of the house." Drayton followed her through the brightly-lighted rooms—table lamps, floor lamps, wall lamps, and even a chandelier—all glistening and glittering. But when he stepped into the view room which was almost all windows, darkness took over. The only light came from the silver glow of the moon, which spread brightness across the valley. Stars were crowded in the night sky.

Marchand turned in his chair, "Drayton, I'm glad you came. We should have a talk. When you were here the other day, I knew it was just a matter of time before you returned." His voice was strained from dealing with pain, but it was calm, as always. Why shouldn't it be? The world couldn't do anything to him. Time had freed him from that.

"Sit down," Marchand said, and motioned toward a wing-back chair. Andrea Marchand took an easy chair on her husband's right. In the pale moonlight, she was little more than a shadow. When Drayton sat down, Marchand said, "You must be tired, chasing down the ghost of Les Tremain. It's funny how it was almost forgotten. Back then, I thought somebody would find his car in a few days and then, poof, twenty years had passed, and it all seemed over and forgotten, but up popped Michael Drayton."

At that, Andrea Marchand got up and walked over to a wet bar. Her bare feet made no sound. She glided in her white robe. In a voice that was stronger than it had been two days earlier and that conveyed a sense of resilience, she said, "You'd probably like a drink."

"Some of Louis's good Irish whiskey on ice. A stiff one, please," Drayton said.

She turned on a light next to the bar. Triangles of light as well as long and dark shadows were cast across the room. Her back was to Drayton and Marchand. Ice clinked against glass. Drayton glanced at Marchand, whom he could see in the light from the wet bar. Marchand was smiling at his wife. Drayton wondered if that was the look of love.

"Leave that light on," Marchand said. "Drayton doesn't like the dark as much as I do." He laughed and said, "I'm trying to get used to it, trying to get used to the dying of the light."

Andrea Marchand gave Drayton his drink and sat in the chair to the left of her husband. It came to Drayton that although he had not hesitated to come to the house alone, knowing that Louis would never harm him, he wasn't as sure about Andrea Marchand. Surely a woman so beautiful couldn't shoot holes in him or spike his drink. He smiled at his ongoing naivete when it came to women.

"Earlier today," Drayton began, "I went back to Marian Mosher's house and looked through a couple of boxes of Les Tremain's photographs." He stepped over to a small table next to Louis Marchand and snapped on the table lamp. Marchand winced at the brightness, and Drayton placed the photograph on the table. Andrea Marchand stood up and stepped to the table. She looked down at the photograph of herself. Tremain had shot the photograph almost straight on, and she was looking into the camera, her nipples erect, as if she was cold or aroused, and she didn't look cold. The water reached halfway up her curved thighs, which accentuated the lighter, almost pearlescent skin of her hips and abdomen. Her stomach was flat, her waist as small as it would ever be. As beautiful as the parts of her body were, the greatest beauty was her skin, which was luminescent and which complemented a feline quality reflected from her eyes.

"Wonderful photography," Marchand declared.

Andrea Marchand stared at the photo and said, "I never looked like that. The photograph is a lie. Les Tremain was brilliant." She picked up the photograph, looked at her husband, and said, "I thought they were all gone. I know the negatives were gone." Without another word, she put the photograph on the table and returned to her chair.

"I knew all about those," Marchand said to Drayton. "Some were taken here by the pool—as this one was—late in the afternoon when the light was flattering."

"Louis introduced me to Les Tremain," she said, from the half-darkness where she sat.

Drayton looked at Marchand, who responded to Drayton's expression, "Drayton, you know me. You can guess how little I gave a damn about society and its marital vows—the most unnatural goddamn convention imaginable." He sighed, smiled, and said, "I was in my sixties, still dangerous, but not exactly a stallion pawing the earth." He laughed at his own image and added, "I told myself that I sure wasn't going to be stupid enough to be jealous. What did I expect this beautiful young woman full of desire was supposed to do?"

Drayton bit his tongue and wondered what Andrea's desires would be like after what her father had done to her. He couldn't imagine, couldn't imagine at all. So, she had gone from her father to a husband old enough to be her father to Les Tremain. And now Marchand was talking about her desires. Tremain had images of Andrea on that old sofa in the mobile home with her father as the drunken beast. And now Marchand was talking about her desires as if he knew what they were. It would take a psychiatrist to even guess at the nature of her *desires*.

"Andie," Marchand continued, "loved us in different ways. I knew Les. I didn't blame her for loving him. Why couldn't she love both of us? Whoever said it couldn't be that way? Some god-damned Calvinist? Society might condemn me, but I've never been greatly influenced by the moral values of a bank vice-president or some money-grubbing county supervisor or any other pillar of the community."

"And she was all right with that?" Drayton asked. "Even after what had happened to her?"

Marchand stiffened but then glanced at his wife, "Yes, of course. I had to help her. She was very young."

"How young? How young were you when you married?" Drayton asked Andrea.

She carefully enunciated her words, "I was seventeen."

Drayton looked to Louis Marchand, who smiled, shrugged, and said, "It's a little late to judge me now, Drayton. I don't think I have time to repent for my somewhat feral lifestyle. I wouldn't know where to begin or how to choose. I'm afraid I'm a lost soul damned to perdition with all those other lost but interesting souls—like Agamemnon, Dido, probably Dante. How about Galileo? Do you suppose he's down there? What an interesting crew—as contrasted to some puerile Protestants or pathetic papists." He grimaced and bent forward, his breath labored. He reached for the oxygen mask attached to the tank by his side. His wife came over to help him. She was gentle, her tanned hand on the wrinkled and slack skin of his face.

In a few minutes, Marchand seemed slightly better, but still short of breath. He said, "Drayton, I don't need to justify myself. God knows I don't give a damn. But think: If I could get past the idea of jealousy, why should I deny pleasure to the woman I love, a woman who is young and full of desire? Is that to be denied?"

"You felt you *knew* her desires?"

Marchand laughed. "I may be old but I can recall desire."

"And you got past jealousy?" Drayton asked.

Marchand shrugged and nodded, "For the most part." He

managed a little smile. "Admirably so. Perhaps as much as is humanly possible. And it wasn't just jealousy. It was partially protection, the way you might protect a child from a cruel adult."

"So you were like a father to her?" Drayton asked. "A second father?"

Marchand answered, "Well, I hope not."

Drayton winced, took a drink of his whiskey, and asked himself what Marchand believed and how. Marchand had another purpose. Aloud, Drayton asked Marchand. "Does that mean you didn't have a reason to kill him?"

Marchand shook his head. "I didn't say *that*. An action can have many causes."

Marchand shifted the ground and asked, "What made you come up here, Drayton?" It was a labor for him to talk. The words were pushed out, and he wheezed. After a pause for breath, he asked, "Why didn't you just go to the police?"

Drayton replied, "I'm not sure, and I wanted to talk to you first. I wanted to find out what really happened. I can't let go of things, and I always want to know what really happened. When this all comes out, it will be a different story." Drayton shrugged. "It's already becoming a different story."

"You didn't know Les Tremain, did you?"" Andrea Marchand asked. Even in the distorted light, Drayton could see that she wasn't smiling.

"I feel as if I do now," Drayton said: "He was complex, but the way bright and talented people often are, but no, I didn't know him the way you two did. And close to twenty years ago."

"Les Tremain was complex—bright and talented," Andrea suddenly said, "And mean sometimes, especially if he thought he had to teach you something. I think that must be common among some of you teachers."

"Andrea was very young at the time," Marchand said. "Young, and with her family life, it was difficult for her."

Drayton looked at Marchand and felt for the first time that he saw something akin to tenderness in the old man. In spite of seeing himself as rational and logical, Marchand loved her too much for his own good. Running out of time, he was still defending her, but why? What had she done other than have an affair that he, Marchand, had arranged. Was it an act of love and decency from cynical Marchand? The old man coughed, reached for his inhaler, and brought the mask to his face.

Drayton leaned back in his chair and waited. He thought about how nice it would be to just get up and walk out of the room and forget he'd ever seen either of them. Instead, he looked at Andrea Marchand and said, "So you told Louis about his friend Tremain and hoped that he would take care of it."

"Don't be naïve, Drayton," Marchand said. "There's not a lot in this town that I don't know about. For instance, I know you talked to Georgie's fellow junkmen today. Charming, aren't they?"

"Did one of those charming men push some cars over on old Georgie?" Drayton asked. "His wife said he'd gotten religion and decided to tell the truth. Then, on schedule, cars fell on top of him and sealed up the truth."

Marchand shook his head, "Drayton, please, you know that's not me. I wouldn't hurt old Georgie. I could control him. He wasn't going to do anything." He paused, "Don't make this any more complicated than it needs to be. Only one person was killed: Les Tremain."

Drayton waited. His knowledge of Marchand told him that the old man was telling the truth, but he'd never seen him in a situation like this, and Marchand was so damned smart that once again he might just be a step ahead.

"At any rate," Marchand said, "I found out about the trouble between Andrea and Tremain. I talked to her about it. I thought about what her father had done to her, and Tremain seemed to be dredging up her sense of disgust—even a kind of self-loathing." Marchand shook his head, "And there was that strain of jealousy I thought I'd completely overcome." He turned to his wife, "I feared for her and what Tremain's behavior would do to her."

Marchand coughed and coughed as if he would never stop, but then he caught his breath, took a breath, and went on, "I'd been following Tremain." The old man leaned forward and gasped for air. His wife got up to help him, but he shook his head and went on, "I'm not sure why. I don't know what I thought I was going to do. I was like one of those private eyes in one of my screenplays. And it was pretty easy to follow him because I didn't give a damn if he saw me or not."

As Marchand talked, Drayton looked at Andrea. She was gazing at her husband as if she were the most faithful and loving wife in the world. It didn't make any difference that all three of them knew that was a lie.

"He'd tormented Andrea by telling her about his Tuesday visits to the beauteous Ellie Boudreau, and I followed him out to Cold Canyon Creek Road a couple of times, saw him hide his Alfa and walk through the woods for his assignation." He took another deep breath from his inhaler and seemed to be thinking back. He said to Drayton, "It may seem hard to believe, but some of it has faded from my memory. I know I'm not supposed to say that, that I'll seem heartless, but, nevertheless it's true." He shrugged and shook his head. "I went out there early that night. I pulled off the road into a small grove of eucalyptus trees. I hid my car and walked over to the gravel road and waited."

Drayton looked to Andrea. Her eyes were on her husband. Drayton tilted his head to the side and asked Marchand. "Why are you telling me all this?"

Irritation crossed Marchand's face as if he was angry that Drayton had interrupted with a silly question. After a few seconds, Marchand regained his composure, smiled, and answered, "Because I want to make sure the story is straight before I leave. You've been stirring the pot, and who knows what brew will bubble up."

Marchand went on, "I stepped out into the road when I saw his headlights." Marchand shrugged, "Don't ask me why he stopped. I guess almost any man would. Fear might tell you to stop. Maybe something as stupid as courtesy."

Drayton took a drink of his whiskey and smiled as he listened to Marchand recount what had happened that night. It was a strange, even studied, confession, and it smelled.

"When he stopped," Marchand went on, but had to pause for a series of coughs. He held his oxygen mask to his face. His wife leaned forward in her chair, but again Marchand shook his head at her. After a time, he began to talk again, "When he stopped, he must not have recognized me, because he got out of his car with the door still open and with his right hand holding the barrel of the shotgun. When he saw it was me, he leaned the shotgun against the car."

"What was he doing with a shotgun in an Italian sports car?"

Andrea interrupted, "A man named Hollis had put a fear in him." She paused, "One night, someone fired shots through his front windows. Each of them." She shook her head, "He started carrying the shotgun then."

Marchand turned from Andrea to Drayton. "He was no saint, Les wasn't." He laughed, "No saint. Anyway. We stood there face to face, the only light the headlights from his car. I told him to leave my wife alone, to stay away from her. He laughed at me and told me that I had practically pimped for her." Marchand paused and closed his eyes as if seeing that night again, "I lost my head for a second and hit him, not hard really, just a reaction, just enough to make him fall against the car."

"Louis," Andrea interrupted, "Drayton doesn't need—"

But Marchand put his hand up to stop her, and then continued. "When he fell against the car, he hit the shotgun and it slid toward me." Now Marchand turned to Drayton, "A reflex action, and I caught it by the barrel, and there it was in my hands as Tremain moved toward me." Marchand's voice was thin, "I'm not sure of exactly what happened, but I think I backed away, and he came at me again, his face contorted with anger. He was a lot younger and a lot stronger than me."

Marchand looked out at the dark night, and then he seemed calm, his voice softer, "I backed away, Tremain cursed me, and then the gun went off, or I shot the gun; however you want to say it." Marchand brought his hand to his lips. "Tremain fell back against the car, his mouth open, blood all over his shirt, and for a split second, I could see his intestines, but then he slumped with his back against the car and slid down to a sitting position. I shouted something to him, his name I think, and his eyes turned toward me, but then he jerked, sort of twitched, and was still." Marchand hesitated. "*Still* except for his breathing which slowly lessened until I wasn't sure that it was there or not, and after a minute, I *knew* that he was no longer breathing."

Marchand hesitated again and looked out at the darkness before he turned to Drayton, and with a smile on his face, said, "He was as still as a man in a coffin. That absolute stillness. That perfect stillness." Marchand shook his head. "Not so bad, I thought. Not so bad."

Andrea Marchand was quiet, her head down. At first, Drayton thought she was crying, but then he saw that he was wrong.

Marchand shook his head. "The whole thing was unreal, as if it were a performance. I wanted to stop, even tried to stop, but I couldn't, as if everything was scripted and I had to play my part."

Outside, the moonlight silhouetted the California live oaks to the east. Drayton leaned back in his chair and took a drink of whiskey,

169

hoping to get the bad taste out of his mouth. He swallowed and asked, "What then?"

After a minute, Marchand looked up. He smiled, "I knew I should move quickly. I put my foot out and pushed him down the side of the car. I didn't want to have to touch him, but then I had to because I had to pull him away, and I pulled him off to the side of the road to the deep ditch that runs along there for the winter rains. I pushed him into the ditch." He nodded. "Weeds grow up there—and he was out of sight—gone. It was all I could do with my bad back." He nodded. "I picked up the shotgun and threw it in the ditch." Marchand enunciated each word, his voice wheezy and faint, "I got in his car and drove it into the opening in the trees and into a hollow of sorts, and I left it there." He looked up at Drayton and smiled. "I thought it would be found in a matter of days." A great sigh escaped him and, in a voice full of finality and resignation, he said, "And I cut through the trees to my car and drove home."

Drayton asked, "And that's where Gagne came into the picture?"

Andrea Marchand raised her head, looked at Drayton, and said, "Louis came home and told me what he'd done. It was my idea to get my father to go out there."

"And clean up?" Drayton asked.

Marchand looked at Drayton with a mixture of remorse and reproach on his face.

Drayton shook his head, started to speak, but paused and sat looking at Marchand and his wife, the two of them like something out of a Renaissance painting—the virgin and her errant priest. A bishop ordering his tomb.

Drayton looked at Marchand and nodded toward Andrea, "That last part makes your wife an accessory to murder."

Marchand shrugged, "Who knows that? Only you, and *perhaps* she said it to protect me. She'd say anything to protect me."

"And vice-versa," Drayton said.

Marchand shook his head, "It doesn't make any difference now." He looked to Andrea and then back to Drayton. "After you were here the other day, I knew it was just a matter of time before you found out the truth, one way or another. I knew you'd hang on to it till you got it straight." He laughed softly, "Obsessive bastard that you are."

Drayton didn't say anything.

"So," Marchand said, "Yesterday, at my request, my attorney

Terry Bix and his secretary came up here. I gave them my written confession about killing Les Tremain. Essentially, what I just told you—except for the part you misunderstood. The part about Andrea suggesting we get her father. Terry and I went over it. Terry made sure it was properly done and his secretary witnessed it." Marchand looked to his wife, "On my death, Terry is to hand over my confession to the district attorney." Marchand shook his head. "There'll be no questions. Nobody but you and Tremain's sister much cares what happened to Les twenty years ago, and I'm a highly respected member of the community." Marchand laughed, "Only because I have a great deal of money." He leveled his gaze on Drayton. "Whatever you might say wouldn't make a difference. And you have no evidence. The only person who really knows anything at all is Andrea's mother, and she's a drunk who already knows that I killed Tremain."

Drayton turned to Andrea, "So, you're not to blame in any way?"

Marchand shook his head and said, "I love my wife. She gave me the greatest pleasure of any woman in my life." He smiled at Andrea, "And she's had some terrible things happen to her. She doesn't deserve any punishment or reproach because she tried to help her husband." He paused and added, "The girl who helped me was a different person than Andrea is now. Back then, she was a girl without much education, a girl who had never been loved. Since that time, I've done my best to open the world to her, I've tried to help her forget, and I certainly have loved her." Marchand shifted in his chair and said, "Please understand that I knew exactly what I was doing that night, there was never a second of doubt in my mind, and I'd do it again. I didn't intend to kill him, but I did." He laughed, "A jury might find me guilty of second-degree homicide."

Drayton took a long drink of whiskey and leaned back in his chair. He was very tired. Slowly, Drayton stood up. As he stood there, he drained the last drops from his glass and said, "I think that's more than enough for me tonight." He felt woozy. Too much had happened. Too much to drink. Too tired. Walking over to Marchand, he extended his hand and said, "I don't know if I can say that it's been *nice* knowing you, but I'm glad I have." He leaned forward and kissed Marchand on his sweaty forehead. Marchand laughed loudly, extended his hand, and said, "Do you know what Andrew Carnegie said to Frick after the two of them had broken their partnership, but not before they'd destroyed the lives of so many workers in order to make a fortune?" When Drayton didn't respond, Marchand said, "Then I'll quote him: *I'll see you in hell.*"

As Drayton let Marchand's cold hand drop from his, the old man said, "Andrea, would you please show my old friend Drayton out? Michael Drayton, Renaissance man."

Chapter 18

Back through the rooms with their blazing light, Drayton and Andrea walked toward the front of the house. Andrea opened the front door, and they both stepped onto the porch, the night clear, the stars bright, and the breeze cool. She shivered and wrapped her arms around herself. She stood in her bare feet, one crossed over the other like a little girl who was cold. Tightening the belt of her white robe, she said, "Thank you."

"Thank you?" Drayton said. "*Thank you*? For what?"

Her mouth slipped into the curve of a smile, "Thank you for not telling Louis that you saw right through him—that you knew he was lying. Thank you for letting him face his death thinking that he had taken care of everything for me—that he'd protected me again." Her laughter was low. "We both know he's a bastard in some ways, but who isn't? But he deserves what you did for him. It's nice that he has a friend who cares that much about him."

"He tells a good story, which I've known for a long time, but I didn't know he was such a bad liar," Drayton said. He shook his head, "Everything he said was so pat, and after a few minutes, I could see what he was doing, what he was trying to do." A small wind kicked up, fluttering the leaves in the trees. "How could I deny old Louis what was probably the most generous act of his life—trying to help someone he loved?"

They both stood listening to the wind, stronger now, moving through the brush, rustling the leaves. When the wind lessened,

Andrea, the smile gone from her face, asked, "But what now?"

"What now?" Drayton asked.

"When Louis's gone, will you go to the police with what you know?" she asked, but her voice made it sound more like an accusation than a question. She went on, "Will you go on with your search for *justice* for Les Tremain?"

Drayton shook his head. He sighed and rubbed his eyes. "To tell the truth, I'd like to wake up tomorrow and never again think about Les Tremain."

"Would you like to know what happened?" she asked, her voice even.

Surprised, Drayton looked at her, laughed, and shook his head, a smile on his face. "If you'd like to tell me. I can guess, but if you want to tell me, I'll take it to my grave." He continued to smile as if greatly amused. "You two were made for each other, if it weren't for all those decades between you."

She nodded. "I'll tell you one thing that's true: I love Louis. I've loved Louis through all of this. His motives may not have been the most honorable in the world, but he always treated me with kindness, and he did more for me than anybody else has ever done for me. No matter what happens, he opened doors for me that nothing can close. I can read intelligently, I can think intelligently, and I finally have some self-confidence." She paused and took a deep breath. "What don't you know?"

Drayton started to speak but stopped, nodded to himself, and said, "You sent the photos to Ellie's husband, didn't you?"

Andrea nodded. "Does that mean I'll burn in hell?"

"Not for that," Drayton answered. "That's probably not even a mortal sin." Andrea stared at him, her dark eyes bright, and she nodded.

Drayton went on, "Ellie and you were each having an affair with Tremain, so you decided to wreck her marriage."

Andrea closed her eyes and took a deep breath. "I was a little crazy." She paused before adding, "Les told me about her, told me I was being too possessive, told me that he was having an affair with at least one other woman. And he pointed out that I had a husband." Stopping, her jaw tightened, and she said, "Les could be cruel. When he realized that I was jealous, he told me about her, what her charms were, how bright she was, what she liked him to do when he made love to her, and he told me knowing it would make me try harder.

And I did. The son-of-a bitch."

At her words, a spike of jealousy stabbed Drayton, and he smiled at himself. Jealous of a man who had been dead for twenty years.

"What about the other woman?"

"Who?"

"The woman you said Tremain sent the photos to—blackmailing her—the woman who talked her husband into leaving town." Drayton took a deep breath. "Did you send those photos too?"

Andrea shook her head. "No, that was Les."

"But you knew about it? You knew about it before the fact?" Andrea shook her head. "No. It was a terrible thing to do."

Drayton nodded and paused for long time before asking, "So you were out there that night? You, not Louis, met Les Tremain on the road?"

She nodded.

"How did you know he'd be there?"

Her face darkened. "He told me—told me what he was doing, told me about his Tuesday night ten o'clock visits." She looked at Drayton. "And I followed him out there one night, and then a week later, I got there before he did. I parked off the main road and walked back through the woods and was waiting for him."

"To do what?" Drayton asked.

Andrea shook her head. "I wasn't thinking that far ahead." She touched her finger to her forehead and shook her head.

"Hollis was after him, so he wouldn't stop for just anybody, but he'd stop for you, one of his women?"

"Yes, *one* of his women," she said. "Frank Hollis had told Les that he'd kill him. I don't think he ever would have, but Les was scared."

Drayton nodded. "What then? I know the mechanics, I guess, but how does that sequence ever develop without someone putting a stop to it? What is it, like some drama you have to act out?"

Andrea stared down at the swimming pool for so long that Drayton turned and looked. The wind rippled the water and the light danced. When Drayton turned back to her, she looked at him, sighed, and closed her eyes. "Les got out of the car," she said. She seemed a little dreamy, as if she was back to that night watching it. "If only he hadn't gotten out of the car. That was the turning point. If only he hadn't gotten out of the car. But he did. He must have grabbed the shotgun when he first saw me in the road and before he knew who it was. He got out of the car with it, but then leaned it against the fender as soon as he saw it was me." She paused and nodded. "I know about guns, which was about the only thing my father taught me other than humiliation and how to hate myself." She paused and looked out at the moonlit fields. "I hated myself for loving him."

"Who?" Drayton asked.

She looked at him and laughed. "My father, and then Les."

"Did you go out there to kill him?" Drayton asked.

Andrea shook her head, "No, I didn't even know why I'd gone out there. I was a little crazy. It was like with my father: it was like I had no control over what I was doing, I just seemed to be drifting. I loved Les and hated him. I hated him, but sometimes—god forgive me—I liked what he did to me." She laughed. "And he wasn't my father or a man old enough to be my father." She took a deep breath and seemed to come back to the moment. "Then he started telling me that I had to be more open to love, that I had to love more people, and he told me about women he loved and what that meant to him. I asked him to stop, but he didn't."

Andrea paused, let out a long breath, and then went on with her story. "Les had brushed against the shotgun and it slid down into the dirt and gravel." She smiled. "I'd learned that you don't treat any gun that way." She laughed. "My father taught me that." She laughed again. "He knew how to treat a shotgun but not a daughter." She looked into the night sky. "I picked up the shotgun and brushed it off, and then I broke it open. Two shells were in their chambers." She looked directly at Drayton's eyes. "I couldn't believe he was driving around with a shotgun with two shells in their chambers." Her face changed again, staring as if she were in a daze. "I snapped it closed." She coughed and said, "He misunderstood, I think because he was already so afraid." Andrea took a deep breath and looked up at the sky before she continued. "He cursed me and grabbed at the shotgun." She shook her head at Drayton as if to make him understand. "God, he didn't know anything about guns." She shrugged. "He grabbed the barrel of the gun. I had my finger on the trigger guard." She stopped and stared at Drayton before repeating. "I had my finger *outside* the trigger guard." Eyes wide, she said, "He pulled the gun toward him and it went off."

Andrea brought her hands to her face. "Jesus." After a long pause, she went on, "The charge hit him in the stomach and he fell against the car, sliding down to the ground and leaning against the front wheel." She shook her head at Drayton. "I *know* I had my finger on the trigger guard." Biting her lip, she said, "The front of his shirt was blood. He clawed at himself." Almost as if calm, she finished. "He looked at me as if he expected me to somehow miraculously undo what had just happened." Andrea shook her head at Drayton. "Then his expression changed, and he was just looking at me without seeing me, and I knew he was gone—and I knew what I'd done."

Drayton waited, hearing the call of a barn owl, and looking at the moonlight on the fields—all those pleasant things.

Andrea seemed to come back from that night, as if she'd gotten through the worst part. She looked at Drayton. "At first I couldn't stop shaking, but then I started to calm down. I looked around." Her eyes closed. "I expected a car to come down the road that minute. I expected to see people, police coming for me." She shook her head. "But the night was the same, just the same, the whole world hadn't changed, and I knew I had to do something, because I knew I didn't want to go to prison. I'd had enough shit in my life, and I didn't want any more. I knew what would happen to me in prison." She nodded and seemed determined, as she must have been that night. She seemed to stand a little taller, ready for action. "I grabbed him by the wrists and dragged him over to the side of the road to one of those drainage ditches." She looked away and sighed. "I pushed him in." She smiled. "I'm stronger than I look." After a brief pause she said, "I picked up the shotgun and threw it in the ditch too."

She hesitated and swallowed. "His car was sitting there running, so I got in it and closed the door." She stopped and shook her head. She laughed. "Just then car lights swept through the car, coming from behind, through the curve and down the hill." A short laugh came from her. "I didn't move." A smile curved her lips, and she shrugged. "Nothing happened. I sat there and the car just passed by." Pausing, she ran her hand through her hair. "I leaned back against the seat. The seat was still warm from his body, which was maybe the worst thing that night, to feel that he'd been alive and warm only minutes earlier, but was now dead in a ditch, and I'd done it." She shook her head. "I almost lost it, but I held on—and I drove his car down the gravel road and into his hiding place."

Drayton waited while Andrea thought.

"I got out of his car and stood there for a long time. I looked down and the keys were in my hand. I didn't know what do with them, so I put them in my pocket." She looked directly at Drayton, light glinting off her eyes. "Then I looked around, and everything was dark, and everything was quiet, which amazed me. Everything was the same as it had been only minutes earlier." She shook her head. "I started through the woods back to my car. I had to walk close to where I knew he was lying, but I couldn't see him. It was so quiet and dark, and I couldn't see him." Her voice shifted. "It was like it had never happened." She repeated herself. "It was like it had never happened."

"But it had," Drayton said and looked at the sensual California night. God, he thought, nature was beautiful but didn't give a damn about anything. Flatly indifferent. Who'd said that?

"But it had," Andrea echoed.

She seemed almost calm now, and stood there as if she were listening, stood there as she must have that night: the same darkness, the same quiet.

"So you came back here?" Drayton asked. "Looking for Louis's help?"

She shook her head. "I was crazy by then. By the time I got back here, I was ready to go to the police. I had done it. I had killed Les Tremain. I couldn't hide that. I had to tell the world. I wanted to confess." She shook her head again. "But Louis said no, said it wouldn't do any good to go to the police, that Les was already dead." She stopped and thought. "He told me I could learn to live with it. He told me it would take time, but I would learn to live with it." She shook her head. "I remember he said, 'We're so adaptable.'"

"Did you?" Drayton asked. "Get used to it?"

"Yes, in a way," she said and nodded. "It's always there, but it isn't always as bad as it was at first. At first I'd think about it, and I would be terrified and horrified. I would start to shake. Then it was less, never easy, but less." She looked at Drayton and said in a very even voice, "And I had already learned to live with terrible things." She reached up and rubbed at her eyes, as if trying to get rid of an image. "And," she said, "I wasn't alone. Louis was there. He knew. He helped me. He still loved me, in his way. And if I had said anything, Louis would have been an accessory." She smiled. "I used that as an excuse to myself." She shrugged. "So I never said anything until now. You're the first person to know other than Louis. And you know more in a way. How does it feel to be talking to a murderer?"

Drayton ignored her question and asked one of his own. "What else happened that night? How did your father get involved?"

Andrea took a deep breath. She had wrapped her arms around herself. Her voice was faint now. "It was pretty close to the story Louis told you." She hesitated. "Except, it was his idea. He said that my father owed me, because of what he'd done to me as a child." She looked up at Drayton and said, "It gets uglier and uglier, doesn't it?"

Drayton didn't answer her.

"Daddy," she said, "knew what to do. I told him exactly where to go. He even knew the road, and he took care of the rest of it."

"Later he got religion and wanted to confess?"

Andrea shook her head. "He was just trying to get more money from us."

"And then he was killed down at the salvage yard."

Andrea didn't respond.

"Was that an accident?" Drayton asked. "Or did Louis take care of things again?"

She shook her head. "No. I don't think Louis would ever kill someone." Drayton interrupted. "You never thought you'd kill someone."

Andrea shook her head. "No, I think it was an accident. Louis knew Daddy, and he knew that Daddy just wanted money."

Again, the barn owl hooted and the wind shuffled through the Manzanita. Drayton stood looking at Andrea with her short hair and dark eyes, the white terrycloth robe around her, cinched tight at the waist, and he thought of the young woman he had seen all those years ago, the young woman coming from the pool, still wet, a towel over her shoulders, nothing more than a beautiful girl to him. But there always seemed to be more than just the beautiful girl. Always more.

Andrea brought her hands to her face, held them there, then dropped them and said, "That's what happened. That's the truth you wanted to know—or as close to the truth as I can get. I can't tell you what to do with it."

Drayton nodded. "That's all almost twenty years old, and soon Louis will be gone, and you'll be an extremely wealthy woman."

"Yes."

Drayton took a deep breath, waited, and shook his head. "I've walked into something. I've walked into something between you and Louis. I'm glad I'm as old as I am. I don't think I would have known what to do with this ten years ago." He shook his head in surprise, and then nodded in acceptance. "No, I'll honor Louis's dying wish. It was probably the most generous and honest thing he's done in his life."

She looked at him. The moonlight glowed on her dark eyes. She asked, "How can I know that you'll hold true to that?"

"The same way that I can't be absolutely sure you won't point a shotgun at me some night in a dark woods."

"You'd be taking quite a chance," she said.

"No," Drayton said, and shook his head.

"Why?"

"Because I believe you."

She flinched, her eyes wide. "Why?"

"I trust Louis's judgment." Drayton answered, and added, "And my intuition."

"Intuition?" She shook her head. "Louis never told me what a good friend you were."

"Maybe he didn't know."

They stood quietly for a moment as an ocean breeze moved through the hillside. Finally, Drayton turned as if to go, but then stopped and said to Andrea, "Call me when Louis goes."

"Good night, Drayton"

Chapter 19
Wednesday

Two days later, Drayton drove down the rough road through the trees that led to Ellie's house, barn, and pastures. He glanced to his left where he'd found Tremain's car just over a week ago. The eucalyptus trees stood tall with white and twisted trunks, their top branches shifting in the wind. Ahead was the bluff.

Tremain's car would have to go. Whatever he'd taken out of the car, he'd put back. Even the photographs. With Louis Marchand's confession out in the world now, Madsen would want the car. It was evidence. Drayton would have to make a statement about where he'd found it. A statement that would fit Louis's story.

Ellie's place came into view. The afternoon sun lighted up the sycamores behind her house. Her two dogs began to amble toward his car, growling, barking, the hair up on their backs, but when Drayton stopped the car and called their names, their tails started wagging. Ellie stepped out onto her front porch. She wore jeans, boots, a long-sleeved shirt, and a straw hat. Dust powdered her jeans. She'd been working. When she took off her straw hat, she hit it against her leg, and dust clouded out. She didn't know anything about what had happened. Not enough time had passed yet for it to reach the newspaper or television.

And Drayton hadn't talked to anybody from the time he had left Marchand's house on the hill until Andrea had called him early this morning. She'd asked, "Drayton?"

"Yes," he'd answered, and he knew who it was before the word was out of his lips.

"This is Andrea Marchand."

"Louis's gone?" Drayton asked.

"Just before dawn," she said. "He died sitting there in his chair on the back porch. He tried to hang on until the dawn. He told me he wanted to see one more sunrise before he *disappeared for eternity.* Those were his words."

Drayton laughed softly. "He told me that he'd see me in hell."

A long pause followed on Andrea's end of the line, and then she asked, "Have you thought any more about it?"

Drayton nodded and said, "I think Louis was right. What's done is done. Things are tied up as much as they'll ever be. Just the other day, an old guy told me that there's never really closure on something like this."

Drayton could hear her sigh on the other end of the line, and then she said, "Thanks. I hope you're right."

"Me too."

DRAYTON HADN'T CONTACTED ELLIE before the call because he wanted to think, and he wanted things to come to their own end.

Ellie smiled at him. "Hello, Michael Drayton."

Drayton nodded. "Hello, Ellie Boudreau."

"Where have you been? What happened?" she asked.

Drayton shrugged.

"How are things?" she asked.

Neither of them moved to touch the other.

"Can we go in the house and have some of your lemonade?" Drayton asked.

In the cool shadows of the kitchen, they sat at the table, their lemonades in front of them, the fogged glasses filled with ice cubes and the pale-yellow liquid.

Drayton looked across the table at her. "It's all settled," he said. Ellie took a drink of lemonade and watched him.

Drayton spoke. "Tremain took pictures of a lot of women. A lot of people didn't like him."

"He was easy to hate," Ellie said. Then she smiled. "But he was easy to like too. I won't lie about that."

"He took some photos of Andrea Marchand, Louis Marchand's wife."

Ellie nodded. "He was seeing her when he was seeing me. He told me all about her."

Drayton nodded. "And he told her about you."

Ellie grimaced.

Drayton said, "She's the one who sent the pictures to your husband."

"Why?"

"I guess she hoped it would get rid of you. Maybe nothing that logical. Maybe just jealousy."

Ellie reached out and touched her cold glass with her fingertips, but didn't say anything.

"She also told her husband," Drayton said. "She told him about her affair with Tremain, and she told him about Tremain seeing you."

Ellie didn't take her eyes from him, but her expression changed.

"Marchand died this morning." Drayton said. "Andrea called me. He'd been sick for a long time. He was on his last legs when I saw him just a couple of days ago."

"How did you end up there?" Ellie asked.

"Never mind," Drayton said. "It's not important."

"Why?"

Drayton drank some lemonade, put down his glass, smiled at Ellie and said, "Because before Marchand died, he dictated a confession to his attorney." Drayton went on. "Apparently, a fairly detailed confession, explaining how he came out here that night. It sounds as if it was as much accident as it was murder. It was Tremain's shotgun, and it went off by accident." Drayton shrugged. "But, it was in Marchand's hands and it was pointed at Tremain." Drayton looked at Ellie, having just thought of something. "Marchand will be remembered as an English Professor, a screen-writer, and, finally, a murderer."

Ellie shook her head and sighed. "Oh, God, what a waste. What a way for Les to go." After a minute, she said to Drayton, "So, old Marchand was who I saw that night? He's who I saw walking toward me?"

Drayton shrugged, but didn't answer the question. Instead, he said, "Your husband had nothing to do with it. He was just somewhere else when you went looking for him."

"God," Ellie said. "Thank God, I should say."

Drayton nodded.

"What about his sister? Les's sister?"

"I've just come from her place. I didn't want to take any chances that she'd hear it on the news or see it in the newspaper."

"How did she take it?"

"She was still crying a half hour later when I left," Drayton said. "But I think now that it's settled, she'll do better." He hesitated. "She offered me the reward that she'd promised." Drayton shook his head. "But I'm not going to take it. It's too much like blood money. I'd never be easy spending it." He smiled. "The truth is that it's not so much an ethical choice. I'd just be superstitious about it."

"What about Andrea Marchand?"

"She'll miss Louis, probably more than any of us can imagine. But she's independently wealthy and a beautiful woman. I think she'll be O.K. Louis was over eighty and sick. Life was no fun for him anymore." He laughed softly. "Easy for me to say."

They both sat in the shaded kitchen, the only sound the breeze in the sycamores behind the house and the low hum of the refrigerator.

"All that time, all that time lost." Ellie said. "And I guess Louis Marchand got away with murder." She took a long drink of lemonade as if it were needed whiskey.

"I guess you could say that."

"Messy people," Ellie said. Drayton looked at her.

"Les and Marchand, and his wife." She smiled. "And me."

"I guess you could say all our lives are messy," Drayton said. "I know my life is messy. I've left a trail behind me. A wife. A job I walked away from. Living out in the woods in a mobile home with a dog and a semi-feral cat."

Ellie looked at Drayton. "So, Andrea Marchand had nothing to do with Les's death?"

Drayton hesitated. He shrugged. "Well, I don't think you could say she had *nothing* to do with it." Drayton told himself that he was protecting Andrea because that was what Louis wanted, and because Andrea had been misused by her father, by Louis, and by Tremain. And besides, what good would it do for Ellie to know? Drayton sighed, unable to answer his own questions.

Ellie stared at him for a long time, and seemed as if she was about to ask another question, but she didn't.

"Ellie," Drayton said. "Do you think that lovers always have to tell the complete truth to each other?"

Ellie sat waiting for a minute, as if she thought he would say more, but when he didn't, she shook her head and said, "Sometimes that's impossible, sometimes the truth is too complicated to tell."

"Complicated?" Drayton asked.

"Slippery," Ellie said. "Like quicksilver."

"Quicksilver," Drayton repeated and nodded. Wind rustled the leaves of the sycamores, and the air in the kitchen was suddenly cooler, but Drayton knew the Santa Ana winds would return.

ACKNOWLEDGEMENTS

My first thanks goes to Lynne, my wife, not only for her love, but also for her superb editorial skills and her fine suggestions about my writing over the years.

Thanks to poet Kevin Clark, good friend and supporter, without whom this novel may not have been published. And thanks to Will Jones, another old friend, who read a draft of the novel and made suggestions.

And thanks for the fine editorial work from the Stephen F. Austin State University Press, especially Kim Verhines, the director, and Emily Williams, my excellent editorial assistant.

Thanks to the San Louis Obispo writing group: Mary Kay Harrington, Kevin Clark, John Hampsey, Glenn Irvin, and Ginger Hendrix, who helped give me an education in writing fiction.

Thanks to California Polytechnic State University, and especially to the English Department, where it was possible for me to teach fiction writing, to oversee the campus literary fiction-and-poetry contest, and to advise students producing Byzantium, the campus literary magazine. And thanks to the students who taught me so much, and continue to do so in my memories.

And thanks to Susann Cokal, Suzanne Roberts, Diane Carson, and Willis Loy for their continuing support.

Originally from St. Louis, Al Landwehr has written and published short stories in national literary and slick magazines since the 1970s. A prize-winning university professor of creative writing and literature, Landwehr and his wife raised their family on the central coast of California. When he wasn't writing in his spare time, he refurbished classic vintage automobiles. After retiring from teaching, he shifted yet more attention to his fiction writing. Eventually, Landwehr put together a collection of his stories titled *The Dancing Horologist,* which contains eight published stories and two new stories, including a mystery novella titled "Merely Players." Fascinated by both the surprising elasticity of the genre and its potential for literary effect, he came to write this longer mystery, *What's Left to Learn.*

CPSIA information can be obtained
at www.ICGtesting.com
Printed in the USA
LVHW050540190322
713645LV00002B/7

9 781622 882342